INVISIBLE
JOURNEY

MARY

USA TODAY BESTSELLING AUTHOR

BUCKHAM

Cover and book design by
THE KILLION GROUP
www.thekilliongroupinc.com

DEDICATION

This book is dedicated to those readers who make it a delight to create. Thank you, each and every one of you. You rock!

ACKNOWLEDGEMENT

It takes a village to create a book and this book is no exception. A special thanks to Tiger Wiseman and Laurie Gifford Adams for copyediting, you are my Grammar and Comma Goddesses. A huge note of appreciation to my amazing Street Team, Mary Buckham's Ninjas, who, by being great Beta readers, helped so much in making sure the story held together — Ramona, Gail, Claudia, Tami, Kimberly, Denise, Marla, Kimber, Sharon, Michelle, Melinda, Virginia, Liette, Denise and Brenda. Thanks to them and all my Street Team members who have loved and supported these stories and spread the word. And, of course, thank you to my husband who keeps me sane — which is a full time job — but is also willing to discuss vamps, Weres and shifters even in a public venue! Any mistakes or adjustments in detail for the purpose of fiction are entirely my own doing.

CHAPTER 1

Life sucked. It looked like death was going to do the same as I squinted, holding a shaky hand up to cut the glare of a brilliant light blaring in my eyes.

I'm Alex Noziak, part-witch, part-shaman, sometimes screw up with an uncanny ability to make things worse. And right now I was lost.

Not only lost, but missing my two IR—I for Invisible, R for Recruits—teammates, Kelly and Mandy. The two I'd brought over to the Underworld with me. The three of us were on a little-hope-for-a-win mission. We had fourteen hours to find an African teen named Aini, pronounced like Ah-nee, who'd been abducted by a very, very bad demon called the Horned One.

Aini was a powerful Seer, or would be if she was allowed to reach age sixteen, which happened in fourteen hours. If we could save her, Aini was the world's best chance at avoiding creatures called the Seekers who made the Horned One just a minor demon bad guy. If we didn't reach her in time, I didn't even want to think about the fall out. It'd be terrifying and disastrous, for the whole world, human and preternatural.

So where exactly were Kelly and Mandy? And, while I was on that subject, where the hell was I?

Or maybe I shouldn't be using the "H" word. In theory I was in *that* place, full of glare instead of flames like I'd learned as a child.

I'd been tasked with getting Kelly, Mandy and myself to the Spirit Realm, but this didn't look like any part of it that I'd seen before.

My dad, a full-fledged Shoshone shaman, had warned me
about too many visits to this Realm and the toll it could take on
a person. Live humans didn't belong here, not for long
stretches—and not going where we intended to travel. This was
the third time I'd been here in the last three months, and I felt
like a piece of worn cotton stretched way too thin.

Duty called, though, and I was the only one of the IR team
who could bring and return my teammates.

First step, figure out where I was. Then find my teammates.

I looked around, adjusting my hand to shield my eyes from
the intensity of the light pulsing against me. Couldn't someone
shut off the damn thing? On second thought, given what the
alternative could be, pitch darkness, maybe I could deal with
light.

Right now my whole body felt like it had the flu—the fear
flu—the kind I got when I was doing something, kicking and
screaming, that I wasn't yet a hundred percent sure I could
accomplish. Heck, I wasn't even thirty percent sure we find
Aini and return in one piece.

Saving Aini was a no brainer. Having to fight the great
Horned One to succeed, that I understood. Possessing the go-
for-broke wherewithal needed to really accomplish that—not
so sure.

But that's what we did—Kelly McAllister and Mandy
Reyes and I. As part of a very small, barely-holding-on-to-our-
sanity, secret agency, we kept preternatural threats away from
humans. Three other teammates, Vaughn, Jaylene and Nicki, as
well as our team instructor Stone and director, Ling Mai, were
back at our Maryland compound, working on a plan B, if this
mission went ass-up. Not if, but when.

Mission after mission, we'd faced impossible odds. This
might be the mission those odds finally caught up with us.

I wasn't a pessimist, more a realist who'd survived more
than one mission by the skin of my teeth, fighting the baddy
preternaturals that inhabited our world, phenomenal creatures,
many very scary, that most humans didn't even know existed.

And now? Now we were in the other Realm, the one
inhabited by spirits, souls and lots and lots of things that went
bump in the night.

Because I was part shaman, which meant I could travel between the worlds, I was leading this mission. Kelly came along because she was our human GPS tracking device being connected to Aini as her Guardian, in some woo-woo way. The theory was if she could communicate telepathically with Aini, we could use that connection as a beacon to find the lair of the Horned One. Mandy? She was part of this op to give me grief and watch our backs. Which was a big fat joke as she was a Spirit Walker.

For those not in the know, Spirit Walkers are also called soulless ones. Most humans are body and soul. Not Mandy. She exists without a soul, which some people can, in the Real World—sociopaths, psychopaths, megalomaniac third-world dictators and the like. Not all are bad, but all have a certain edge to them, which Mandy does, in spades. But in this world? Here, having no soul was like tacking a neon FOR RENT sign on your forehead. She was a walking ticket out of here for any soul with enough guts, pun intended, to possess her.

And she was our protection? Yeah, right.

Not.

Three blind mice heading into a house full of cats stood a better chance.

On the other hand, someone had to do the hard, no glory jobs. That was the bottom line.

So first steps first. Find my teammates. Then find Aini and bring her back to where she belonged, where we all belonged. Then, if we had to, eliminate the Horned One. Oh, and did I mention we only have a couple of hours to accomplish all this? No sweat.

So where were Kelly and Mandy?

Had I messed up my transition spell so badly? Or was something already at work on this side to divide and conquer? Or maybe, just maybe, I really was alone.

Shuddering at the thought, I glanced around, ignoring what I didn't want to deal with: finding, much less rescuing Aini on my own defined a fool's errand.

Doing nothing wasn't helping either, so best to get my bearings and get moving.

I was sitting against something solid. It could be a partition in a room, since there was a sense of enclosed space, but unlike any space I'd ever seen before. Shimmering white walls, so brilliant they vibrated with an incandescent glow. Unreal. Nothing was squared off, but pleated, layers of whiteness folded in upon itself. A tent? No, something less flimsy.

I'd been in a prison, but it wasn't like this. A loony bin? Not politically correct but this place had that kind of feel, like a nightmare that had only begun.

"Kelly?" Shouting was like whistling in the dark, but maybe they were just around the next corner. "Kelly? If you can hear me, call out."

That's when I heard it. Two sounds actually, one deeper than the other and only one that I was expecting. The deeper vibration pulsed like a beating heart—low, thrumming, steady. The CD I'd left behind to tether the three of us to the Real Realm. Our means of finding home.

That was good news because it meant I was still connected with my human shell existing in the Real Realm. Kind of freaky, but there wasn't time to focus on it because of the other noise. A child's sobs. The heartbroken resonance humans made when it felt like the world had ended. I remembered weeping that way when my mom left and I knew she was never, ever coming back. I'd go to the hayloft in the barn and blubber until I couldn't breathe.

Who was crying now? And why?

Not Kelly or Mandy as I felt sure neither was near. Kelly, being a former kindergarten teacher wouldn't let a child weep like that, that's for sure. Not if she was around and could stop it. And Mandy? She wasn't my favorite person in the universe, but I couldn't see her turning her back on a child. So what was up?

Screw it. Time to find out where I was and what I was up against. I scrambled to my knees, which took some doing. Every muscle in my body screamed pain. I wasn't surprised. Ever since joining the IR Agency pain was the new norm. My norm.

Given that the fledging IR Agency, of which I was a charter member, was created to battle really nasty, very vicious, bad-guy preternaturals, meant that when we fought, we frequently got hurt. In fact, people tended to die.

Like Wyatt. A fledgling recruit who'd been killed just last night.

I hated that Wyatt died. He had his whole life before him but never got a chance to live it. He deserved to fall in love, hold his own child in his hands, lean against someone he adored in the twilight of his years. Now? Nada. I was even missing his funeral. He died and only a handful of people knew why and how. A silent sacrifice.

I swallowed a lump of grief, only too aware that it hadn't even been a full day since we'd come up against the Horned One the first time. Only then he'd been inhabiting a human's body, a man named Kincaide, who ran a security agency where my oldest brother Van worked. Or used to: not now as Kincaide had killed many of his own men and nearly killed the rest of us, including Van.

Have I mentioned that being an IR Agent isn't the easiest occupation in the world? And that was before the last minute call from Bran. Talk about poor timing.

Bran, my lover, sometimes friend, and biggest complication in a complicated life.

Just as I was getting my game face on to do this whole mission to the Underworld, he called and 'requested my services' which he'd said the IR Director, Ling Mai, had approved. Guess she'd forgotten to tell me.

As for Bran? Requested my patootie. He didn't make requests. He's all Alpha male from the tip of his dark arrogant brow to the toes of his handcrafted Italian designer shoes. He's a creative genius, designing clothes that make me drool, which is saying something because, before I met him, my idea of dressing up was getting out of a pair of jeans and into khakis. That's what comes from being raised on a pig farm in Mud Lake, Idaho with four older brothers. Clancy's Bar and Grill doesn't have a dress code and neither did I, until Bran.

On top of being Midas rich and a celebrity in the haute couture field, he was also a warlock, more specifically a mage master—enemy to blood-born witches.

Then he calls right when I needed all my concentration to get not only myself, but two others transported between Realms. No wonder I mucked things up. Bran could mess with me from across an ocean.

He seems to think we are fated to be together because of some old prophecy. I think that is a bunch of bullpucky; meaning he has an excuse to get into my pants. Not that I mind. Not in the least. He might be as arrogant as a demi-god, and as inflexible as steel when he thinks he is right, but he is all lip-smacking sexy and man, oh, man, he can kiss. And make love in the most imaginative ways for hours on end. Even thinking about how imaginative, and how many hours, made my skin flush and a simmering heat build low in my belly.

Whoa. I didn't even know I could feel these kinds of emotions in this Realm. Who knew? Maybe they were another test—one designed to second guess my willingness to take on the biggest bad-ass I'd faced yet and in his place of power to boot.

For the sake of Aini I would. Except. . .

If I'd been able to put off the mission for one more day, even a few hours, maybe I could have found Bran, face-to-face, and instead of arguing I could have had one last kiss, one last chance to tell him words I'd never shared before, one last moment to memorize his face, the sound of his voice, the crook of his smile.

Was that too much to ask? Selfish? Probably. Hadn't all soldiers who'd gone into battle felt the very same way? Knowing how fragile life was, how easily it could end? Yet they still went. Could I do less?

Squeezing eyes shut against the light, I sucked in a deep, braced-for-bear breath, rose from knees on the floor, to hands on knees, to a quavering upright position where I stumbled back until I could prop my sorry-assed self against the nearest wall. Only then did I exhale and crack open my eyes.

Standing might be overrated. Last time I'd traveled to the Spirit Realm the effort hadn't zapped me like this, but then I hadn't brought out two others with me—two living humans to a place they didn't belong.

The earlier crying had stopped, or maybe I'd just imagined it as the space around me looked empty. Totally, eerily empty, like a high school gym after a basketball game, when there was still a sense of people around, their energy vibrating unseen, but nothing remained except silence and trash.

Was I someplace other than the Spirit Realm? I'd been here before, but it didn't look or feel like this place. From what my father taught me, the Spirit Realm, where beings traveled to when they left their mortal bodies, was not simply one place or one level. It was multi-layered, which is one of the reasons it was so hard for those still connected to the physical or Real Realm, where I lived, to travel here. The Spirit Realm led to the Underworld, one of the lower levels. Too many layers and very few guideposts. If a live being found herself lost here she'd be trapped until her physical body truly died.

Great. Another cheery thought to shove away until I could deal with it—like never.

Squeezing my eyes shut again helped a smidge with the vertigo winging through me. But only a smidge. Light hummed beyond my closed eyes, creating a dizzying swirling that made me want to sink back down. Or throw up. It was a toss up.

Until one noise grew louder, the other quieter.

The loud sound was a steady thrum, a drumbeat I recognized.

Slowly, as if expecting only bad things, not that unusual since I'd become an IR Agent, I peeked. Not that it did any good. Just that freakin' light and a fresh wash of pain shimmering through me.

Nothing else, even as I sensed a waiting presence. Something, somewhere, waiting for me.

Call me a chicken but I was beginning to think chickens were the realists of the world.

Even having the extra boost of some shifter blood streaming through my veins wasn't helping my body. A few missions back, my brother Van—a blood-born shifter—had bitten me. Not while he was in his right mind, and not enough to kill or turn me into a wolf, like he was. For that I was thankful because my genetic mix was messed up enough. What had changed, so far, was that I tended to have enhanced hearing and vision, more strength and stamina, along with the ability to heal quicker than I had before. Which was an A-plus bonus in my book.

If there were bad ramifications, I hadn't learned of them, yet. But I had no doubt I would, and soon.

Eyes wide open, I brushed my hands against the faded jeans I wore—worn, well-loved and not-fancy. So something here was familiar. Like that fainter second sound I'd heard. A child in trouble.

Maybe I'd already made it all the way to the Underworld?

My heart nose-dived because there, where we intended to go, lurked sure death.

That sent cold shivers racing across my skin. Could I have really messed up? Been too wiped out after the recent battle? Too distracted by Bran's call and our argument? So arrogant as to believe that I could cross three of us over to this side?

Was I really and truly dead?

A sharp pang sliced through me. Anguish? Or relief?

Dead or alive, I still had a mission. Find Kelly and Mandy first. The crying child if I could and eventually Aini held by the Horned One. Pushing off from the wall where I'd been standing like a tottering drunk I staggered forward into that pulsating light.

That's when something slammed against me, throwing me backwards against the ground with a hard thwack.

CHAPTER 2

Before I could catch my breath, or even figure out what was happening when two, then three dark shapes swept toward and through me.

My muscles clenched, adrenaline spiking. I threw my hands out to protect my head, which only exposed them to a stinging cold as the attackers slammed against my skin.

Like cold, icky showers, the shapes flew around and around, swinging closer the second I inched away from the floor. Standing and running away, even if I knew where to go, was out.

These were wraiths. Had to be. Dark spirits—angry and greedy in death as they had been in life—that attacked living beings for no other reason than they could. Nasty, slimy creatures.

One-on-one I could cast a quick banishing spell, but I didn't have any of the necessary ingredients that could help me—the leaves of an ash or rowan tree, blessed oils, heck, even table salt could help in a pinch. Plus fighting multiples meant my using magic could backfire. If you give a wraith any entry into your being—physically, emotionally or magically—they pounced and next thing you knew—you could become a necromancer. One more dead than alive; neither human or spirit but with an affinity for reaching other dead beings. Yuck!

Not a good thing.

Wraiths hung out where death lingered—battlefields, in the midst of epidemics, the hospital wards of terminal patients—any place they could weaken and feed off the living. Feed until there was nothing left to suck dry.

Fear jammed hard tension through my spine. Doing nothing led to a form of madness because wraiths never gave up.

Flat on my back. Alone. With no weapons. Nothing except my wits.

Think, Noziak, think.

A fourth and fifth wraith joined the three earlier ones, tumbling and swirling until all I could see was blackness storming around me, chills raining down upon me.

Maybe if I called on the light of magic, different than the light streaming through the room, I could threaten these creatures into dispersing. Wraiths, being dark, hated both magic and light.

Threaten was too strong a word. More like water to cats, enough agitation might convince them I wasn't worth their effort.

Hard as it was, I shut my eyes to visualize a circle of bright white light, filled with warmth and gentleness twining around me. It took a little focus but the image came—a sunny August day, snuggling beneath my favorite afghan as a child, the heat of fresh baked chocolate chip cookies eaten near a fire.

Murmuring low, I started the chant.

"Light come forth.
Clear the darkness.
Guide and protect.
Light to dark."

Nothing. I needed movement to activate the spell.

With a scream—part fear, mostly desperation—I shot to my feet, swatting my arms as I pivoted counter clockwise, aware of the angry brush of the wraiths as I bared my whole body to them. But I kept murmuring the chant.

Repeating the important elements, I raised my voice.

"Clear and guide.
Light to dark.
Protect."

By the time I had turned a double circle the fear squeezing my chest began to ease.

The wraiths pulled back but still swarmed, creating the hum of angry bees. Noise I could survive; possession I couldn't.

I kept calling out loud, raising my chin in the four directions as I turned.

"East to the morning light.
North to the warrior spirits.
West to the waning light.
South to the heat.
Beat back the darkness.
Scatter and protect."

Easing open my eyes to mere slits, I caught one wraith swishing away. The others? Just the opposite. I could feel their anger, their frustration, their desperation as they pummeled against me. Both eyes open now, I tried again.

"Dark to dark, seek thy home," I shouted, getting desperate. *"Be gone. Be gone. Be gone."*

The last words I screamed at the top of my lungs and, with a final shriek that raised the hairs along my skin, a harsh explosion, smelling of ash and iron, blinded me.

By the time the sooty cloud sifted away, the shapes were gone.

Thank the Great Spirits!

Breathing hard as if I'd been racing, and feeling my own sweat cool me, though the room was warm, I sighed.

"Impressive, Alex Noziak," a male voice slapped against me so close I jumped. "I expected no less from you."

There wasn't a soul around. Just that glowing, empty whiteness.

Another wraith? Or something else?

"Who are you?" I shouted, hands clenched and raised before me. "Where are you?"

"Here." A form shimmered in front of me, more a faint shadow than a body against the glaring, undulating walls. At least the shadow held the hint of being human at one time, a silhouette of a body. "Does this help you?"

"Not really." Was he kidding? There was something familiar about his voice though, even if all he looked like was a puff of pale beige smoke. I took a stab in the dark. "I know you, don't I?"

"We've met before."

Like that helped. At least it meant he wasn't a wraith, as I hadn't ever tangled with them before—thank goodness. Then I remembered. My first visit to the In-Between Realm, someone helped me. Well, technically I had to twist his insubstantial arm by promising a future favor to get him to find a friend, if that's what I could call Franco. Pain in the patootie was more like it.

I'd assumed the favor-granter was a ghost, which was better than a wraith or a ghoul.

"You need my help again," Ghost Guy said. He sounded so sure I had to check myself. "You know the rules. I assist you— you owe me a favor of my asking."

"Don't think so," I mumbled. On both counts. Owing a strange spirit one favor was bad enough, no way was I going to make promises I didn't know if I could keep a second time. Except it'd be nice to know where I was and where Kelly and Mandy were. As long as a question wasn't seen as a favor, I might be okay.

"Can I ask you something?" I said. "Without creating an obligation?"

"Depends."

Fat lot of good that answer did. "What if I ask you something and, if it doesn't give you an IOU over me, then will you answer it?"

He paused before saying, "That should work, but the minute you ask the wrong question—"

"Don't answer it and we'll both be fine." Or I would. Owing a spirit or ghost a promise could have really bad repercussions. For all I knew I was chatting with Genghis Khan, Jack the Ripper or Hitler. "So do we have a deal?"

"Yes." I thought he nodded but it was hard to tell watching a shadow.

I cleared my throat before I said, "Am I dead?"

"Not yet."

That was a cheery comment, but at least I had an answer. On the other hand, was I that close to dying that the issue was up for grabs? And why wasn't I freaking out because of it?

Exhaustion probably. Best to get back on task.

"Do you know where my friends are? The ones I came with?"

"Yes."

Amen and halleluiah! That meant they made it over to this Realm. Then the tone of his single answer struck me. "Are they alive?"

I'd actually stepped closer to him, fists balled, as if I could punch out a spirit. Get real.

"For now."

Not liking that response. Not at all. It was one thing for me to accept death, another to think of my teammates dying.

Before I could wrap my tongue around my next question, or demand more, he said, "You've been sent here to find something important to you."

Did he mean Aini? Or the Horned One?

"How'd you—" I blurted out. Probably not the best reaction, to blab too many of the details as to why I was here, in case he was on a fishing expedition, plus no telling who was listening. So I scrambled to make it clear I wasn't verifying his hunch or asking for his help. "Good guess, knowing I wouldn't be in this Realm without a reason."

"Not to worry." He spoke as if he could read the secrets of my mind, which was downright creepy and raised the hairs along my arms. Maybe he was more ghoul than ghost, which didn't make me feel better. Ghouls made fae look like nice folks. Ghosts, being all spirit, I should be able to handle as a shaman. At least in theory, but a ghoul? They were something different, a little nastier, a lot trickier, closer to wraiths and I had absolutely no reason to want to mess with them again.

The child's sobs, which had disappeared when the wraiths appeared, started up again. "Who's that?" I grabbed at the distraction to stop dark thoughts better left buried and peered around at the emptiness.

The ghost shrugged his shoulders as if it was no concern of his.

"Is it a kid?"

"A goat?" came the lazy reply.

"Very funny." I eased myself deeper into the white room, angling my head to get a bead on the crying child. This way? No, over there. Not that there was a clear location but I was getting a stronger feel for where the sound originated.

Walking forward wasn't easy. The very floor vibrated with reflected light, so each step was an act of faith that I'd find something solid beneath me and not something else, like a trap or an ass-over-teakettles plummet downward. Or more wraiths.

"What are you doing?" Confusion stained the ghost's voice as he hovered near me. Not close enough I could reach out and touch him, as if I was that stupid, but close enough to make sure I was very aware of him.

"The child obviously is hurting." I inched forward, trusting more to a shuffle-slide move than a step-by-step approach.

"He's not your problem," Ghost Guy said, in a voice so flat and void of emotion I wondered if he'd ever been human, or if he'd forgotten what made a human less than the angels but more than a lot of other beings. Things like empathy and the willingness to act on that natural instinct to protect the young and vulnerable.

"So you know who's crying?" My tone accused as much as confirmed.

"His name is Benjamin." That half-shrug again, which was very unnerving on an unsubstantial being, sort of like watching a garment on a clothesline riffle invisible shoulders.

Another shuffle forward.

Good thing I was looking closely or I might have missed the small shift in the ghost's hooded head. Now I had a direction to go. I ignored Ghost Guy and followed the crying. It wasn't helping me locate my teammates, but no way could I ignore a child in need.

One mini-motion forward at a time I stepped until I found a darker bundle in the lighted space. "Benjamin?" I spoke quietly, not sure if I was trying not to spook the child or myself.

The sobbing stopped and the shadows moved as a head peeped out of a pile of tattered rags. He couldn't have been older than five or six, about the age I was when Mom left.

Kneeling down so I didn't startle him, I repeated, "Are you Benjamin?"

A loud sniff was my only answer. This close I could see thick, corn-silk colored hair that looked matted, as if someone had chewed it. Huge eyes. A grubby face with tear streaks mapping the only clear patches on his skin. A Charles Dickens character had nothing on this kid.

"My name's Alex," I said.

"That's a boy's name."

Okay, so the kid had some bite left in him. I could respect that.

"Yeah, I was supposed to be a boy."

"Your ma and pa didn't want you?"

Talk about a punch to the solar plexus. Since my mom left, I always assumed she didn't want me. And my dad? At one time, I'd have had no doubts. But after learning how he stood aside, knowing he held the power to keep me out of prison if he spoke up, but didn't, well, I guess he didn't really want me as I'd once thought.

Still, my open emotional wounds weren't what were important now.

"Is that why you're here?" I asked, at a loss of how to help. "That's why you were crying. You miss your parents?"

"Yeah." He wiped one tattered sleeve beneath his nose. "I can't get out."

I glanced around. "You mean out of here?"

"Ya daff?" he said it as if any idiot knew that. "Course from here."

I rose to my feet, looking toward Ghost Guy who'd been strangely mute this whole time. Quieting my voice so it was barely audible over the heartbeat thrum that continued to echo all around, I spoke to Ghost Guy, sure he was near. I knew I was pushing the no-question-asking issue, but since I'd gotten this far why not risk a little more.

"Why can't he leave here?"

"You haven't told me why this child matters?" he said, less hostile, and all sure of himself, than he had been so far.

"It's not a hard concept. Benjamin's just a little kid who needs help. Is it that hard to understand my wanting to help him?"

"You can't."

Red flag to a Noziak. I took a deep breath before asking, "Why not?"

"Because he's been here for a hundred of your years. Maybe more. He must find his own way out. You have a different challenge."

My stomach knotted at the images he painted, but especially of a child alone and waiting for that kind of time. It made no sense. But then what had lately. So I grabbed the easiest question tumbling around my head. "What if I *am* his way out?"

Careful, Noziak, don't get sidetracked from your mission.

No answer from the ghost, so I tried a different approach. "Where is *out* from here?"

Ghost Guy glanced behind me. "Where you must go."

I hesitated. Not because his words scared me skin-deep, which they did, but because there was a wealth of words left unsaid. Taking this child on my journey could be the stupidest thing to do, but leaving him didn't feel right either.

"Does. . . does Benjamin, need to go in the same direction I'm going?"

"Possibly."

"Make it a simple yes or no." Like it was ever that easy.

"Yes." There was a hesitation there, as if he debated telling me that much.

"Is it in the same direction my teammates are?"

"Yes." This one more reluctant.

Tough. His affirmation was enough for me to squat back down to Benjamin.

"Would you like to leave with me?" I said, knowing, deep down inside, that it was the right thing to do. I also knew this made no sense. No sense at all. Now if I'd been big-hearted Kelly, then it would make sense. But I wasn't and I had to find Kelly and Mandy, not take on a child who could only be a liability. Then there was facing the Horned One if we crossed paths. Putting a child within reach of that monster wouldn't do Benjamin any favors. So who the heck was I, thinking I could help anyone in this place?

On the other hand, could I leave this child here? Trapped. Alone. Scared. How many more years, or hundreds of years, would he remain trapped here?

What had my witch mentor once said to me? Trust the vibes you get, energy doesn't lie. Too bad she hadn't also clarified that energy could be a pain in the backside.

Right now the energy vibes screamed that I could help Benjamin. My head shouted the opposite. Talk about being between a rock and a hard place. I cleared my throat and crossed my fingers that I'd get a clear sense of what I needed to do next as I spoke to Benjamin again. "You want to leave?"

Squinting his eyes as if he wasn't used to kindness, he finally nodded his head.

"Do you know where you're supposed to go?"

"Yggdrasil." He slurred the word, or maybe it was my being distracted by the goose bumps running up my spine. It sounded like *IG-druh-sill*. The word meant something, something primordial, and scared me without having a clue why. Surely Yggdrasil was not the Realm of the Horned One.

I swallowed as I offered Benjamin a stiff smile and stood again, turning to speak to Ghost Guy. Which was like speaking to a black hole in a hoody.

"This Yggdrasil place." I stumbled over the word. "Is that where I'm supposed to go, to meet my teammates?"

"Yggdrasil holds answers you seek without knowing you seek them."

I hated mumbo jumbo vague answers. What was Yggdrasil? Where was it? Could it get me closer to Kelly and Mandy? Or farther away? .

"Is Yggdrasil where I need to go?" My tone emphatic.

A silent nod this time.

Stay or go? I looked at Benjamin before I asked, "Is Yggdrasil dangerous?"

The nod this time was slow and ponderous.

Of course it was dangerous, why should I expect otherwise?

"Then I shouldn't bring a child there?" Help me out here Obi-Wan Wanna-Be.

"I didn't say that," came his neutral reply. He was damn lucky I didn't wrap my hands around his neck and shake him. Just the thought that there'd be nothing to shake kept me from trying the move as I exhaled a deep breath.

"Look buddy." I tried to keep my voice to a whisper, only too aware of Ben squatting next to me, his large, liquid eyes gazing at me like I had all the answers. As if. "Assume I don't know anything about where we are." Which was the truth. "Would you bring a child trapped in a sterile room for who knows how many years to this Yggdrasil place?" I raised a hand to stop the ghost from doing the head nod thing, as I wasn't finished. "Or would you leave him here as the safest, best option for him?"

"Because a place is dangerous does not mean it's not the best place for some to be."

"What a load of hogwash," I snapped. "Yes or no? Take him or leave him?"

"It's your choice. You must make it."

Screw him.

Why were choices always hard? Why couldn't there be some choices that were such no-brainers that a decision could be made in a snap. Like the choice between eating broccoli or venison? On second thought, I shuddered at the thought of either.

Would I regret taking this child to a place he might be hurt? No doubt about it. On the other hand if I left him here, could I live with that?

No. My mom could leave a child behind. I couldn't. Not if there was something I could do.

I reached one hand out for Benjamin, not knowing if I was going to make things worse for him. Sure I was asking for a boatload of trouble for me.

But when he slid his tiny fist into mine I knew I was doing the right thing.

When he stood, he barely reached my waist. I made sure my hand was secure around his before I glanced at Ghost Guy, who wasn't looking too pleased. How could a vague shape look angry? I don't know, but he did and that was before I said, "Fine. Show me the way."

"And if I say no?"

Men? Always making simple things complicated. "You want me to leave here. I'm supposed to find something. Yggdrasil." I didn't think that's where the Horned One hung out but who knew. "I'm ready to go. To find my friends. Then—"

"With him?"

I had no doubt my look mimicked Benjamin's duh expression of a few minutes ago. "Yes. With him."

When Ghost Guy didn't move, I stepped forward, hoping I was headed in the direction we needed to go, hoping more that my shapeless mentor would get the hint and direct me.

Ghost wavered in front of me, making me pull back or shuffle through him. Yuck.

Then he appeared to reconsider or came to a decision. "If you must. Choose a passage."

"Where?" We were in a closed room. Not a lot of . . . as my mind churned three dark squares appeared behind him. Or he was so insubstantial he was just a mist before the murkier rectangular shapes.

He chuckled, which should have been a comforting sound, but wasn't.

He wafted toward the nearest door.

Even though my decision was made, my stomach twisted at the thought I could be putting Benjamin in more danger if I took him elsewhere.

"Are my friends this way?" I pointed to door number one— a silvery gray color. The second door was white and the third black.

"It's all about choices," Ghost Guy spoke from beyond the doorway. All I wanted was a straight answer. Was that too much to ask?

I stepped up to the silver door and cracked it open. A loud roar, like an angry lion greeted me. I slammed that door shut so hard I was surprised the knob didn't come off in my hand. Behind the second door dampness seeped out, reminding me way too much of being trapped in the underground tunnels beneath Paris. The fact I died at the end of that mission, even though Bran brought me back to life, made me close the door with a silent click. No Bran this trip, so no way to get a jumpstart back to life.

Sucking in my breath, I slid the third door open just a bit. No horrible odor or sound. Good. Opening it a little wider I couldn't see a lot but so far so good.

"I choose this door," I said, my voice steadier than my nerves.

Ghost Guy disappeared through the door, so that was the way I was headed.

It looked like following a ghost who pointed out that I needed answers was my only option.

And if all I did was bring Benjamin to a better place, that could work, too. Maybe I wasn't meant to fight a big battle just yet. Sometimes it was the small skirmishes that made a difference. Maybe my contribution was on a smaller scale. Like helping one lost child.

Yeah, I could live with that.

Besides, I'd be acting instead of standing around waiting and, as a bonus, I wasn't beholden to Ghost Guy for another favor. Yet.

I sucked in a deep, lung-filling breath, squared my shoulders, and notched my chin higher. Being foolhardy didn't mean I wasn't scared down to my toes. But out there, wherever there was, was where I needed to go.

That didn't mean that the first step beyond the door was easy.

CHAPTER 3

Kelly McAllister woke in stages, clawing her way out of a dark nightmare filled with graphic images of horned demons, some grinning, some screaming, all threatening.

She heard her own groan before she opened her eyes. Only once before had she felt this bad; in grade school when she'd come down with a horrible flu that became pneumonia. The doctors told her parents they were lucky she hadn't died.

In hindsight they might have wished she had, once they learned about her curse of turning invisible when stressed, too emotional or afraid.

All water under the bridge now that she knew her "parents" were not really hers, they were foster parents who never shared the truth of her real origins. Not important now as she had a whole lot of other issues to deal with, starting with a splitting headache, a stomach that roiled and a sense that something bad was around the next corner.

Given Alex Noziak had transported her to the Spirit World, bad was a given.

As she looked around, she was surprised to find herself curled on the hard ground of what looked like a forest glen. Gnarled old trees, maybe live oaks, grass the color of fresh spring and a silence so profound it made her sit up faster than was wise.

She whimpered as she clutched her stomach, willing it to settle.

"Finally," said a voice somewhere behind her. A voice she recognized which eased the tenseness rushing through her.

"Mandy?"

"You expected someone else?"

Mandy was obviously in a snit. Kelly had no idea why, but that didn't really matter. Getting to her feet did. When it looked like she wasn't going to be able to do it on her own she raised her hand. "Help me up."

It was meant to be a request, but came out more as a demand.

Mandy appeared before her, obviously not dealing with a hangover and yanked Kelly upright with a little more force than needed.

Once stabilized, Kelly glanced around, slowly, so she didn't topple back over. "Where's Alex?"

"Not here."

This attitude was going to get old quick. But after years of parent-teacher conferences, and in-fighting in teacher lounges, Kelly had learned the lesson of when and where to pick her battles. This wasn't one of those times.

"Since we're supposed to be together, it'd make sense Alex would be here. Somewhere." She used her best soothe-the-cranky-child voice.

It must have worked, as Mandy rubbed the back of her neck, looking less in-your-face Chicana and more a fellow frustrated IR agent. "I have no idea where she is. While you were. . . anyway I looked around and couldn't find any sign of her. For all I know she never made it. Or was here and took off."

Not likely. Kelly knew Mandy and Alex were oil and water, but Alex was the one who brought them here. She wouldn't just abandon them.

Unless something came up. . .

Alex was a Noziak and Noziaks were all about duty and responsibility. That slammed the image of Van to mind. Van being Van Noziak, Alex's older brother and now Kelly's lover. Or he had been before Kelly agreed to this mission. Sure Van believed in duty and obligation, just not hers.

Shove the thoughts away. She'd promised herself she wouldn't second-guess her decision, or Van's response which wasn't that supportive. Okay, he was downright upset with her. But when she got back, if she got back, they'd work it out.

They had to, as she was beginning to think he might be a little more important to her than she'd told him.

Head back in the game. Where were they and what happened to Alex?

"Maybe she had to go somewhere. Do something." Kelly glanced around again, not expecting to actually see Alex behind one of the trees but appreciating that they could be stranded some place far worse. "This is kind of nice. Someplace I'd like to spend my afterlife."

"No, you don't."

The edge in Mandy's voice had Kelly eyeing her hard. Mandy stepped away, shoulders rigid, her skin pale as she titled her head one way, then another. Usually Mandy was all attitude and cockiness. Probably one of the reasons she butted heads with Alex. Kelly would never tell either woman but they were so much alike, it was no wonder they rubbed each other wrong.

"What's going on?" Kelly asked, very aware of the silence. This place should have bird song, the whisper of a soft breeze through the grass, or the warmth of summer sunlight. But it didn't. Instead it held a waiting expectation, like an empty room in a horror movie.

Mandy turned away. "We've got to leave this place."

Not what Kelly expected. "Without Alex?"

"Alex can take care of herself."

Kelly stepped forward. "We're a team. We don't leave Alex."

"And if she left us?"

Not that Kelly believed it. On the other hand, she could see Alex haring off to save the world on her own. Another Noziak trait. "If she did, I'm sure she had a very good reason."

"How much time do we have to get to Aini?" Mandy asked, pushing Kelly's buttons since she, herself, should have thought about the time element they were up against to save the girl. It was why Kelly was here, being the Guardian of Aini. The only one who could reach her telepathically.

Kelly glanced at her watch. "Thirteen hours and twenty-two minutes."

Mandy shook her head and said something in Spanish under her breath. Not a word Kelly recognized, but she got the message loud and clear.

Time for a compromise. Plus, they were in the Spirit World, or Underworld, though it looked way too pleasant to be that place. "Let's wait for a little bit. See if Alex shows up? Who knows what we'll run into if we go wandering around?"

"Are you crazy? Can't you feel them?" The whites in Mandy's eyes became more pronounced. Scaring Kelly.

"Feel who?" She looked around again. The trees looked not quite so welcoming. The grass less beckoning.

"Trust me on this. We've got to go." Mandy whispered the words, making goose bumps tiptoe up Kelly's arms.

"Go where?" She'd lowered her own voice as if someone, or something, was listening.

Mandy tilted her head again. "What?"

"I asked—"

Mandy raised a hand to silence her, then pivoted in a ninety-degree turn. "This way."

"Wait!" Kelly grabbed at Mandy's arm but the Hispanic woman side-stepped her.

"What part of 'we've got to go' don't you understand?"

"We can't just go racing off in any ol' direction." Kelly widened her stance as she fisted hands on her hips. "You have no idea where we're going."

"We can't stay here," Mandy repeated as if a mantra.

"Because?"

Mandy gave one quick shake of her head and lowered her voice. "They mean us harm. We don't belong."

"Who are 'they'?" Goosebumps tip-toed down Kelly's arms.

It wasn't news that they weren't in Maryland anymore. But she knew that's not what her friend meant. Something was frightening Mandy. Something or someone. Bad. And that didn't happen often.

But if they left, how would Alex find them? And how sure was Mandy about the direction they needed to go when Kelly's whole reason for being here was to use her ability to connect with Aini. A connection that, hopefully, acted as a map to help find her.

Kelly held up a finger to signal a quick timeout. She'd follow Mandy if she had to—the other woman had at least been to this Realm before—but they weren't going anywhere before Kelly started acting like an agent instead of a scaredy-cat.

She stilled herself, closing her eyes and reaching deep inside to the place where she'd heard Aini before. Or Aini's voice. Before the young girl had disappeared.

Aini? Can you hear me?

Nothing.

Please Aini, if you can hear, let me know.

Still nothing.

"We don't have time for you to stand around and meditate." Mandy grabbed her arm and started tugging.

That's when Kelly heard it. Or felt it. Like the whisper of a thousand voices, or the scrape of a snake's scales sliding slowly over rough rock.

"What's that sound mean?" Kelly asked, watching Mandy already moving away.

"Nothing we want to meet," came the cryptic reply.

It wasn't the words as much as the urgency driving them that had Kelly hustling behind her teammate who was picking up her pace.

They'd already lost Alex. Last thing she planned to do was lose Mandy.

CHAPTER 4

Stepping from the brilliant white room, I guess I expected more light. But I was wrong. Instead there was darkness so profound I couldn't see my own hand as I raised it and waved it in front of me, my other hand still clutching Benjamin's small, sweaty one. How was I supposed to follow Ghost Guy if I couldn't see a thing?

I heard a sniffle beside me. I didn't blame Benjamin, I wanted to sniff, too.

Instead I lied. "Don't worry, we'll be fine."

How many times had I said that lately as things went downhill at Mach speed?

But Noziaks didn't buckle at the first speed bump. No, we continued head on until we could find the end of the cliff and then jump off.

Ghost Guy looked like my only way out of this section of the Realm, so following him was my goal. That was a clear, concrete goal. Getting to Yggdrasil was the next goal since that sounded like it'd lead me to Kelly and Mandy. If I reached them, we might be able to save Aini.

One step at a time.

I pushed immediate worries about my teammates to the back of my mind since I already had my hands full. As far as I knew, they might still be back at the IR Compound. My spell casting didn't always work. With my luck, I'd crossed over alone.

Which meant once I dropped Benjamin off at the Yggdrasil place, finding Aini became my solo mission. At least alone meant I wouldn't be taking anyone else down with me.

Sometimes illusions were all that kept us moving forward.

It was so dark that moving was near impossible. I stumbled to a halt, twisting my head, but the door we'd walked through had disappeared. Straining to hear something, anything, I was glad Benjamin didn't utter a sound. Saying warm and fuzzy things was not my style. If Kelly were here, she'd be soothing and making all well with her voice alone.

As it was, the silence vibrated with stillness. Sort of like when you listen to something really loud for so long that when you stop you can still hear the ringing in your ears. The room we'd been in had no sound in it. There had been that drumming, but now even that was more a quiet murmur, as if getting farther away. So what was happening? The only thing I noticed was the sheen of sweat drying on my skin, as if I'd been running, hard. But I hadn't been. I'd been standing frozen in place, trying to decide which direction to move in the darkness.

Maybe it'd be better to go back into the room? Light was less scary than dark, but as I pivoted in a three-hundred and sixty-degree turn there was absolutely no sign of the doorway we'd just passed through.

And this was a better choice than a raging lion or dank catacombs because?

"You lost?" Benjamin asked, his voice a thin waver.

"Nah. Just thinking."

Panicking was more like it but that wasn't going to help.

This was pissing me off. Yeah, common sense said be afraid, be very afraid, but since I'd started at that point, anger seemed an okay next step. Besides, I was still a Noziak and rash, foolhardy, and risky beat standing around having a pity party any day.

"Hey buddy?" I shouted to the ghost, or at least where I thought he might be since I couldn't actually see him. "You suck as a guide!"

I didn't really expect to hear a response, but I did. Not from him, but a different sound. A faint rustling, like paper rubbed against paper.

What now? Move toward the sound or away from it?

"What are you doing here?" a woman's voice demanded out of the darkness. Scared the bejeebees out of me and made me jump. Only Benjamin's small hand growing cold in mine kept me sane.

"Who are you?" I shot back, realizing I'd been asking that question of a lot of different people lately.

"Flee while you still can," she whispered, as if able to sense, or see, something I couldn't.

"Flee where?" I raised my one free hand before me. "I don't know where we are or how to get out of here."

"They will find you."

By the power of the Great Spirits, this was getting old. I wasn't trying to piss off anyone. For once.

"All I want to do is leave here," I said, impressed how calm I was able to keep my voice when that's not how I was feeling at all. "Tell me how to do that and I'll be glad to disappear."

"Follow the blood."

That's all she could give me? Blood in a pitch-dark space? Maybe if I'd been a full shifter like my brothers, I could smell the blood, but I couldn't. Besides, a blood trail didn't sound like a win-win route.

Then I realized I'd either been in the sootiness long enough for my eyes to adjust and start to figure out shapes, or the light was changing. Before, where there was nothing, now there were figures in the distance, moving figures, as if watching a herd of deer far away on a misty morn—more movement than shape. The rustling paper sounded louder.

Fear locked my throat and made every hair on my body stand up. Something told me those things, those shapes, were not the welcoming committee.

I still couldn't make out who'd been talking to me, and still couldn't see Ghost Guy anywhere.

"Are you still there?" I whispered through a tight throat, feeling stupid talking to the nebulous air but it wasn't like anyone I knew could see me. If I did find my guide from Hell, I'd give him a talking to about how he sucked.

"Leave," she hissed the word in my ear, upping the creep factor. A lot.

"Show me." Then I noticed it. Instead of a vague sense of hard-packed ground beneath my boots, I could now see a flat gravel and sand surface. One stretching before me and clearly showing an uneven trail of stained rust that looked long dried. And the smell. A copper-metallic scent with a sickly sweet note to it, which it shouldn't have been, since the blood looked old.

I'd say I'd found the blood.

Now what?

"I'm scared," Benjamin whispered.

"I know, kid. But don't worry." No sense the both of us freaking out, but that was TMI, too much information, for him.

The woman's voice had gone silent. Ghost Guy had evaporated. And that rippling, swishing sound inched closer, as did the shapes that seemed to be creating it. A wall of people. Or something. They were wearing, or covered in, a darker black than the surrounding light, but dabbed with splotches of white.

I rubbed my eyes, trying to figure out what I was looking at. Costumes? I couldn't make out faces, only the chalky patterns that, as they neared, started looking more and more like bones.

A scream dried up in my throat. Those *were* bones. Walking skeletons with the rustle coming from bone rubbing against bone.

That settled it. I'd follow the blood path before facing skeletons.

My Native American ancestors respected spirits because we believed every living, breathing being contained spirit. But that respect didn't extend to death, and animated skeletons screamed death with a capital D. Besides, the path took me away from the bone people, which was a win-win in my book.

"Come on, Benjamin, this way."

He followed without a sound.

Had I ever been that trusting?

CHAPTER 5

I jogged down the blood-streaked path, not going toward something as much as away from something—the skeletons creeping along behind me, my stride short enough to keep Benjamin at my side. Good news? They moved with a stiff lurching gait, which meant with each hard footfall I created space between them and us. Bad news? I still had no idea where I was or how I was supposed to be finding Yggdrasil, which might or might not unite me with my teammates.

"We goin' tha' right way?" Benjamin asked, his words breathless and mirroring my own thoughts.

I slowed down. No need to kill us. Yet. My gut said that possibility was only too real and too imminent. "Yeah, this path will take us where we need to go."

"To Yggdrasil?"

"Yup." So what if the single word sounded a little winded? Give me a break. I was trying.

"Will I see me mum and dad again?"

Damn, why did kids always ask the straight to the heart questions? The ones that plunged a knife into vital organs. I hated to lie, but I'd taken on his welfare and the second I'd done that, I'd made a promise to him. Lying betrayed that promise. The one that said I'd see him get to someplace better.

Instead of answering I copped out, opting for parents' age-old ploy. I changed the subject. "You really want to see your mom and dad?"

"Uh-huh." The two syllables sounded like a single word, it was uttered so quietly. I had to lean down to hear it.

I put a little more backbone into my response. "Then I'll do everything I can to make that happen. I don't know if I can, but I'll try."

Right now that was all I could promise, and it seemed like a huge stretch, as we continued following the trail, the blood not being a great omen.

As we walked, the sounds of our steps echoing around us, I noticed the light and shapes surrounding us morphing. Instead of a vague darkness, walls had begun appearing. That was good. Wasn't it?

Wooden beams stacked upright along each side and overhead to create a tunnel, row upon row, but colored orange etched in red. A tunnel of blood-orange color—like a mineshaft but illuminated by the walls themselves instead of any specific light source. The path looked like gravel, only with blood stains saturating each small, sharp rock. And that smell. It intensified, enough to make me want to wrap my sleeve across my nose. But Benjamin wasn't complaining so how could I? Then again, maybe he couldn't smell what I did.

Was the blood an illusion? Could be, but it sure felt real. As real as the pounding of my heart, even though I'd slowed my pace. My breath chugged in and out. Fear kicking through me as if any minute something horrible was going to jump out at me.

"Wake up, Noziak," I whispered, not too loud lest I woke up something better left undisturbed. Or started Benjamin crying again.

Suddenly we rounded a corner and the path forked. To the left, more of the eerie orange tunnel. To the right, a wooden bridge with mist muting its shape but not its colors, all silvers, blacks, and whites, as if all pigmentation had leeched from the world.

Both paths showed the bloodstains—one in rust, the other softened into charcoal smudges.

What now?

I glanced behind me. No skeletons, but no road signs blasting, 'this way out' either.

Beware.

The voice echoed around me. That familiar woman's voice.

"Mom?" The single word slipped out, making me want to kick myself. As if my mom, who'd abandoned me, and my family, when I was five, would give a rat's backside as to what was happening to me now.

Be very careful.

Okay, this was just getting creepy. Last time I heard this voice, the one that might or might not be my mom's, was in the middle of fighting a Snobble troll. Or was it a Were tiger? Didn't matter, the result was the same: I accessed a freaky-ass ability I had to amplify others' preternatural abilities. An ability that screwed me every time I used it. Which wasn't often for that very reason.

Alex. Don't—

I released Benjamin's fist to jam both my hands over my ears. Immature? Yeah. But better than losing my sanity. So why did I feel like my five-year-old self, hiding behind the barn, whispering promises to the sunburnt wood. *I'll be good. I'll eat all my peas. I'll never, ever, ever fight with my brothers. Just please, please, please come back.*

But she never did.

That was the summer I stopped believing in happy ever afters, fairy tales with good endings, and magic. Which was why accessing my magic was so iffy now. I also stopped believing in a mother's love. Now was not the time to start.

By the time I lowered my hands the voice had faded.

Finally, something working for me.

"Your mum here?" Benjamin whispered, swiveling his head right and left as if looking for the source of my reaction.

"No," I replied, feeling very, very lost and alone. "She left me a long time ago."

Time to refocus on business. Getting us somewhere.

Eenie, meenie, miney, mo. . . did it make a difference? Fine. . . right it was. At least the gray misty route was something new and maybe my skin would quit crawling if we left the red-orange tunnel. As long as the bridge wasn't too high—I hated heights.

"Come on Benjamin." I snagged his hand again. "Let's get out of here."

He didn't hesitate to hold on to me.

It took about twenty steps to realize that new was not necessarily better. We'd crossed from gravel to a wooden walkway, so it was a bridge. Each measured tread across the weathered planking echoed in my ears. I couldn't tell if we were a few inches above a murky swamp or hundreds of feet above a sheer drop. A hovering mist blurred the world beyond the railings and soon thickened, driving a fear that grew thicker and thicker in me.

"Ghost Guy?" I'd whisper now and then, just to see if he might be playing blind man's bluff with me.

He wasn't.

"We all alone?" Benjamin's voice wavered.

"Looks like it, kid."

Just when I decided I'd had enough of eerie, scary vapor I realized my steps were becoming slower, as if I'd used up every ounce of energy in my body. And my head started burning. The hot stick in a fire kind of burning.

What now?

I stumbled, caught up against the wooden rail of the bridge and hung on.

"You sick, lady?" Benjamin asked, his hand still hidden in mine.

"Don't know." The words sounded slurred even to me as I slid from a standing position to a half-crouch, almost eye-to-eye with Benjamin now. "Gotta take a breather." I offered what I hoped was a smile and not a grimace.

"Lady?" he cried out, but the word sounded so far away.

Just a minute. One minute to close my eyes. To stop everything twirling around me.

"Don't go—"

Too late. I felt my head hit the wooden planking then everything went dark.

CHAPTER 6

"You sure you know where we're going?" Kelly asked Mandy, working at keeping the fear out of her voice.

The green grove lay far behind them. They'd been walking for what felt like days, instead of an hour. A precious hour they couldn't afford to lose—not with Aini in danger and no idea what was happening to her.

Aini?

Still no answer. Kelly kept trying, throwing out her soundless cry like an ocean-going boat emitting echo sonar. If Aini answered, they'd have a better handle on which direction to head. If she didn't? Kelly elbowed that thought away. It wouldn't help her keep going, and she needed all the help she could muster right then.

The one positive something that Alex had explained before they set off on this mission, was that, in this Realm, they wouldn't be hungry or thirsty. Since their bodies didn't need sustenance they didn't have to worry about those pesky details. Which was a nice thing to know because nothing else seemed to be going their way.

The path they'd taken had quickly morphed from nice and meandering to an uphill slant, just enough to have them breathing heavier and eliminate chit-chat because it took too much energy. Now the route was more mountain goat climb than path. Kelly couldn't see that far ahead with thick, acrid smoke blanketing the area in front of and behind them. As if somewhere fires burned, not bright and cheery but smoldering, creating deep, swirling whorls of gray, and darkness. She rubbed her arms. Not that it was cold, far from it. The place

gave her the creeps and the more they climbed into the
unknown, the worse it became.

When Mandy didn't answer Kelly's question about where
they were headed, Kelly stopped, forcing Mandy to halt or
leave her behind, something Mandy wouldn't hesitate to do.

"This can't be right." Kelly leaned over to brace her hands
on her thighs. Maybe if she tried a subtle approach, Mandy
would slow down and not take affront.

Mandy jerked to a halt, glancing over her shoulder. "And
you know this because?"

In some ways Mandy was right. Kelly hadn't ever been here
before, and wouldn't again if she had her druthers, but
following Mandy blindly without knowing why she was
heading in the direction she went, meant they ate up precious
time. Besides, Kelly had dutifully attended Sunday School
classes every week and had learned a few things.

"If this. . ." She glanced around, unsure if she should even
speak *that* name here, so she decided to err on the side of
caution. "If *you know who* is supposed to be so ancient and
powerful, wouldn't he be hanging out some place with—" She
waved her hand before her to indicate what she was and *wasn't*
seeing.

"With what?"

"More people, souls, whatever." Sure it was a nebulous
impression, but her gut told her something was wrong, other
than the fact they were here, without Alex, and lost. "We don't
have that much time to play tourist in no man's land." She
wished she sounded surer, and less breathless, though if Mandy
thought she wasn't being directly attacked, she might actually
listen.

Mandy eyed the grayness in front of them, slowly shaking
her head. For a moment Kelly thought she'd forgotten her
when Mandy mumbled, "You sure?"

Was Mandy talking to her? Progress, even if the question
made no sense. "No, not a hundred percent, but climbing the
smoky mountain here doesn't sound anything like where the
arrogant being, whose name I won't mention and who attacked
us last night at the compound, would reside."

Mandy turned back to Kelly, deep groves dug between her eyes, as if suddenly seeing her. "What are you talking about?"

"We're lost. I think we should try a different route, and you asked if I was sure." Yes, Kelly spoke as if addressing a confused child, but there was something off here. What, she couldn't quite pinpoint, but Mandy wasn't acting like her assured, go-for-broke self. "You okay?"

"Of course I'm okay," Mandy snapped back, clenching her jaw and sounding like she was chewing glass. "If you're so sure you're right and I'm wrong, you lead."

Great. Now she'd pissed her off, which wasn't Kelly's intention. "We're supposed to be teammates." She put a little stiffness in her own spine, as she looked behind her. "Not too far back we passed what looked like a tangent route."

"A what?"

"A path that cut off from this one."

"Then why didn't you say so?" Mandy jammed a hand through her thick black hair, reminding Kelly for a second of Van, when he was really, really frustrated with her. Which was a lot.

Time to slam the door on those thoughts again: they weren't getting her anywhere.

"Why are you sure that path is better than this one?" Mandy challenged.

Wrong approach. Kelly might come across as meek and mild but she wasn't stupid. Nor did she appreciate being treated like the ugly, red-haired stepchild. "Didn't any one ever tell you heaven is up and the bad place is down?"

That stopped Mandy cold, then she started laughing. Not a happy sound, but more like a cross between a groan and desperation. "You serious?" she asked at last. "You do know there's absolutely no basis in fact to your up or down theory. That the sunlit sky above probably was a whole lot more appealing than a deep, dark cavern and that's all?"

"Yeah, I know that." Or her adult self did. The scared child inside of her wasn't so sure. "Point is, I think we need to reconsider our route."

"You mean lose time backtracking."

"It's not that far." A lesson Van, and Alex, had eventually learned about Kelly was that she could be determined, stubborn even, when she knew she was right. And this was one of those times.

Mandy seemed to be debating with herself, cocking her head in that way that looked as if she was listening to something Kelly couldn't hear. At last she shrugged and said, "Fine, we'll do it your way. For now."

Kelly released a breath she hadn't realized she'd been holding, already turning to scramble back down the hillside. "Thanks."

"Not a problem," came from behind her. "As long as you know, if you're wrong, not only does Aini die for good, but we do, too."

CHAPTER 7

Traversing down wasn't any easier than climbing uphill. The ground became slippery, though there wasn't any sign of rain or moisture. And the smoke had become denser, until Kelly found herself crossing her arm over her nose and breathing with her mouth. Until she started coughing.

"According to your Heaven and Hell theory, I'd say heading downward is bringing us closer to a version of Hell—the smoke and brimstone one," Mandy croaked between her own hoarse hacking.

"Not helping."

"We keep going this way, we'll die of asphyxiation."

And going back the way they'd just left? No telling if the smoke was now as bad there. But standing still wasn't getting them anywhere either.

Kelly started to wave one hand, pointing back up the hill because talking was too difficult, when she spied a swirl of cobalt blue through the denser gray smoke.

She stepped toward Mandy, brushing shoulders as she pointed toward the change in air color.

Bless her, Mandy didn't turn tail and run, though it might have been tempting, but instead eased in front of Kelly, accepting her role as bodyguard on this mission. Not that Kelly was okay with her move. Not until they knew what the blue swirls meant.

A tense few seconds later, they saw a woman step from the blue.

Tall, taller than Kelly's five-six height, the woman was stunningly beautiful, though in a way that Iowa-born and raised

Kelly had never seen before. The stranger was naked but didn't look unclothed as her whole body was tattooed in one continuous pattern, sometimes showing pale white skin, other places the ink so dense it acted like a second skin. With each step she took, the tattoos undulated in a curving sensuous motion. A sexual and eerie movement all at once.

"Stop right there," Mandy managed to say, though it might have sounded more threatening if she hadn't ended in a fit of coughing.

Kelly adjusted her stance so she was now clearly shoulder-to-shoulder with her teammate. They were both still vulnerable, but sometimes showing a united front helped back down a threat. A playground lesson Kelly learned only after she'd become a teacher.

"We mean you no harm," she said, spacing each word between short breaths.

"You do not belong here." The woman's voice sounded as exotically liquid as her appearance, but at least she'd paused. Her body language wasn't telegraphing aggression, or Kelly hoped it wasn't since she kept glancing at the strange woman then looking away. She wasn't sure that she should be gawking given the whole no clothes thing. Being raised by strict fundamentalist parents never prepared her for this kind of situation.

Suddenly she found a small smile deep inside. She was in the Underworld for Pete's sake, seeking a kidnapped teen. There was nothing normal about any of this.

"Go back the way you came." The woman didn't seem impacted by the smoke, which wasn't fair at all—looking beautiful, in control and able to inhale without scouring her lungs—the woman had it all.

Kelly found herself shaking her head. "Not sure. . . *cough.* . . we can." She offered a weighted shrug before adding. "Can't breathe enough. . . *cough.* . . to. . ."

The woman raised one hand above her head like a ballet dancer, the motion looking as if her arm weighed nothing at all.

What was more important, the smoke whirled, tornado style, and then in an echoing explosion of blue, it disappeared.

Just like that.

It should have been an improvement but what Kelly saw behind the woman wasn't.

A stone pathway replaced the slick mud path she and Mandy stood on. White sandstone, or maybe marble of a great age, created slanting walls on either side of the path, stepping back in space through a series of metallic wrought arches. Ornate, complicated arches ending in a gateway wide enough to allow entry for one person at a time.

It sure wasn't like the gate to Kelly's backyard in Dubuque. This one resembled an interwoven design, like tatting, with all spokes appearing ethereal and restrictive at the same time. It also looked like. . .

"What the h—" Mandy whispered.

"Don't say it," Kelly broke in.

"It's a freakin' spider web."

Kelly really, really wished Mandy would take the words back, because once said, they lingered and grew until there was no denying that the entrance was exactly that. A trap.

Clearing her throat, Kelly placed one hand on Mandy's arm and slowly, so as not to arouse too much attention, edged backwards.

"Thank you," she said, to the Painted Lady, remembering her manners even as she knew her forced smile wobbled around the edges. "Now that we can breathe, and see, we'll be going."

The woman barely twitched her lips, but it wasn't in a smart-move smile. No, it looked as sinister as that gate. One that might have been exquisite and beautiful, but also very, very dangerous.

"You must come with me now," she murmured, her voice offering no alternatives.

Except there were two of them.

"Count of three," Mandy whispered, obviously on the same wavelength as Kelly. Yikes, she didn't know if Mandy meant run or fight.

"One."

"Go or stay?"

"Two."

Kelly's muscles locked. Attack the woman or high-tail it away? If she did the opposite of Mandy, they'd both lose.

"Thre—"

The word died in Mandy's throat as a phalanx of warriors materialized behind Kelly and Mandy, cutting off any hope of retreat. And like the Greek word that created the term, these soldiers bore arms—pikes, spears, lances—all leveled at them.

"Kels?" Mandy's voice sounded shaky. Which meant Kelly wasn't alone as a tsunami of fear swept over her.

"Yeah?"

"What now?"

The lady's creepy smile ratcheted up. "This way." Her sweeping gesture pointed toward the spider web gate.

"We move forward," Kelly said, her first step feeling more like a hard, jerking robot walk.

Before she went any further she cast out a silent call. *Aini?*

Still nothing.

CHAPTER 8

Surging up from darkness, I found my face pressed against weathered boards, someone shaking my shoulder.

"Wake up, lady. Please wake up."

Who? I groaned, feeling like the first time my brothers introduced me to orange juice and vodka. They thought it was hilarious as I loved orange juice and had no problem guzzling what they were giving me, sure the stories I'd heard about drinking liquor were all overrated. Until I stood up. Made it to the barn door where I emptied my stomach several times, then staggered to the house, each step an effort as the world spun and twisted around me.

Yup, just like that again.

I propped myself up on one elbow, but could only see swirling mist and darkness. That and a pair of very young eyes clouded with concern staring at me from a distance of about six inches.

"What happened?" I croaked.

All I got in response was a widening of Benjamin's eyes. Guess that meant two of us were clueless.

So I tried an easier question. "Where are we?"

"Goin' to Yggdrasil. You promised." He flung the last words like a vow betrayed and that helped stiffen my backbone enough for me to crawl to my knees. It was coming back to me. Benjamin. A white room. Wraiths. Missing Kelly and Mandy and Aini. Waiting. Somewhere ahead.

Maybe.

"Don't worry, kiddo," I slurred, staggering to my feet, very glad the bridge rail was there to steady me. "We'll get to your Yggdrasil."

"You promised," he repeated, the last word high and wobbly.

I patted his shoulder because it was the only thing I could think to do. The lethargy eased but not the memory of it, or the lingering shakes it left in its wake. Like a cowboy on the last day of a rodeo, I needed every ounce of focus to move step by step forward.

I had no idea what had hit me but man, it packed a wallop. I didn't know what brought it on or if it'd happen again, which was a whole new worry to juggle. What if I'd slid off the bridge? Or left Benjamin all alone out here?

Enough. Deal with the here and now. That's all I could do.

"Yggdrasil this way?" I asked out loud, before I caught myself. Benjamin expected me to know that. So I cleared my throat and tried again. "That's right. Straight ahead. Yggdrasil isn't far."

It couldn't be or I'd never make it. And if I didn't make it, what would happen to Benjamin who kept glancing up at me as if waiting for me to betray him. A killer look it was, too.

We kept shuffling forward, the mist wrapping around us like cold silk, giving me the shivers. At least I tried to blame the setting for the shaking gripping my muscles and not the tightening in my stomach that screamed we were lost and alone. So very alone.

Then I heard it. A sound. A young voice muttering, "I hate 'im. Hate 'im. Hate 'im."

Just ahead.

I pulled up, hesitant to move forward, not willing to turn tail and run. Not yet. Because the words held the gut-wrenching note of disappointment, and not just any disappointment, but a small child's heart breaking.

What was this place? The Realm of mourning children?

On the other hand, a voice meant we weren't alone.

Unless it meant a trick, a ploy to make me go closer?

Releasing the tenseness riding my shoulders with a steel grip, I strained to see into the mist. Nothing. Not a hint.

Suck it up, Noziak. Only sissies and wussies back down when the going gets tough.

But only fools jump in without an exit plan.

A quick glance behind me created my plan. If the voice wasn't a child in distress then I'd have us high-tail it the way we came. If we ran into the skeletons, then. . . well, I'd deal with them if that happened.

"Shhh." I used my index finger against my lips as I leaned toward Benjamin, who was all eyes staring up at me. "Stay here. I'll be right back."

"No!" he grabbed my shirt with a death-grip.

Great. Nothing like risking a child on the chance another child needed help. But what choice did I have?

There was that damn word again. Enough with the sucky choices.

"Come on, then." I peeled his fingers from my clothes and held the hand tight. For his sake, of course, though touching another helped me, too. "Just stay behind me. Okay?"

He nodded. I took it that he'd heard and would obey. What an innocent optimist.

Inching forward, I felt like a long-necked heron scenting trouble. Which is just what I expected to find.

With each step, the child's voice sounded louder and more intense. "Hate. Hate. Never listens."

I licked my lips and managed a weak croak. "Anybody there?"

The voice stopped. Cut off completely.

Which didn't make me feel a whole lot better.

"I'm not going to hurt you," I whispered louder, hoping who, or what, was ahead got the message—the whole I-won't-hurt-you-so-don't-hurt-me bulletin.

Must have, as there was a sudden scrabble, the sound of someone clamoring to their feet, then small footfalls receding.

The kid had run away.

No way was I going to give chase. That would take foolhardy to a new level. At the same time I sure hoped this was good news. If he could run away, it meant there was something beyond where we were. For a while I was beginning to have my doubts.

What now?

"Onward and upward," I murmured, quoting one of my favorite kid books. If the phrase worked in Narnia, it should work here. Right?

Benjamin released my hand but followed me so closely he kept bumping into me. Which was okay. I'd prefer that to leaving him behind, lost in the fog.

Just as I began to breathe again, a small shape materialized out of the mist right in front of me. A small human, painted all in green with smears of red splotched across his body. The child, because he couldn't have been older than eight or nine, wore a raffia skirt and waved a very long, and very sharp spear. The huge whites of his eyes gleamed from his green painted face, showing as much fear as rushed through me.

Where the heck were we? In a Halloween nightmare?

"Who you be?" he shouted. I guessed he was a "he" by the rasp of his voice.

I jerked to a halt and eyed that spear. "Name's Alex. Who're you?"

The only answer I received was a few jabs of the spear in our direction. Not an attack but more a feint. I figured if push came to shove I could subdue a kid. Noziaks didn't hurt children. Not in a million years, but we did protect those who needed protecting—which meant Benjamin.

"Okay." I stepped forward to splay my hands before me. Universal symbol of no harm, no foul. Right? But green kid here didn't seem to have gotten the memo. "I won't hurt you." Well, unless he attacked me or tried to hurt Benjamin. "Can you tell me where we are?"

"Narkara," came the one word reply, which sounded much like an oath.

I was hoping for more than a name. But as long as I was talking to the kid he wouldn't be killing me. More wishful thinking?

Plus I knew we weren't in Yggdrasil yet if this was Narkara.

I cleared my throat, not too loudly as the spear was still too close, and too sharp, for comfort. "We're trying to go to Yggdrasil. Is this the way?"

No response.

A different tactic maybe.

"Can you tell me a little more about Nakara? Like how you got here?" And how to get out of here?

Patience, Noziak. Baby steps.

"Yama put us here." I heard the implied word "idiot" but ignored it.

"And Yama is?"

The spear thrust up. It didn't exactly jab at me but was getting awfully close. "Lord of Justice. Yama be praised."

Okay. Still not too clear, but maybe I was closer, plus he was speaking in English so I could understand him, even if the details were fuzzy. Raising my hands a little higher I wrapped a strained smile on my face before asking, "Any idea how to get out of here? To Yggdrasil?"

I drew an imaginary house with two fingers, not having a clue what Yggdrasil was, but something had to be better than nothing, plus Benjamin seemed to associate the place with home so that worked for me.

This time the spear did jab me as the green kid jerked forward. Poked into my arm like testing for doneness.

"Ouch!" I wanted to shout more than that, but he was still a child. That and I didn't want to panic Benjamin, wrapped behind me so tight the green kid probably couldn't see that there were two of us.

"Look, I'm not the enemy. I just want to leave here. If you can help, great, if not, I'll just be on my way."

He released a cry that made my blood chill and suddenly several more shapes appeared behind him. All green with that red paint drip look, bald-headed and shirtless. Only they looked older, bigger and a lot more badass.

Great. I was heading to Hell and ran into a green punk gang. Why wasn't I surprised?

"Hey guys. No problems." I nodded, stepping backwards and scooting Benjamin further away from the threat with the move. "Just talking here." Their expressions said it all: they weren't buying my words or my tone. Before I could turn and skedaddle back the way we'd come, another sharp stab between my shoulder blades had me wheeling around. Behind me another cluster of green and red guys huddled, a few smaller ones in front, larger ones to the back, all waving those spears as if they'd like nothing better than to shish-kebab us.

Where had they come from? And what had I done to any of them?

One aimed at Benjamin as I squeezed him between the bridge rail and my body, my gaze hopscotching between the two groups on either side of us.

Logically I knew now wasn't the time for getting pissed off, no matter how tempting, but they weren't going to hurt Benjamin. Not without blood being spilled, preferably theirs.

I squished the two of us tight against the wooden rails, one with squared off sides that added more bruises to my back, as I weighed our options, which were between nil and zilch.

I was happy my voice didn't shake. . . much. "I have no reason to fight you. So if you let us go back the way we came, we can all be friends."

All right, maybe not best friends forever, but this was as close a win-win as I could think of with all the spit in my mouth dried up and the mist chilling my skin. They murmured among themselves, arguing I'd say, as the tones became shriller and more strident. This time I couldn't make out the words.

I cast a quick glance behind me to see if jumping was an option. It wasn't. As if I'd asked for more trouble, the fog cleared enough to reveal that the bridge wasn't above a swamp, or a drop of a few hundred feet. It was a sheer thousand plus foot plunge into a ravine so far beneath me, it made my head spin.

Plan C—escape over the side—just disappeared.

What about magic? I was supposed to be some all-powerful witch right? Actually I wasn't. I was more of the hit-or-miss variety witch, but there was no time like the present to try one of the simpler spells. A containment or freeze spell. Nothing to harm anyone, but something to allow us to get around the two groups edging closer.

I stilled myself—as much as I could facing not-so-happy green guys with spears, and reached for any ley lines nearby to feed into my magic.

But there weren't any. Not so much as a small ping of energy. Probably because we were suspended in space.

I'd do this the old-fashioned way. Spell casting. Harder with no herbs, salt, or runes drawn about me, no time to enact a ritual to help center me and the spell, but something told me these spear-happy dudes weren't going to give me enough space to work efficiently.

Breathing in a deep breath, I left my eyes open. I had no weapons on my body to negate the spell so this might work.

"Air to wind, earth to dust.
By water and by fire.
Trouble to heed and trouble to find.
Compel. Coerce. Constrain.
I thee call. I thee command.
Threat be gone. Power be bound."

Nada.

A good gob of spit as a weapon would have been more effective. Where were we that magic didn't work? And what was I going to do now?

No way did I want to risk hurting Benjamin by fighting my way off the bridge. No way.

CHAPTER 9

So much for magic. Last time I even considered myself a passable witch. What was it with magic that every time I tried to use the stuff it either backfired big time or left me standing in a tight spot with nothing happening?

A body blow slammed against me from the left. One of the bigger guys had made his move as I splatted against the rough planking of the bridge floor. At least Benjamin wasn't hurt. Yet.

"What the Sam h—" I shouted, still hoping for a win-win scenario. Given how close my face was to the edge of the bridge, and the drop over the side, anything involving me not going over was a good option.

Several of the mid-sized green guys grabbed my legs and started pushing.

Toward the open bottom gap in the handrail.

I scrambled for a finger hold. Nothing but splinters.

So I twisted and rolled, taking them by surprise. Especially when I kicked out. Hitting shins, knees, anything I could reach while raising myself on my arms and bracing my back. "Run, Benjamin," I shouted, but heard no movement. Poor kid was probably frozen with fear.

I could relate.

One of the green guys I was pummeling with my feet doubled over, grabbing his crotch.

Good. Growing up with brothers was paying off.

But the bridge was only so wide. And there were a heck of a lot more of them than there were of us. More than I could take. Why the others hadn't moved yet wasn't clear.

Voices started shouting. The kind of low-rumble increasing in volume, like a Saturday night bar brawl that lasted long after closing time.

Not looking good.

I offered the closest green kid a weak-ass grin. "Can we talk this over?"

"He doesn't understand what you want," came a deep baritone voice from somewhere near the back of the crowd on the right. "But I do."

Saved?

Not the way things had been going since I woke up in this crazy Realm. But the voices lowered by a notch—less let's-kill-her-now to a more we-still-want-to-kill-her-why-can't-we volume.

A tall man stepped forward and when I say tall, I mean basketball height tall. The Knicks would snatch him up in a heartbeat. He also wasn't slathered in green paint. No, this guy was coated in red, dark rich red with black dots smeared beneath his eyes, a funky triangular hat covering his head, and a trio of feathered arrows skewered through his lips.

Ouch.

I swallowed, but since he was the first one to step forward with anything except outright hostility, who was I to squirm? With a quick look at the others still clustered around, spears aimed at me, I gave my best let's-be-pals smile at Red Guy.

"I don't mean any harm," I said, glad to hear that my voice didn't rattle even as my insides felt like they were ready for a rhumba contest. I shifted to a sitting stance. Still vulnerable, but it braced more of my back against the handrails. I pulled Benjamin next to me to make him less a target.

"Why are you here?" Red Guy demanded. No idea why I could understand some of these creatures and not others but I'd take my wins where I could get them.

"I got lost." I realized the stark truth behind my words the moment I uttered them. I was lost, and had been for a while. Going on a suicide mission was just one more manifestation of what I'd been stumbling through for some time. Coerced into joining the Agency. Fighting Weres, djinns and power-thirsty druids bent on world domination until I'd lost track of where one battle had ended and another began. Yeah, *lost* pretty well summed up the last few weeks.

Not that this was the time for a pity party.

Red Guy lowered his head as if sniffing my words. Or me. "Where are you going?"

What was it with the deceptively simple sounding questions? The ones that I had no answers for?

Instead of responding directly, I scrambled to my feet, taking advantage of the lull in their trying to kill me and grabbed on to what I'd been saying since I'd woken up in that white room. "I'm trying to get out of here. Taking this child to Yggdrasil. Looking for two friends lost in this Realm, who don't belong here either."

Not sure the last information was needed, but maybe if Red Guy thought I had back up he might take pity on Benjamin. I didn't expect the same favor for me.

"Here?" he asked. "You wish to leave here?"

Of course he would focus on that one word.

I shrugged then stilled as the sudden movement had caused the littlest green kid near me to jump back.

"Here," I repeated in the solid, solemn tones of an evangelical preacher. Not that I'd ever heard one in person but I watched them on TV. "This place." I fanned my fingers to indicate the space around us instead of using my whole hands. "I want to find my friends."

I was bone-tired, drained from the last give-it-your-all fight, with only a few hours before being thrust into another no-win assignment—this one.

I didn't want to go to this Yggdrasil, wherever that was, even as I wanted my teammates. A momentary lull in the fighting. Bran. A few more smiles and a lot less bruises.

Talk about an ostrich-in-the-sand illusion.

"No one leaves here. Not without my say."

That was a splash of ice-cold water in the face.

Red Guy just laughed at my expression that clearly wasn't my best poker face. A rolling echo, like a football stand roaring in the distance, until it was abruptly cut off and he pointed a very long, very red finger toward me. "We are in Narkara. This is *all* there is that matters."

That made me scuttle back against the railing until it bit into my spine, again. There was no place to go. But I had to start somewhere.

"What about Yggdrasil? We were told to go there." I glanced at Benjamin, at the turmoil in his eyes.

The green guys around me, brows furrowed and faces pinched, started murmuring. I took that as a good sign. I hated being the only one confused. Plus as long as they were kept occupied, they might forget to kill us. The only one who didn't look lost was Red Guy.

Please, let that be good news.

After a very strained pause came giant Red Guy's reply. "Follow me then."

He had that whole say-nothing-while-talking thing down.

Everyone else seemed to understand the reasoning behind the command, because that's what it was. En masse, the greens pivoted and shuffled off in the direction the red man pointed.

Maybe this was just a really, really weird nightmare and any second I'd wake up. Or maybe he'd just given us permission to continue our journey. Wouldn't that be a nice change?

In the meantime, it wasn't like I had a lot of choice in what to do. Remain where I was? Or move with the group? If we migrated away from this blasted bridge, maybe we could escape.

I shook out the tension in my shoulders, aware of a few more bumps and bruises, but nothing that would keep me from walking. Fighting, yes, but movement I could do. With a ragged grunt, I tucked Benjamin up beside me, wrapping one hand around his shoulder to show him I wasn't abandoning him though that might be what he wanted right then. So far my choices had just made things worse for the both of us.

"After you." I gave a shallow wave to the basketball dude who replied with a con-artist's wide smile. No words. No explanations. No "good-decision" remark.

He just turned and started walking which, given the length of his legs, meant I had to double-time for us to keep up. But I did.

I hoped it wasn't the last bad decision in a long line of iffy ones I'd made lately.

CHAPTER 10

Kelly and Mandy were in a great room, a very large, very grand, very cold room, filled with elongated statues wearing armor from centuries ago. Assyrian maybe, or even further back in time. Kelly wracked her brain to remember the quote she'd used on a college history paper.

'I am powerful, I am all-powerful .... I am without equal among all kings.'

That was it. King Esarhaddon. And Professor Tintian didn't think she had a head for dates and names. Take that Tintian!

What she wouldn't give to be back at the U of I right this minute.

"There." The gorgeous Painted Lady gestured to a flat marble bench to the right side of the room. Not up against a wall where they could cower out of sight but close enough that anyone in or out of the hall could see them clearly.

The squad of soldiers marched in behind them, making no sound, which was much, much scarier than if they jingled and jangled. As it was, Kelly's nerves were about to snap and she bet Mandy felt the same way.

The two of them edged toward the seat, looking around to see who, or what, would pop out of the woodwork next. Not that there was any wood to be seen. Everything in this room was harsh, sterile and cold. She couldn't spy any lighting, but there didn't seem to be a need for it as her eyes ached with the strain of so much luminosity, as if light bounced off the marble walls while being swallowed by the blue-black shadows.

"Where are we?" she mumbled to Mandy, sitting close enough that their shoulders touched. A small measure of solidarity.

"No idea." Mandy didn't seem inclined to say anything else, but surprised Kelly when she added, "You reach Aini yet?"

"No." They were batting zero for two. Plus they were running out of time. Kelly pointed to her watch, a newer model than the one she'd had since high school. That one she'd lost to some desperate foot soldiers in Africa weeks ago. At least those warriors made noise and were alive. These?

Mandy glanced at Kelly's wrist and gave a raised-brow look followed by a shrug. Not anything either of them could do right this minute.

"How much time?" Mandy mouthed.

Kelly held up nine fingers to indicate nine hours to find and save Aini, then closed her eyes for a second, wishing Alex was around. She wouldn't sit still, twiddling her thumbs, waiting to be interrogated or acknowledged. Or saved.

But thinking of Alex made her think of Van. He'd been right that Kelly's haring off to the Underworld was a bad idea. A fool's wish to make a difference. Fat lot of good she was doing here, waiting for a catastrophe to happen while Aini was in mortal danger. Aini and possibly Alex, too.

Popping to her feet as if goosed, she surprised both Mandy and the Painted Lady, but doing nothing wasn't helping.

"Excuse me," she said in her best teacher-to-new-school-administrator voice. "I'm afraid we have some urgent business to attend to and would really like to be on our way."

Mandy groaned beside her as the Painted Lady cast a lethargic glance at the two of them but said nothing.

Kelly stepped forward, equal parts determination and desperation driving her. "We're not simply tourists passing through."

Mandy lowered her head as if to separate herself from Kelly. But what's the worst that could happen? The lady could say no and they'd be right back to where they were.

"We have to find someone. A very bad man." At least she thought at one time he might have been a man. "And if we can't find him, and stop him, a young girl will die before her time."

No point mentioning all the others who would die if the Horned One succeeded in using Aini. The Painted Lady didn't look like she'd care about a few more hundreds of thousands, or millions, no longer breathing.

Unless they'd create a traffic jam in this place?

Kelly wanted to kick herself with that last thought. Obviously the strain was getting to her.

"Who is this one you seek?" the Painted Lady asked, not as if she really cared, but more as if bored and looking for a distraction.

Kelly glanced at Mandy. Should she go for broke and tell? Or was uttering *his* name going to bring a whole lot more hurt down on them?

Mandy was shaking her head, the whites of her eyes showing, her lips a thin line.

That would be a no then.

But what *would* Alex do?

Probably tackle the Painted Lady then try to take out as many soldiers as possible.

A better question was what should Kelly do? After all she was supposed to be Aini's Guardian—chosen to protect this Seer who was also a girl with a whole life ahead of her. But only if Kelly could find and save her.

Raising her chin and squaring her shoulders, Kelly looked directly at the Painted Lady, whose eyes were as black as her skin swirls.

"We're looking for one called the Horned One," she said, hearing each word drop like ice upon the marble floors, shattering the silence.

A second ago Kelly could have sworn she and Mandy were the only two living things in this room. Now? She wasn't so sure.

It was as if a huge, collective breath had been inhaled and held.

The room was so still that when the Painted Lady spoke at last, Kelly flinched.

"You speak of Dryghtyn?" It was said in the same tone Kelly's mother had used when discussing the divorcee who'd moved in next door when Kelly was seven and Kelly had shared that she'd talked to the new lady. Disgust. Repulsion. Wariness.

The last emotion strongest of all.

Kelly wracked her brain to remember what Alex had said about the other names of the Horned One. Or was it the Librarian, the all-knowing font of knowledge, who sold what she knew for a price to the highest bidder.

"I think Dryghtyn's one of his names," she said at last. "But I can't be sure."

Talk about a political non-answer. Plus there was that whole piece about a Clavis of Dryghtyn, which Kelly was supposed to be, or so she was told. Since she had no idea what it meant to be a Clavis of anything, she'd chosen to ignore the title awarded her, hoping it would not come back to bite her, hard, on her backside.

Mandy stood up beside her. Kelly didn't know if that was a good sign or not. Either her teammate had decided to support Kelly or planned to use her as a shield should the Painted Lady hurl a thunderbolt at them.

As a palpable presence stretched between them, Kelly decided to take another page from Alex's playbook: once committed, there's no backing down.

"If you can tell us where this creature is? This one called Dryghtyn," Kelly pronounced it like dry-tun, just like the woman had. "If you can point us in the correct direction, we'll leave and you can be done with us."

That sounded fair.

Didn't it?

Or maybe not?

The Painted Lady reared back as if slapped and released an unearthly howl, a scream that started low and ended on a sound that had both Kelly and Mandy backing up until they almost toppled over the bench.

"Should we run?" Kelly murmured out loud, wondering what she'd unleashed.

"Where?"

Good point.

Kelly gave a quick corner-of-her-eye glance at the soldiers, who might or might not have corporeal bodies but their weapons, all too real, warned her they were the biggest threat. The biggest known threat.

Mandy suddenly grabbed her arm. "This way," she cried, scampering around the bench and heading to the furthest corner with Kelly in tow.

"Where—"

"Run!"

Kelly got it. No time for talk.

Their shoes rang on the floor as the Painted Lady shouted something in a language Kelly didn't recognize. Guttural and harsh. Or maybe it was the echo of her heart thudding against her chest, clawing to get out.

Mandy seemed to know where she was going though as she skidded to a half-stop before she demanded, "Where to?"

Like Kelly would know?

"I need more," Mandy continued, as if talking to someone.

Kelly glanced over her shoulder. Their hostess was no longer standing still. With her arms raised and her face a mask of fury, she marched toward them, her warriors right behind her.

"They're coming."

"I'm trying," Mandy bit off as she pressed her palms against the wall, patting it down.

What was she doing? And why?

Kelly turned her back to Mandy, falling back on her IR training because they didn't have anything else.

She stepped forward on her non-dominant leg, balancing her weight and tucking her chin as she raised her hands high enough to protect her head and neck. Attack or defend, either way she was ready.

Missy, Miss? You there?

Aini?

Talk about rotten timing. But that must mean they were close. Or close enough. And it meant Aini was still alive. Hallelujah!

I'm here, Aini.

Need you.

Coming, sweetheart. As fast as I can.

"Mandy?"

"I'm try—" A growl, then a curse. "Here? Why didn't you—"

Kelly glanced over her shoulder, expecting to see someone with Mandy. But no one was there.

Including Mandy.

CHAPTER 11

Eventually the mist disappeared and I could clearly see that the bridge was higher than I'd realized up to this point. It hovered over a chasm that made the Grand Canyon look like a bike jump. There were no supports below and the thin trickle I could spy, that might be a river, was so far away as to be almost invisible. And no suspension cables above. Man, would the bridge engineers back home in Idaho want a look at this.

Have I mentioned that when I get scared I focus on the stupid details? Easier to deal with than certain death or disaster. And I'd had a lot of practice with both recently.

But the fact this bridge was straight out of my worst-places-to-be list also kept me focused on where I was and how easy it'd be to topple over the side.

On and on we walked. No one talking. Not even when I asked questions. Especially when I asked questions. Sure I earned a few grumbles, but after a while I saved the spit in my mouth and just trudged along.

Benjamin at last piped up, keeping his voice low. "We goin' to Yggdrasil?"

"In a roundabout way," I hedged. "You know, sometimes the shortest distance between two points is an angle."

"Huh?" He looked at me, tangled hair falling into his eyes.

"Yeah, that sounded stupid to me, too."

After that, we fell silent but kept following the crowd of green, and one large red, painted bodies around us.

I'd done such a good job of putting one step in front of the other that when the green guys in front of me stopped, I smacked into the back of the closest ones.

"Sorry," I mumbled, quickly adding a palm out gesture. "I didn't hit you on purpose. It was an accident. No harm meant."

Thank the Great Spirits that Red Guy was there and stepped in before I earned a spear to the gut. I glanced around, noticing the bridge had at last ended, as if it had just petered out onto dun-colored sand.

At last, no more scary height to face.

"You come with me," he spoke to me alone, jerking his chin in the opposite direction from where he'd pointed the green entourage. Which was fine by me. A better chance to run if there was only one threat to escape from. We were off the bridge, which meant no leaping to our deaths. I could work with that. Relief made me shaky.

When the last green body shuffled away, the smallest casting me a stink-eye look over his shoulder, Red Guy turned and started walking away from all of us after repeating, "You follow me."

What now?

This wasn't just a nightmare: this was the nightmare that wouldn't end.

Before I knew it, Red Guy's back was disappearing in the distance, getting smaller and smaller. A distance that looked like the Gobi desert, all beige-colored dunes and shades of tan.

It reminded me of the last time I'd been in the Spirit Realm, fighting a crazy djinn who was evil through and through. Was the guy I was jogging to catch up to the same kind of creature? Or worse?

Should I take the chance to disappear with Benjamin?

Shouldn't we be high-tailing it in the opposite direction? Stay? Leave on our own? A quick glance around nixed that idea as the horizon in every direction was the same; flat, empty and the same dull color. Having grown up in high desert country, I knew only idiots went into that kind of landscape alone as a seriously stupid way to commit suicide. If I didn't have Benjamin, I might have tried it anyway, but no way would I risk his life.

Bloody choices again. This one was easier though. Follow the guy who saved my hiney back on the bridge or the spear-jabbing others? See? No brainer.

I started jogging after the silhouette, now just a black dot on the horizon. I'd like to think my shortness of breath was because we were running, but it wasn't. It was fear squeezing my heart in a vise as I realized that no matter how hard we ran, the Red Guy was the same distance in front of us.

I shuddered to a stop, aware Benjamin was huffing and puffing, too. At least Red Guy stopped at the same time, otherwise we'd be on our own in this desert world.

Maybe that was his intention. Let us follow him like hopeful fools only to abandon us when it suited him. Why hadn't I just stayed in that eerie white room? Every action since then just got me, well, both of us, deeper and deeper into trouble. And now? Dying in a desert ranked up there with dying by falling from a bridge.

"Hey!" I shouted, my voice bouncing across the emptiness. "Wait up!"

But the minute we started moving again, so did he.

Now I was just getting pissed off. Anger being easier to deal with than terror and that's what coated my skin with a sheen of sweat.

Unfortunately anger was as useless as tits on a bull. It wasn't going to get Red Guy to change. Or pop us out of this place. So I inhaled a deep breath to slow my heart beat and reached for Benjamin who was quivering. With a grunt and a heft, I lifted him to my shoulders and started walking again. He was light but any extra weight slogging through a desert wasn't easy. But if Red Guy wanted to play games, what was I going to do?

Even as I was thinking of exactly zero answers to my own questions, I spotted something beyond Red Guy. A darker shape on the horizon. A shape that gradually stopped looking like fingers reaching from the hard packed ground and morphed into a tree.

Good grief! How could a tree survive here? And why did my heart start beating faster? And sweat break out along my arms? Not exertion sweat but the cold, clammy kind. Fear crawled over me as I bit my lip to keep it from trembling.

Had to be the effort exerted to keep Benjamin curled around my shoulders. The gritty taste of my bone-dry mouth. The impossible situation. But in my heart, I knew those were excuses.

That tree was something different. A break in this nothingness, and I was getting scared that if something didn't keep me from it, this non-place was where I'd die.

"Run, Alex!"

This wasn't the woman's voice. No, this was Bran's.

I twirled around, stumbling as I scanned in every direction. Nothing.

Was he here, too? Which meant he was dead. Bran couldn't die—a thought slicing me in two. He was too alive, too solid to think of him as rotting into dust.

But if he was here, why couldn't I see him?

"Run!"

"From what?" I shouted back, earning only an echo and a sharp look from where Red Guy stood and waited. "Where to?"

If I was going to run, now was the time.

With a curse for invisible warlocks, one in particular, I pivoted and started hoofing it in the direction I'd just come. Each step slower than the last. The sand softer, snagging my boots, slowing me down, the weight of Benjamin making every move harder. But all I could think was *keep running.*

Away from Red Guy. More from the black speck on the horizon. From whatever it was.

I'd covered maybe twenty feet when Red Guy suddenly blocked my path.

Staggering back, I switched direction.

Red Guy again.

No matter where I turned he was there, his face growing darker and darker.

"For love of the Spirits," I huffed, exhausting myself, sure any second I'd drop Benjamin before face-planting in the sand. Instead I sank to my knees, reaching one hand up to brace Benjamin who hadn't uttered a word.

"This way." Red Guy pointed toward the tree, as if waiting for a rat in a maze to get her act together. Me rat. This, the maze from Hell.

"What is that thing?" I whispered, nodding my head toward where he was pointing, my hands on my knees, chugging in one ragged breath at a time.

"Your destiny." He hadn't even bothered looking at me as he answered. Which gave me a second to get my game face back on before he announced, "Your journey begins there. Come. Now."

Begins? So what had I been doing in the meantime?

CHAPTER 12

"Mandy? Where are you?" Kelly shouted, hearing the Painted Lady and her warriors bearing down on her.

"Here." Mandy's arm slid from the solid wall. Not between chunks of marble but from the middle of a slab four feet wide in each direction.

Kelly blinked. Frozen. Petrified.

The arm waved. "Grab hold."

And go where?

"Hurry!"

That part Kelly already knew. The other?

Closing her eyes, not completely but in the way you did knowing a racing vehicle was bearing down on you and there wasn't anything you could do to get out of its way, Kelly grabbed Mandy's hand.

Before she could inhale, Mandy yanked her forward, just as the sound of spears and staffs hitting solid stone rang out, not far behind as she pushed against resistance, a ghostly silver murkiness, like a membrane. No going backwards, only forwards. Shoving, shoving, shoving, Kelly popped out and tumbled forward into an awkward sprawl.

"Where are we?" She opened her eyes wide, not that it helped. In fact she wanted to close them again, but Mandy was already tugging her upward and forward—into a world of ice.

Not just any ice but layers and layers of blue ice, as if waves dashing and foaming against a shore were caught and suspended.

"Where. . ." Kelly tried to say more but her teeth had begun to chatter.

"We don't have much time," Mandy threw over her shoulder, zig-zagging down slender crevices between the towering blueness surrounding them.

"Before?"

"Before we freeze to death."

Of course, why hadn't Kelly thought of that? So she slipped and slid behind Mandy, aware of a slow rumble growing behind her.

She ignored the roar as she rubbed her hands over her arms, puffing on her fingers, anything to warm up. Instead, small crystals formed where her breath hit her skin. They tinkled as they fell and splattered against the ice floor.

Who was it that described one of the levels of Hell as icy? Dante maybe—if he hadn't, maybe he should have.

"Almost there," Mandy breathed at last, her words swallowed up so quickly by the density of the ice forms surrounding them that Kelly wondered if she'd just imagined them.

As Mandy zipped around another serpentine corner with Kelly following on her heels, Kelly's feet hit a patch of slickness, skating her feet right out from under her. Landing with a hard thud on her tailbone, the air blasted from her lungs.

"Come on. We don't have time to be playing," Mandy snapped, pausing for only a second before disappearing from view.

"Love you, too." Some people didn't think Kelly could get snarky, but she could, especially when she was exhausted, at the end of her rope, and so cold her whole body shook. Using elbows and knees to crawl to her feet, assuming if she placed a bare hand on any of the ice it'd freeze solid, it took a minute to get to slogging forward again.

"Mandy?" she called out, hearing only her own voice echoing. No sound of footsteps ahead of her. But behind her?

She paused, looking in that direction, taking a second to catch her breath. What was that noise?

Then it hit her. The soldiers. The rumble was the hammering of heavy steps pounding toward her. They'd crossed the barrier and now were in the ice caves.

With a pivot a ballerina would have envied, Kelly jogged forward, each foot-fall jarring bruised bones. A sign of being alive. Right?

But where had Mandy disappeared to?

Increasing her speed to match the tattoo of her heart, Kelly hurtled forward, bracing at every turn, expecting to go sling-shotting through the air again. But still no Mandy.

Call out? Pinpoint her position for the threat bearing down on them? Or hope that Mandy was just around the next curve? Staying quiet. Stealthy.

So much for thinking her old naïve self had been totally eradicated.

Where was Mandy? What happened to Alex? And Aini? Would they get to her in time?

I'm coming Aini.

No response. Not good.

Blindly racing forward, Kelly skittered around an outcropping that looked like a finger raised in a rude gesture and all but splatted into Mandy.

"Where've you been?" Mandy snarled before turning her back to Kelly.

Which was probably for the best as Kelly didn't know if she wanted to stick out her tongue or throttle her teammate. Instead of choosing, she bit back a slew of words that would have earned a good mouth washing with soap from her foster mother. Alex would have given her a high five.

"Where now?" she managed to ask, her lips so numb she expected them to fracture.

"Somewhere. Here. There's. Supposed. To. Be." Each of Mandy's words bit off as if talking took too much effort. Kelly leaned forward to catch the last word.

But it didn't come.

"How'd you know about this place?" Kelly jumped in place to keep warm and help hide the sounds of the soldiers racing closer.

Instead of an answer, Mandy kicked at the nearest ice pile, earning small chips flying in every direction.

Frustration? Or fear?

"Anything I can do?" Kelly pushed closer.

"Get the hell back."

If they got out of this. . .

"I *am* trying." Mandy smashed a balled fist against the ice this time.

Now Mandy was wigging out, talking to herself again. Kelly hadn't said a word, not that it wasn't tempting. Everyone had their breaking point, though. Looked like Mandy just hit hers. Which didn't bode well for getting out of this mess.

Mandy started pounding with both fists. Kelly grabbed at her. "Stop. Stop."

But Mandy wouldn't. It was as if she were demon-driven.

This time Kelly wasn't taking no for an answer. "Mandy? Listen to me." When the other woman wouldn't, Kelly did what she never expected to do. She raised her hand and slapped Mandy across the face. The loud thwack made both of them rear back.

"What the hell was that for?" Mandy rubbed at the red handprint marring her cheek.

"I was trying to help."

Mandy rolled her eyes. "By smacking me?"

"Only way I could get your attention."

"Next time, just ask," came a grumbled response as Mandy turned back to the ice wall, shaking her head.

Refusing to feel like a chastised child, Kelly stepped closer, noticing the puff of air as she shouted, "This is me asking. What's going on? We're at a dead end." She waved her hand over her shoulder. "A whole lot of bad is coming at us and you're acting like you're one step from the loony bin?"

"Loony bin?" Mandy actually looked like she bit back a grin. "Isn't that politically incorrect?"

So Mandy thought this was funny? Freezing to death, lost and trouble coming?

She bit her hand into Mandy's shoulder. "I don't care if it is. What's going on? Who are you talking to, because I know it's not just me? And why in God's Green Earth are we here?"

"Here as in the Underworld or—"

"Talk to me." Then hearing the marching soldiers clearer, she added, "Now!"

Mandy sighed as if pulling oxygen from the far reaches of her toes. "You won't believe me."

"Try me."

"We don't have—"

"Try, damnit."

Mandy clutched her hair as if wanting to pull it from the roots. "*Dale! No sé.*" Then she released her fingers. "What's to lose?"

Kelly wasn't sure what Mandy just said in Spanish but she waited, a lesson she'd learned with scared five- and six-year olds. Even when they really wanted to talk, they had to do it in their own time.

Unfortunately, she and Mandy didn't have a lot of that. Come on, Mandy, spit it out.

"My brother." The words were spoken so low Kelly had to lean in to make sure she'd heard them at all.

"What about your brother?" Was now really the best time to get into family dynamics?

"He's telling me." She looked up at the wall of blue in front of them. "Or trying to tell me, how to escape."

Her brother? Had Mandy really lost it?

Mandy glanced at her out of the corner of her eye. "*Ser un punto!* I'm not crazy. He's here."

"As in. . ." Kelly looked around, half-expecting a spirit to materialize at any second. "Here? Like right here?"

"Of course. What else could I mean?"

Kelly shrugged because it felt like a huge mine shaft had just opened under her. Thankfully Mandy turned back to the ice wall.

"Alejándro said there was a door here. But where?"

"Alejándro being your brother?" The cold must have been seeping into her brain cells, because even the simple questions sounded stupid and slow.

"Of course."

Okay, so Mandy had a brother named Alejándro. Who must have died if he was in this place. Right?

Inhaling a deep breath Kelly decided to focus on the most important issues first. "What exactly did. . . did Alejándro say?"

She couldn't roll the word like Mandy did, but her teammate didn't seem to care right then as she threw her hands upward, a helpless, hopeless gesture. But she answered, "*No es fácil.*"

"In English?"

"Life's hard."

As if that helped. "Anything else?" Like something helpful.

"What he says doesn't make sense at all."

Like their being there? With scary, dead warriors coming? Tempted to shake her teammate, Kelly instead sucked in a deep breath and pushed. "Like what? Can you be more specific?"

Mandy scrubbed both hands across her face. "When cerulean turns to teal and turquoise becomes cobalt, the path is there."

Great. Who talked about color theory when lives were on the line?

Judging by Mandy's look, she felt the same way.

"Okay, okay, let's not panic." Yet. Kelly stepped closer to the wall, repeating, "Cerulean turns to teal. Turquoise to cobalt." Her gaze flashed over the wall, high and low, then she stepped back, muttering, "Cerulean? That has some green with the blue, right?"

"How the hell do I know?"

Not helping.

Then she saw it. Above their heads. "There!" She pointed. "Where that one vein meets the other. That's cerulean."

Mandy angled her head back. "If you say so."

"And there, look where the vein almost peters out. That's more teal."

"Looks the same to me."

She was right, the colors were very close, but at least they had a start. The width of the two seams was no more than three or four feet.

"Let's assume that's the width of the door." She stepped closer to the section of wall beneath the cerulean/teal marker. "So where's the turquoise?" It had to be close around here. "It's a darker color of blue, but could have some green in it."

Mandy held her tongue. Probably a good thing as desperation surged through Kelly. "It has to be here. Somewhere."

"There." Mandy materialized right beside her, stubbing one finger toward the floor. "Is that it?"

"Of course, who thinks of looking down?" There it was, like an arrow, smudged and faded beneath layers of ice. The green-blue morphing into a darker blue with the arrow was pointing away from the wall with the cerulean and teal.

Like a child on a scavenger hunt, but one with a clock ticking down—and fast—Kelly paced the length of the arrow, ending up at a fissure of ice, so narrow she could barely get the tips of her fingers into the seam.

"This can't be right," she murmured, blowing on her fingers to try again. "Did he say anything else?"

"No."

She whirled on Mandy. "Then ask him again," she demanded. "We're not getting anywhere with our thumbs stuck up our backsides."

Mandy swallowed then stepped back and went still, closing her eyes. The silence broken only by the rumble of the threat coming closer.

Not saying anything, Kelly used her hand to wave Mandy on, as if that was going to help. So she turned back to the cobalt wall.

"He said we have to ask for a wish," Mandy said. "Something we really want."

"Wish? Other than getting out of here?" Sure Kelly was being a little snippy, okay, a lot snippy. But what did *wish* mean? "Are you supposed to ask? Or me? Or both of us?"

"I tried." Mandy sounded defensive. "But got nothing."

"Fine." She stepped closer to the wall. "Let's both try. Can't hurt."

"And if we don't have a wish?" Mandy asked, joining her anyway, shoulder to shoulder, inches from the ice.

Kelly didn't want to point out how sad those words sounded. How lonely and isolated. But they didn't have time. "Find something," she snapped, wondering what her wish was? To find her birth mother? A woman who abandoned her with only secrets and no answers. To remain an IR Agent? Since they probably wouldn't survive this mission, that didn't seem to matter as much as it once did. To save Aini.

Should have thought of that first.

Thinking of years of Sunday services, the scent of wooden floors, neighbors and friends side by side, flowers of the season stashed in nooks and crannies, Kelly put herself in the Baptist church of her childhood. That's where she'd prayed time and time again to lose her ability to turn invisible.

Come to think of it, that wish hadn't happened either.

But instead of being where she should pour out her wish to save Aini, she was in the stark and functional bedroom she'd been in just last night. The one she'd shared with Van. She could feel his touch, gentle and urgent, hear the beat of his heart as she pressed kisses to his chest, listened to his breathing increase, the heat of his skin brushing against hers.

That was her real wish. They'd left one another in anger and regret. There was no way to go back and erase those memories.

But if she could have just one more moment. A chance to part from him with kind words. A hug. A kiss.

That's what she wanted. Only that. With Van.

She was so deep into her thoughts she didn't hear the ice splinter, hear the shouts of the Painted Lady as she rounded the nearest corner, or feel the slam of Mandy's fist to her back, tumbling them both forward.

Into darkness.

CHAPTER 13

Before I could struggle to my feet and follow Red Guy again, he disappeared. Poof. One second there. The next nothing. Benjamin's weight vanished from my shoulders. And the sand surrounding me dematerialized as if a strong wind tossed all the grains away.

What the?

I was alone. Again. So alone the wind whistling around me felt like it was actually knifing through me.

What was going on?

"Benjamin?" Nothing.

"Bran?" Still nothing.

The dun-colored desert had disappeared, replaced by a blackness so thick I raised my hand to my face to make sure I was really here. Wherever here was. I'd been in choking, palpable darkness before, after leaving the white room, but this felt different—rattle my bones kind of difference.

I waited until my heartbeat slowed. Getting my breathing under control was harder. My hands clenched at my sides.

Patience was not my strong suit. Okay, I didn't have it in my genetic makeup, at all. So waiting around, lost in darkness, was not my thing.

What now?

"Kelly? Benjamin? Someone? Anyone?"

Nada.

I could do a quick protection spell. . .or . . . I could do a seeking spell.

Idiot! Why hadn't I thought of this before? Yeah, the magic might not work, but if it did, I could find Kelly and Mandy.

Centering myself in the darkness, I took a few deep, cleansing breaths and began my chant. Last time I'd used this particular one I'd called Bran to me. So did not want to do that this time. Not only would he be a very, very unhappy warlock, he could be trapped here forever. So didn't need that.

Focus, and get on with it.

I started the chant slowly, using it to anchor me in the darkness, reaching out to Kelly. If Mandy was with her, fine. But it was Kelly I connected with easier and once I found her then we'd find Mandy. Then save Aini.

Weariness coated my thoughts so I paused, inhaled and started again.

"Light to darkness. Spirit to earth.
Friend to friend.
I seek thee. I summon thee.
Bring me to your side."

Who knew darkness could have a palpable feel to it? Not scary, but waiting. I shook out my shoulders and chanted louder.

"Bound together dark and day.
Time forward meet time reversed.
I seek thee. I summon thee.
Bring me. Bring you to my side."

A loud, long boom erupted near me—an explosion times ten, shaking where I stood so hard I threw my hands out to balance myself. Didn't work.

Like a downed ponderosa pine, I toppled to my knees.

This couldn't be good.

That's when something slammed against me. Heavy and fast.

I face-planted and rolled, wanting to escape whatever I'd drawn to me as soon as I could. Nothing like being attacked in pitch-blackness to activate every primordial fear. Adrenaline jackknifed through my body as someone screamed.

A woman's scream.

Mid-roll I caught myself. "Kelly?"

"Alex? Is that you?"

"Yeah. Where've you been?"

"No idea." Her voice was near, and shaky. "Where are you?"

"Follow my voice."

The sound of jeans brushing a hard surface inched closer.

"Talk or I can't find you." She sounded stronger and a little miffed.

"Right. Sorry." I extended my hand in the direction I thought she was coming. When my fingers met her head, she squeaked.

"Scare me to death," she whispered, then added, "maybe I shouldn't say that in this place."

I found a rusty laugh, then quickly sobered. "Where's Mandy?"

"She was right behind me." Kelly had scooted close enough that our knees brushed, both of us now sitting. "She should be—"

"What the *Joder!*"

That thud and the oath, in Spanish, gave us our answer.

"We're here," Kelly reassured, until she added, "wherever here is."

"Getting damn tired of that," Mandy grumbled, a few feet away. "Can't someone turn on the lights?"

"You figure out how to do that, you let us know." Yeah, I sounded snarky. Bite me.

"That you, Noziak?"

"Anyone else you know in the Underworld?"

Instead of a smart comeback, there was a strained pause as if I'd stepped into something better left alone.

Kelly jumped in playing peacemaker. "Let's focus on what's important. We're all together. At last. That's good news, isn't it?"

"Should be," I mumbled, getting in one more poke at Mandy before I was ready to turn to the most pressing issue. Finding out where we were and how to get out of here. That was quickly becoming my new norm.

"Have you been here the whole time? Sitting in the dark?" Kelly asked. I could sense her looking around as if expecting to see something, anything. I didn't have the heart to tell her that this darkness was not like we were used to, back in the Real Realm. There, if you close your eyes for a moment, then open them, you can usually see more than you expected—outlines, shadings within the shadows, faint illumination. Not here.

I focused on Kelly's question though. "No. I just got here a little bit ago."

"Oh." The single word whooshed from her like a balloon deflating.

I scrambled to my feet, brushing my hands against my pants as if eliminating any crud I might have rolled in here. "Let's figure out how to leave here." I spoke out loud, pretending I had a clue. Which I didn't.

Next to me I heard Kelly rise to her feet. There was something about standing to face a threat, which this darkness was, that gave a person a psychological advantage. At least it did for me.

"Mandy? Can you stand?" I peered at where I assumed she was.

"In a sec."

"You hurt?" Kelly saved me from what I was going to say. Something along the lines of 'whenever you're ready, princess,' or maybe, 'get your sorry ass in gear. We don't have all day."

"Not hurt. Listening," came Mandy's response.

"Listening to what?" I lowered my voice. Not that it did any good—there was no noise here. Other than the three of us.

Kelly reached out and laid a hand on my arm.

"Is it Alejándro?" Kelly asked.

"Who the hell is Alejándro?" I wanted to know.

"Her brother," Kelly whispered near me, but since it was so bleeding quiet in the darkness, her words echoed through the space.

"Our way out." Mandy wasn't quieting her words, even as her voice receded as if she was walking away.

What was going on?

"Where you going, Reyes?" So much for her guarding our backs. Couldn't do that if she flitted off somewhere.

She didn't answer, which only pissed me off more.

"Reyes, get back here."

Nothing.

"Don't be too hard on her." Kelly sighed next to me. "We've been running from one problem to another, and the only reason we're still alive is her listening to her brother."

"She has a brother?"

"Yes."

"Is he. . . dead?"

"Well, I'm assuming he's dead since he's here."

What next? I'd rather take Red Guy over this crap.

There was no way we were going to get separated because Mandy was off to have a family reunion.

I understood the ties of family. Mine mattered more to me than anyone. Well, there was Bran, too, but I wasn't ready to admit that fully. Not yet. So I got it.

But that didn't mean we split the team up. Plus I had to find Benjamin. I hated the thought of him lost, again, and all because of me.

"Come on," I snapped at Kelly. This time I was the one holding her arm, dragging her along behind me as I high-tailed it in the direction where I'd last heard Mandy's voice. "Reyes? You here?"

A faint sound, far away. Crap. One minute Mandy wanted to stay put, the next she's disappearing. This was not how a team operated.

"Stay where you are." I called out—a demand, not a suggestion.

I picked up my pace, hoping I wasn't heading us over a long drop in this darkness. "Reyes?"

"Here."

Closer. Good. "We're coming."

I could hear Kelly's breathing increase as my own did.

Mandy must have wised up, or heard the thinly disguised threat in my tone as she started directing us by voice. "Over here. Waiting. You coming?"

As if we were the reason she stood alone. Sheesh.

"Almost there," Kelly answered for us. Probably because she knew Mandy wouldn't care for my words. Smart, Kels.

We almost slammed into Mandy, who'd gone quiet again, but we were close enough we could find her with outstretched hands and only a stumble or two.

"Don't do that again." I wasn't being sweet and understanding. Leave that to Kelly. "We're a team. We stick together."

I swear she snorted then mumbled something about Paris. Sore point, but I wasn't going to justify why I'd ended up striking out on my own for a bit. A small bit, before I realized how stupid that was.

When Mandy spoke, she was back to business. "You figure a way to get us out of here yet?"

Like that was my job? I might know magic but I wasn't a miracle worker.

"I thought your brother was doing that?"

"He can't," came the low, don't-push-the-point response.

Great. Back to square one.

"Maybe if we hold hands," Kelly offered.

"And do what? Click our ruby red slippers together?" Mandy said.

What a bitch. Before I could step closer and smack some sense into her, Noziak style, Kelly sighed. "No. I was thinking if we held hands it'd be easier to stay together. Given the darkness."

I was actually glad for the inky blackness right then. Made it easier to hide my smile. Take that, Mandy. Snark met kindness and kindness kicked your ass.

Then to bring home the point, I grasped Kelly's hand. "Great idea, Kels. Give me your hand, Reyes."

She did, though I could have sworn she wasn't any happier about the situation than I was.

"And now?" she asked.

I opened my mouth but before anything could come out, the ground started shaking beneath us, like when I'd arrived.

"Hang on!" I shouted as a whirlwind of smoke, grit and what felt like chalky powder enveloped us.

Not again.

CHAPTER 14

Red Guy was shouting at me as I came to, back in the bleak desert area of wherever I'd ended up this time.

He'd just have to wait. I had enough to deal with as I looked around for Kelly and Mandy.

Thank the Great Spirits, Kelly was there, flat on her back, a dozen feet away. I could see the rise and fall of her chest, so she was alive.

Mandy?

A little further away, curled in a fetal position.

Crud in a bucket. If she was hurt, I'd never hear the end of it.

"Lady? Lady, you here?" Benjamin's voice jumped me back to the present. That and his wide-eyed gaze staring at me from inches away.

"I'm here," I mumbled, realizing how iffy a statement that was. Hadn't Benjamin been on my shoulders? Now he was before me. And where had he been while I'd been gone? And Red Guy, I was supposed to be following him. But where? And why?

"Come with me," Red Guy growled, snagging my attention. Could he read thoughts? Or had I spoken out loud? "You and them."

He'd started walking ahead again, shaking his head.

"Yggdrasil," Benjamin whispered to me as if I'd forgotten what we were doing. And I had. Somehow it didn't seem as urgent as getting back on track with our mission. Find Aini. Save her. Stop the Horned One if needed. Survive. Or not.

So maybe being here, finding this Yggdrasil place, was a better option. At least a safer one. If we could do it quickly. I knew it was what Benjamin wanted, as if a child really knew anything.

On the other hand, sometimes they did. They kept life simple. If you're hungry, you eat. If you're tired, crash. And if you thought you could find your mum and dad in a place called Yggdrasil, then you went there.

"Okay, kiddo." I crawled to my feet. "Let me get my friends and we'll get going."

Benjamin's smile was the best thing I'd seen in. . . well, in however long I'd been in this Realm. For that alone I'd keep walking across this dry, dusty landscape toward a spot in the distance.

It took only a few shakes to wake Kelly up, which meant I could breathe again. Once on her feet her first comment was, "There's a boy behind you."

"Yeah, that's Benjamin."

"Is he. . . is he like Alejándro?"

"Kind of." Technically Benjamin was a spirit, but since I didn't have a clue what Alejándro was, other than dead, I really couldn't answer.

The two of us crossed to Mandy who was already sitting up, coughing as if she'd swallowed half the desert.

"You found a kid?" she said, rubbing her eyes as if not seeing very clearly.

"Well, actually, he found me."

"You left us, found a kid and now we're stuck with him?"

Kelly stepped forward, keeping her voice pitched low. "He can hear you."

Yeah, and so could I. "The kid has a name. It's Benjamin, and we're taking him to his parents."

"So you scrubbed the mission to play nursemaid?" Mandy wasn't holding her punches. I was thankful Kelly stood between us, a strategic blocking position—her face looking as confused as Mandy's.

"You sure?" Kelly asked, glancing from me to Benjamin.

"Far as I know, where we're going will get us closer to *you know who*." Okay, it was a stretch but Ghost Guy had said where Benjamin needed to go was where I needed to go. Like I could trust a ghost. Or myself to know anything.

"Far as you know," came Mandy's echo-response, but there was less heat in it than I expected.

I turned to Kelly. "Have you connected with Aini?"

"Yes." Her words sounded sad. "Very faint, but it was her."

"Good." I looked at Mandy but spoke to them both. "If Kelly keeps touching base with Aini—" I raised one hand, knowing mind-to-mind talking wasn't exactly an exact science, but that's the whole reason Kels was along on this mission, to use her ability to connect with the girl as our roadmap. Not the easiest way, but the only way as far as we knew. It wasn't like there was a clear map to the Underworld— "and if Kels finds it harder to connect, rather than easier, we'll stop and reassess our direction and our options."

I only wished we had an X-marks-the-spot guide. I had heard of a few clues where to look from our IR guru-of-all-things-and-places-preternatural, Fraulein Fassbinder, who shared with me before we left on this mission—down versus up and past a Guardian at a gate, but the rest of my knowledge was vague at best.

Kelly looked steadier though and that, more than my words, brought Mandy around. "Fine."

Not a gracious or a rousing endorsement, but I'd worked with less.

"We've got to get going then. Our tour guide is literally leaving us in the dust."

"What guide?" Kelly asked, looking around.

My guess was she couldn't see him.

"Not important." I gentled my tone as much as possible as I watched Red Guy disappearing into the distance. "But we're running out of time."

She sighed and then squared her shoulders. "Lead. We'll follow."

I looked at Mandy. "You ready then?"

She gave a jerky nod.

"Wait up," I shouted to Red Guy, hoping he could hear me. He didn't even shrug his shoulders. Not that I expected much more from him.

I snagged Benjamin's hand again as the four of us started forward. One step after another. Surely if we could see the tree, the place called Yggdrasil couldn't be that far. Could it?

Boy when I was wrong, I was really wrong. You'd think after a while I'd learn that lesson.

I focused on reaching the tree that was becoming clearer and clearer to me as we walked toward it. Each footstep became slower than the last one, as if my legs met the earth with a hard thud. That and I became more aware that I was in the middle of absolute nowhere, with a creepy Red Guy who didn't even talk to me, a frightened child, a worried Kelly, and a moody Mandy. With no back up.

Head down I just kept moving forward.

As we drew closer to the tree, the fear riding me grew stronger. I could taste it in the back of my throat, feel it in the pounding along my temples, the stiffness of my neck and shoulders.

Whatever this place was, I was less and less sure about being here. A quick glance at Benjamin, though, shook me. His face glowed with the biggest smile, one brightening his eyes and making his steps higher.

"What are you seeing?" I asked, bracing myself for his answer.

"Me mum and dad." He pointed one pudgy finger ahead of us. "There. Near me gram. And Mr. McGinty is there, too." Benjamin paused, as if confused, then looked at me. "He used to sneak me sugar plums 'n' butter scotch toffee after church on Sundays."

"Sounds like a nice guy." I squinted into the light around me while blinking back moisture in my eyes. Had to be dryness. That's all. I didn't see anyone.

"He was nice." Benjamin nodded his head, then paused. "'fore he caught the pox."

That stopped me. "What kind of pox?"

"I dunno. It kilt him."

One word did it. Like a good swift kick from a mule's hoof, I rocked back on my feet.

Oh, yeah, on an intellectual level I knew we weren't in Oz, but that didn't mean I was ready to accept that Benjamin was really not a little boy. Only a small, lost soul who had waited a hundred or more years to find his family.

I squeezed Benjamin's hand tighter, as if the power of touch alone could make him something he wasn't. Fully alive.

"Ow," he murmured, before glancing ahead. 'What're we waitin' for? They're right there."

I followed the direction he was tugging me, bile coating my mouth. I wasn't seeing what Benjamin saw but that didn't mean he didn't see it.

Kelly and Mandy stumbled behind me, as silent as the empty desert.

Maybe I was the blind one here. Not a comforting feeling as each step took us closer to this Yggdrasil place. Or tree, because that took up my whole vision. Did Kelly and Mandy have the same heebie-jeebies as I did? Only it was more than that. Sort of awe and fear jumbled together.

High, bare branches reached into the dusty tangerine-tinted sky. They strained against the massive roots plunging deep and clinging to the earth. The tree was so large that Red Guy looked small beside it. Small and insignificant. As if all that mattered was the tree and not the puny human-looking being standing in its shade.

Though there was no sun to cast a shadow.

Maybe I was meant to swing from one of those gnarled braches. Or meet the spirit of the tree. My Native ancestors knew all living beings possessed spirits, but that didn't mean they were all benign ones. There was a reason some trees were called widow makers.

Moisture dried in my mouth, but I knew I had to go toward that monster-sized landmark. Metal shavings to a magnet, the tree being the magnet and I being the helpless filaments.

When had the tree morphed from pinky-sized on the horizon to filling the landscape?

"What is it?" I whispered as I drew near to Red Guy, my neck straining as I looked up and up, but couldn't even see the higher branches. I hadn't released Benjamin though he tugged against my hand as a wiggling puppy would who wanted something just out of reach. No idea where Kelly and Mandy stopped but I didn't sense them close behind me. The tree demanded all my focus.

"The tree has had many, many names among your kind." Red Guy studied my face as if waiting for something.

I hadn't really expected an answer, especially when I caught sight of the way he looked, once he twisted to stare at the trunk, an expression of awe exploding across his face, until his creased cheeks looked like they bled red.

"It's beautiful," Kelly whispered, suddenly next to me.

Beautiful? Talk about rose-colored glasses. Power was not beautiful and this monster was powerful, in the way old, ancient things are—each limb, gnarl, and knot-hole echoed with authority. Its presence clawed deep inside me, a hollow wonder overlaid by apprehension. The ocean was old and powerful and created the same sense of dread deep inside me. Sometimes it looked benign but it wasn't.

When I wasn't much older than Benjamin, my dad took my brothers and me to the Pacific Ocean, along the Oregon Coast. At first I loved the newness, the curling breaking of the waves against the beach, the tide pools teeming with life. Then a rogue wave smashed into me, sucking me out into cold so bitter it stole my breath away. One second the ground squished under my feet, the next I tumbled over and over in waves that didn't give a rat's ass about me.

If my father hadn't been a shaman, and my older brother Jake close enough to lunge for me, I'd be dead.

Which was why beautiful wasn't the word that came to my mind now. Deadly, yes, but not beautiful.

So many questions crowded my thoughts, it was hard to grasp one at a time but I sensed Red Guy waited, having more to share.

I latched on to what seemed the easiest issue first. "You mention my kind? You mean humans?"

"You are neither angel nor archangel. Not demon, nor of the preternatural, though your blood is tainted by them." He spoke as if reading from a large, heavy book.

Tainted? This coming from a red giant with skewered lips? As if.

But I bit my tongue. I knew my brothers would double over in hysterics at the very thought of my doing so, but they weren't here, and a wave of sadness rolled over me.

I looked at the tree, a touchstone, too aware of its presence, its strength, its aliveness. Suddenly, it didn't seem so much scary as inevitable. Sort of like being called into the principal's office, and knowing there was no escape. Or the sound of the metal prison doors clanging shut behind me that first day in the Idaho State Prison.

Yeah, more like that final boom, the kind that shook your whole body. And world.

Red Guy had mentioned names and, as a magic wielder, I knew names mattered. Calling something, or someone, by their name created the first step to understanding, or ownership. Licking cracked and dry lips I murmured, "What are some of the names the tree is called?"

"The Norse are the ones who call it Yggdrasil."

Go figure. So we'd been looking for a Norse place?

"The Mayans believed this tree is the *axis mundi*, which connects the Underworld planes with the sky and the terrestrial world." The words rolled from Red Guy like the most profound poetry that could move you to tears by words alone.

Okay, maybe we were getting somewhere. So we hadn't been to the Underworld. Yet. I wasn't quite sure how this tree was going to get us there, connected or not. A ladder maybe?

Or even if I was up to going, to head into another fight-to-the-death. You had to cherish life to do that and right now, I really wasn't sure.

Kelly stepped up. "Why are we here?"

Red Guy turned to spear her with ancient eyes I could tell weren't really seeing her or me. It was as if they looked through us. But he did answer. "This is where those who seek answers, those answers they need to hear but have refused to face, come."

"What are you talking about?" Now I was totally confused but aware of a pressure squeezing me, an awareness that what I was hearing mattered. If only I could figure it out.

"This is where life and death meet. Where all spirit begins."

For love of the Mother Goddess, couldn't he speak in plain language? Or maybe he was, but I was blocking what he said.

I eyed the massive trunk before me, getting a hunch, and not liking it. Hearing truth, the kind of truth that upended everything I'd assumed, knew or believed before this, was not an easy thing to accept. "Are you saying this is the Tree of Life?" Even as I uttered the stiff words, an ice-cold chill scurried over my skin without a breeze anywhere.

"I told you already, it has many names."

This was getting too out-there for me. It didn't matter if I dealt with magic and dead spirits back on the earthly plane and here, too—standing next to the beginning and, some said, the end of all life, was too much to take in.

I stepped back, scrambling for breathing space. Tugging Benjamin backwards with me, even as his sweaty palm strained against mine. But I wasn't letting go. Not until I was certain what that tree meant.

But just like the optical illusion of always seeing Red Guy in sync with us as we walked, but always at the same distance, it didn't matter how many steps I took in any direction, the tree in front of me remained massive, blocking out everything else.

Kelly remained in one place, looking with awe at what scared me so bad I would have screamed, but no words would come. Mandy stood apart, as if waiting for more information before she moved. Not an act-first, think-later Noziak approach for her.

Shuffling backwards faster, like a child afraid of the bogeyman, I tripped over my own feet and sprawled on my back, choking in dust and cringing as the tree leaned toward me. I pulled Benjamin down beside me as he cried out. "Ow! I want me mum!"

"In a second." I wanted to soothe but how could I, feeling the power, the fathomlessness before me. I wasn't sending Benjamin toward that.

My focus was on the tree and what it meant.

That's when awareness crashed against me with the force of a twelve-bore shotgun fired right to the gut.

"No!" the scream tore from my throat. Awareness blasting through me. Awareness that morphed into certainty.

I didn't care if Kelly heard me. If Mandy had proof at last that I was a flake. It was as if a giant spotlight speared me and there was no cringing, running or hiding from it.

My mind raced, my heart stuttered. This place meant one thing to Benjamin, but something totally else to me. Something I hadn't wanted to face.

I wasn't ready to die. That's what the tree whispered to me. What I feared.

My death. There was still so much left to do. So many things I needed to accomplish. My Dad. I hadn't said goodbye to anyone. Hadn't accomplished anything. Bran.

I wasn't ready.

Sure I'd taken a suicide mission. Every battle we'd been in and still faced meant we could die. That I could die. I thought I'd accepted that. It's what Bran and I fought about. His wanting me somewhere safe, my pointing out that nowhere was ever going to be safe—not a car, a plane, walking across the street.

But this? It wasn't a route to the Underworld, a means to an end—this was a final notice. To avoid death, I had to accept life.

It was that profound and that simple.

Life *was* messy—relationships, expectations, emotions. All my life I'd skirted around them, investing in just enough to get by, but no more. I'd used my family as a shield, and an excuse. They were tied to me by blood so I expected them to be there for me. Not my mother, but everyone else.

But then I'd become an IR agent. Initially as a means to escape a life in prison sentence, but slowly, in incremental steps, my life had changed. I started to make friends—okay, a friend—Kelly. Took a lover—Bran.

Yet I'd still held myself back—expecting, waiting for them to abandon me. I'd focused on the next mission, the next do-or-die action, avoiding the part of living that scared the crap out of me—caring, committing, loving. Living truly, wholly, took courage. The kind of courage I'd hid from since forever.

Red Guy appeared beside me again, his voice a husky whisper stirring across my skin. "Now you have found what you came to find."

Talk about a hard shoulder-slam reality check.

My shoulders sank, even as he added, "there will be more for you to learn. Your journey has only begun."

CHAPTER 15

Tears streamed down my face. Sobs wracked my body as I twisted where I was, sprawled in the sand, searching for the new voice. New as in not coming from the Red Guy, Kelly, Mandy or even Benjamin. Or farther afield, it wasn't Bran, or the woman I refused to believe was my mom.

"I told you I would return for you when you needed my help."

Gulping air to slow my blubbering, I shuddered. Ghost Guy. The bastard. He knew I'd end up here, cringing in the dirt, begging to live. He knew.

"Of course I knew." He materialized, not looking like much but the background dun colors. More a shimmer of texture than a human-like form. "I told you so."

Four words that never, not once, made anyone feel better.

I slowly and cautiously picked myself up out of the dirt, creating a cloud of ochre dust around me as I swiped at my clothes, wiping one sleeve across my face, avoiding the expressions on Kelly and Mandy's faces, the fear still trembling through me.

Action. Noziaks acted. We didn't contemplate. Time to remember that.

I knelt down to Benjamin, who'd remained at my side, his hand still curled within mine. His gaze still trusting.

Had I ever been that way? Wrong question. Better question was could I ever be that way again? Could I ever believe someone would really, truly accept me, warts and all?

Kelly did, no idea why. Bran did, too. And, like a chicken facing the chopping block I'd skittered away. But maybe, now,

I could make different choices. Make it up to him. Show him what I'd feared to show him up to this point—my heart.

Baby steps. Help Benjamin. Then, maybe, if I could, help myself.

"You still see your mom and dad?" I asked, hardest words I think I'd ever said.

He nodded, all big eyes and solemn look.

"And you want to go to them? Be with them?"

"Yes, lady."

And I knew what I had to do. Choices. It always came down to choices.

I hugged him, squeezing him more for my sake than his, wanting to believe his small, chunky body was solid. But it wasn't. Only now did I accept what I'd undertaken for him.

He'd been waiting for hundreds of years to reach this place. These people. And to let him go tore me apart.

I sniffed, just once, and opened my eyes wide so the damn tears would slow down, but my voice held reasonably steady as I said, "Then this is goodbye." Only then did I release him, remaining on my knees in the dirt.

He didn't say anything, just turned and skipped off, calling. "Mum. I'm comin'."

I didn't think my heart could break any more. But I was wrong.

Benjamin stopped, just for a second, turned and waved at me.

Then he was gone.

CHAPTER 16

I didn't cry. Not in public. And I certainly didn't kneel in the dirt and blubber.

Kelly appeared beside me, reached out her hand, then let it fall. She was right. I had to face whatever was happening on my own.

When I could, and it took a few tries, I staggered to my feet, sniffing hard and rubbing a dirty sleeve across my face. Not that it was helping a lot, but the grit helped knock some sense into me. Only when I was sure I looked as funky as Red Guy, only in dirt browns and blotchy beiges, did I turn to glance at my companions.

Kelly stood to the side. I hadn't asked her if she could see the two spirits in front of us. Mandy could. Her expression combined wariness, distrust and suspicion. She didn't even spare a glance for me.

Didn't blame her. I was supposed to be team leader, not an emotional basket case imploding in front of her. Tough. I still reeled from being scoured from the inside out. I'd deal with Mandy later.

In front of me, Red Guy nodded at Ghost Guy. Nothing I hated more than a smug expression. Especially one at my expense.

"You two know each other?" I growled. Should have figured. Bastard one meet bastard two. Why did I feel like I'd been set up?

Maybe because I had been. You'd think I'd get used to it after hanging out with Bran when his way and my way didn't mesh. Which happened a lot.

Funny how awareness of him kept washing over me. Not the laugh, laugh kind of funny either. More like a when-will-this-feeling pass kind of spasm.

"We know of one another," Red Guy answered, moving to stand on one side of me as Ghost Guy stood on the other. Kelly stepped away, closer to Mandy—a smart move. The tree flanked my back. No way was I ready to face it again. Not until I controlled the tremors still pulsing through me.

Kelly whispered, "You okay?"

"I will be." And I meant it. Enough of spirits jerking me around, as I looked at the spirits in question. "You two finished?"

"You're talking to someone." She didn't say it as a question.

"Getting directions. I'll explain everything in a sec."

One thing at a time. Set these two straight. Find how to get to the Underworld. Rescue Aini. I spoke to my spectral advisors, tired of half-answers and vague directions.

"You said I wasn't dead." I shot a harsh glance at Ghost Guy, who actually opened his empty socket eyes wider. Very creepy.

"And you are not."

I jerked my thumb over my shoulder toward the tree. "Then why'd your pal lead me here?" And where exactly has Benjamin gone?

"You are human."

Like that meant anything? I couldn't be dead because I was human? Or I waltzed to the tree of all trees because I was human? I threw my hands wide, fed up with all the crypto-babble.

"The gift of humans has always been choices," Red Guy spoke, a sound so deep it vibrated like a bass through me. Or the sound of a prison warden warning me to keep my nose clean while in his facility. Fat lot of good that did.

And that bloody word. *Choices.* Embroider it on a pillow, for land's sake but quit shoving it in my face.

"I didn't choose to come here and get the innards scared out of me." I tried not to sound like a pissed-off kid, no matter how much I felt like one right then. Good thing I wasn't crossing my arms or stamping my feet, always a dead giveaway, pun intended. And I hadn't really spoken the truth. I hadn't chosen to be here, but to save Aini, not this whole journey into self-realization. Leave that to the granola eaters.

Ghost Guy and Red Guy both nodded, like they were dealing with a particularly cranky toddler in spite of my best intentions. It was Ghost who answered. "You are in one of several worlds. Your choice is to descend deeper to find who you seek on the chance you can return to the earthly Realm. Or to release your shell and remain here. Permanently."

Live or die? That's what I'd been juggling?

Since when?

On second thought, wasn't that why Benjamin disappeared? He chose his parents. I cried that I wanted to live. Technically I blubbered that I didn't want to die so by default that meant to live. Didn't mean I got to, with the whole finding the Horned One and taking Aini from him. But it looked like I might, which was a whole lot more than I'd expected up to this point.

Living meant more than simply breathing and occupying space. It meant committing and risking and getting hurt. Not as the only option but because we didn't get connection and high-fives and love only by existing. There were always two sides to balance out life. Seemed like lately I'd been only focusing on what I didn't want and couldn't have. I'd forgotten what I did want and was willing to challenge myself to obtain—and that didn't mean a fancier car or a big house. It meant having teammates, even the ones that rubbed me the wrong way. And family, even when they tried my patience. And love, most of all love, even when it meant I had to compromise sometimes.

I felt stupid, but also liberated. "I didn't know I had a choice."

"Clearly," rumbled Red Guy.

Good thing he looked like such a scary-assed dude or I'd have smacked him. Accepting that I'd always had a choice didn't mean I wanted to have the process, and my fears, rubbed in my face.

I could have sworn Ghost chuckled as he shook his head. "You sought clarity." He paused, then added in a sterner voice, "Not always an easy process."

"Now you tell me." I steeled my spine enough to turn around and look at the center of the universe, the Tree of Life, only to find it had vanished.

One second there. Then? Presto. Gone!

CHAPTER 17

Pivoting so fast I made myself dizzy, I hunted in every direction. I had to be losing my mind. It'd been right here. Now nothing. No branches. No huge trunk. No gnarly roots. Just sweeping vistas of brown on brown. "Where'd it go?"

"It is no longer needed," Red Guy said. "The tree is the center, the beginning, the place where you start. Now you must walk the path."

What? But I'd just found the tree and my reason to keep going. Did it have to disappear so soon?

"I need it," I choked out, then grabbed at only one of the reasons I wasn't ready for its disappearing act. "We have to get to the Underworld. Wasn't the tree our way?"

"There is more than one path to that which you seek," came his mumbo jumbo response.

Enough with cryptic males. If I was going to be dead, then let me be dead. But since I'd chosen life, or it'd chosen me, time to get on with it. Find the Horned One and straighten out a few things. Like how Aini was returning with us. And Bran? His name kept crowding into my thoughts. It always came back to him. I shook my head. Scarlett O'Hara was right. I'd deal with him later. There were only so many grenades a woman could juggle at once, and I was at my limit.

Before I could say anything, a strange whistle started coming from Red Guy. Louder and louder. Then I noticed him fading, starting with his face.

"Wait!" I shouted, which did nothing. "Where's he going?" I demanded of the ghost, when Red Guy dulled to a light pink.

"To where he belongs."

"But—"

I stood there, feeling like an idiot turned inside out as Red Guy wasted away, not saying a word. Then disappeared.

CHAPTER 18

It wasn't like we'd become BFFs, but now I was stuck only with Ghost Guy, which was like getting stuck with one of the seven plagues of Egypt.

I eyed him, half expecting him to pull the disappearing act like he'd done to me already.

"You wish something?" his voice so reasonable I wanted to scream.

"I want out of here." I shouted the words as if that'd make them happen faster. "No, on second thought, I want to get to the Underworld. With my friends." I jerked a thumb toward Kelly and Mandy.

Okay, using the friend word with Mandy's name was stretching things, but it'd take too long to explain teammate and all that.

Ghost smiled, then angled his head. "You only had to ask."

And here I thought he was going to do that whole for-a-favor routine again. My shoulders eased a micro-inch.

"Now you shall owe me two favors," he continued before I'd even inhaled a deep breath.

Of all the low down, sneaky, black dog behavior. But I didn't say anything. Not a word. Just stood there with my hands balled, glaring.

He shrugged, his tone so smug I wanted to lunge at him and stomp. "You expected something else?"

"Not from you."

He offered a wimpy smile. "Two favors. Agreed?"

"What kind of favors?" I back-pedaled, suddenly realizing that in many of the original fairy tales, the ones full of darkness and bad things happening, a favor could mean the loss of a first born, or death and disembowelment, or even something worse. Better late than never to figure out the fine print in any arrangement I was making with this guy.

Not that I had a lot of choices. It was favor or remaining lost in a dun-colored world and leaving Aini with the Horned One.

"I'm not an unreasonable man," he said, as if I'd called his integrity into question.

"You're not any kind of man." I glanced around to see if there was an exit sign anywhere.

There wasn't, but then my brothers always chided me for being too optimistic. What I did notice was the light fading, as if someone was cranking on a dimmer switch. I shivered. How to make an empty desert world scarier? Make it a dark, empty desert world. No thank you!

"You crush me," Ghost Guy spoke, snagging my attention, not looking crushed at all. Smug, yes, but nary a hint of hurt feelings.

"I notice you're avoiding the direct question." I faced him, hands now fisted on hips. Yeah, I can get in-your-face belligerent when someone is messing with me. Growing up with brothers taught me that lesson early and well. "Spell out exactly what a 'favor' means to you."

He glanced away as if weighing his answer. He looked away so long that when his gaze finally shifted back to mine, I expected some major revelation. Instead I got, "I'm looking for something."

Aren't we all? Hadn't I just learned that hard-won lesson?

I narrowed my eyes. "What kind of 'thing'?"

"Something that belonged to me. Before."

I couldn't believe this. It sounded like ghost dude left something behind on the earthly plane and now expected me to play fetch and return. If I was lucky it'd be a baseball trading card or favorite poker shirt. Too bad I wasn't that lucky.

So what could he have left behind? A heart? A person? Something I really, really didn't want to have to collect? The last was a guarantee.

"Wait a sec." I shook my head. "Material items can't cross from the temporal plane to the spiritual."

I might be behind on knowing the finer points of shamanism but that issue I did know. Why? Because last time I'd been here, I'd have given my right arm to have brought along a weapon strong enough to kill a djinn. Think wicked bad-ass genie with no redeemable traits. But I didn't get my wish and almost got Mandy and me both killed.

"For most items, you're correct." Now he sounded like a stuffy butler. But what worried me was that key word, "most."

"Explain."

He might have the rest of his existence here on this plane, but I wanted away from it. Now. We had a mission to finish, and, like an itch between the shoulder blades, I was more and more aware of the passage of time with all the fading light happening. Aini's time was running out. And if it did, humans were next. Not a warm and fuzzy feeling at all.

I still had no clear idea where to find her. I knew the general where—the deeper levels of the Underworld. But I needed more than that, and I needed it now.

Ghost Guy said, "All you are required to know is that it *is* possible to transit *some* items through the barriers."

"Not an item that's going to set off bells and whistles?" I wasn't sure who was really in charge of this Realm, and I didn't fancy finding out. "Or harm another?"

"Transporting the item will cause you no harm here."

Why did I feel like there was a whole lot he wasn't saying? Probably because after even a few months as an IR Agent, I was learning that it was the gray areas in life that caused you the biggest problems.

And, like that, an image of Bran forced its way into my thoughts. Not that I'd say he was a gray kind of guy—more black and white. His way or the highway. That and the whole dark and dangerous vibe he had going on. If he wasn't a powerful warlock, he'd make a good vampire. Lookswise at least. Especially with those Celtic blue eyes of his. And the way he could stare right through you. And the way being in his presence ten minutes made you want to jump his bones or smack him.

"Spirit to Alex." The ghost mentally nudged me back to the pressing present. "Do we have a deal?"

Fight, flee or freeze? My primordial brain screamed wait-just-a-minute. A carte blanche, open-ended deal meant trouble. Even as I weighed the choices, I accepted that there were none. Aini's life, and the lives of who knew how many if the Horned One was allowed to succeed, against an *unknown* favor sometime in the future?

Like I was really going to say no? That didn't mean my yes was very gracious, or very loud.

"And they said you'd never agree." He arched his brow, not a good look for him.

What did he mean, 'they'? But before I could ask, he said, "Ready to go on?"

"To the Underworld?"

"Of course."

No 'of course' about it. Not in this place.

I glanced behind me and waved Kelly and Mandy forward before I turned to the ghost. "All three of us need to go."

"That might—"

"Do it or no deal," I growled.

He paused then gave a reluctant head dip.

"Ready?" I asked my teammates. Kelly offered a wobbly smile, a nice contrast to Mandy's thin lips and tense jaw. But she did nod.

I turned back to the ghost. "I'm read—"

Before I could finish, I catapulted through time and space, pulled six ways from Sunday and pummeled into a body that felt too small, too fragile and in way too much pain.

I screamed. And screamed. And screamed, as heat blasted through me—acid etching my blood. Firing every nerve into hyper-sensitive.

And between one harsh, pain-washed breath and the next, I woke up.

Then wished I hadn't.

CHAPTER 19

I looked around, sure that Ghost Guy had royally messed with us as I'd been smacked down in the middle of what looked like an airport terminal. I lay sprawled on a hard, and not too clean, scuffed, yellow-flecked linoleum floor beneath a set of cracked plastic chairs. From my vantage point, flat on my back, I could see legs and feet, shoes actually, scurrying past, and hear the metallic, blurred sound of announcements floating overhead. But the messages were in a different language.

Yup, I was in Hell for sure.

So where were Kels and Mandy?

Using the seats to tug myself upright, at least upright enough to flop down into one of them, I bit back a groan. There had to be a less violent way to move around in these realms. At this rate, my muscles and bones weren't going to survive too many more pop-here-pop-there journeys.

Massaging my leg muscles, I checked out my surroundings. People, lots and lots of people, mostly adults but some teens, flowed around me in a focused catatonic Stepford Wives way. No one looked right or left, they simply moved as if there was someplace else they needed to be. The terminal, or this part of it, looked industrial gray, everything muted with faded, washed-out colors. Come to think of it, the people appeared that way, too. As if leached of any spark of life.

Which made sense, given where I was.

Enough with getting my bearings, more importantly, where were my teammates?

I lumbered to my feet, aware of the dryness of my throat, the lack of give in my muscles. One too many pummelings lately.

"Kels?" I called out, it sounding more like a croak.

Since I could pretty much see every spot within a three-hundred and sixty degrees radius, it was clear Kelly and Mandy weren't around here.

If that ghost screwed me over, he could take his second favor and shove it.

I expected that small lick of anger to give me some energy. It didn't. What it did was cause those people closest to me to all swivel their heads at the same time to stare at me.

Talk about creepy.

They didn't approach me, which was good because I seriously would have launched myself from sitting to standing on my chair in seconds flat.

No, they simply glared at me out of vacant, filmy-colored eyes. Not white but murky pale.

I so had to get out of here.

Standing and stepping forward made facing demons and killer druids seem easy. But like any airport I'd ever been in, there seemed to be a silent code communicated by total strangers passing one another. No speaking, no direct eye contact, just slide into the flow and go with it.

But where?

Like an automaton, I advanced. Most of the people around me looked like everyone I'd seen at any of the dozen airports I'd passed through recently—wearing jeans, saris, *burkas;* carrying backpacks, briefcases and purses. But no one had any roll-on luggage. Or held the hand of another. Everyone was alone. Isolated.

Enough. I wasn't here to do a kinship or social structure study. I was on a mission. Time to get my head in the game. First step—find Kelly and Mandy. Second step—find Aini. Third step—rescue her. Fourth step—get out of here in one piece.

Now I moved with purpose, my stride longer, looking for what stood out in a scenario of sameness. I should have bumped a few shoulders but didn't. Instead I brushed through people, as if passing mist.

Don't think. Focus. Or lose it.

As I walked, I noticed this area of the terminal kept expanding. I know I felt that way when I needed to rush between planes; the gate I arrived at and the one I needed to depart from were always as far away from each other as possible. It was that sensation—the more I walked, the greater the distances became. But nothing stood out. Until—

There. Ahead and to the right. Someone standing absolutely still, a woman, enough of an anomaly to snag my attention. I wanted to call to her, or give a leap of excitement but held back. No idea how an emotional aberration that large would be construed around here.

Except the woman didn't have Kelly's blonde ponytail or Mandy's thick, black hair. This woman wore some kind of close-knit head covering and what looked like a hospital gown. One of those flimsy cotton ones, tied in the back— not what one would wear to an airport.

As I came up closer to her, I hesitated, sort of sliding around until I stood in front of her.

She raised her head, her gaze snapping to mine, confusion and some other more dangerous emotion deep in the brown of her eyes. I was still processing the fact that her eyes weren't the opaque whiteness of everyone else's when she took me by surprise and spoke.

"Where are we?" she asked, her voice raspy.

Why did everyone think I knew the answer to that question?

I shrugged. Not the best of responses, so I added, "Far as I know, we're in the Underworld, or close to it."

Furrows dug deep grooves between her brows as she glanced down while raising her hands from her sides. My gaze followed hers until I noticed what she was looking at—ragged gashes like hash marks across her wrists—blood red against the paleness of her skin.

Cripes. What happened?

"I couldn't stand the pain any longer," she whispered, as if I'd spoken out loud.

My stomach dove as her words sank in. "Suicide?"

She nodded, a weak, slow movement. "I only wanted the pain to stop."

Then, as we both watched, the blood disappeared, pale scars appeared and she let her arms drop.

When she looked up, I could already see the film starting to cover her eyes.

No, wait, I wanted her to stay, to help me, but she couldn't. Already her color began bleaching, her body outline fading. In only seconds, her gaze no longer met mine and she shuffled off.

She must have just died. That's why she initially looked confused. And that other emotion? Fear. Then relief.

Brushing dampness from my eyes, I found myself wanting to lash out, to cry, to pound a wall with my fists. That's when it hit me. The sensation washing against me, since I first opened my eyes in this terminal, was one of resignation. These people might not know where they were, but somewhere, deep inside, they accepted that they belonged here. At least for a while.

I hoped the childhood stories I'd been told about a waiting room for souls was real. That this wasn't really Hell, but maybe a first level. Which made sort of a twisted sense. Just as there were degrees of badness, of evil, that there might be degrees of Hell.

That woman, driven out of her mind with pain, made a choice. One that landed her here. But I'd like to think her choice was not a one-way ticket to an eternity of—

"Alex!"

Mandy's cry startled me. Scared me, to tell the truth, as I pivoted around and spied her, leading a stumbling Kelly beside her.

What the—

As they neared, I noticed how Mandy's arm wrapped around Kelly's. How Kelly kept moving her head as a dog did when listening intently. A frown stained Mandy's face.

I didn't need to ask anything before Mandy said, "She's blind."

CHAPTER 20

On a scale of one to ten, being on a mission to Hell with a blind teammate ranked as an eight or nine.

"What do you mean she's blind?"

"Just what I said." Mandy glowered at Kelly then at me. "I found her like this."

"I'm right here," Kelly spoke up. "Not deaf. Only blind."

"Like when you turn invisible and then come back?" Kelly had a really cool ability—invisibility—with a wicked side effect—being blind for twice as long as she'd been invisible. Not lately though. Her gift, if that's what it was, had been wonky. She couldn't use it. Then, last night, while battling the Horned One, she'd been able to wink out of sight again, and stay away longer than she ever had before. So what was going on now?

Kelly shook her head. "No. It's different."

"How?"

"I don't know. I just know it's different."

Because I heard the exasperation skimming the surface of her words, I bit back my own frustration.

"You weren't blind before? I mean when you were alone with Mandy?" Not that it'd make much difference. The more important question was when would she be able to see again?

"No. Up until now, but when we came here, then yeah," the last word eeked out. "I heard Aini's voice as I was hurtling through the darkness. Then pow! I landed like a sack tossed off of a high building. And I was like this." She waved a hand toward her face. "Maybe it's temporary and I'll be able to see any moment."

"This sucks," I murmured, trying to figure out what to do next while keeping a stiff upper lip and all that. The very fact Kels didn't know herself if the blindness was a blip or a big deal warned me to stay calm. Running around like a headless chicken wasn't going to help her or any of us.

Time ticked past, but leading a blind person through the levels of Hell was not a smart option. Leaving her behind wasn't either.

"Is *this* Hell?" Mandy asked, her in-your-face tone reverberating around us, earning some of those blank stares I'd noticed earlier.

I lowered my voice. "Far as I can tell, it might be one of the levels."

"And that means?" This time Mandy's voice ramped up to angry. Like this whole lost in the Underworld issue was my problem.

"It means we have to figure out where Aini is." My tone wasn't any less caustic than Mandy's, but I was damn tired of being the non-functioning GPS for the Underworld. My task was to get the three of us here—which I did. Not as cleanly or straight forward as I'd have liked but we were here. And, if we survived, to get us back.

Before Mandy could snap a retort, a sound washed around us. A shushing murmur, like rubbing sandpaper against wood.

I looked around, then wished I hadn't.

The people, or souls, were no longer just glaring at us, they were pressing closer.

All the spit in my mouth evaporated.

"What's going on?" Mandy demanded, nudging Kelly closer to the two of us.

Heck if I knew. But I didn't say it.

Then I remembered what Mandy was—a Spirit Walker. Which meant if any of these spirits realized that fact, Mandy was in deep trouble.

A squishy arm brushed against me, sending a chill sliding through me—like grabbing an icicle with bare hands. Only creepier.

"Mandy," I whispered, trying to keep the panic out of my voice, "squeeze in behind me. Kelly, put your hands on Mandy's shoulders."

"Like a train?" Kelly asked.

"Yeah."

"Why—" Mandy started but I cut her off.

"Just do it!"

I heard her mumble, but not loud enough to set off the beings closest to us. Making Mandy a sandwich between us might keep the spirits from passing against, or worse, into her.

"What now?" Kelly asked, fear evident in her voice. Which set off the spirits again.

I evened my words until they were as bland as discussing dishwashing liquid or the sex lives of banana slugs. "Emotion. Attracts. Their. Attention."

"The—"

"Yes." I bit off, hearing the rising panic behind Mandy's single word. "Let's start walking," I said out of the side of my mouth as I shuffled forward, trusting Mandy to follow and Kelly to hold on to her. "This way."

"What's that way?" Mandy murmured. At least she was moving.

"No idea. Just hoping it'll take us away from here."

Even though she was the caboose of our mini-train, I could feel Kelly shaking, which seemed to agitate the closest people. I knew it was hard for her, not seeing what we faced but feeling them with each whisper against her.

"You have a feel happy song?" I tossed out, for Kelly's sake as much as mine and Mandy's.

"Like *Don't Worry, Be Happy?*"

"Sing that and I'll gag," Mandy admitted as we continued our slow shuffle-step-slide forward.

"Maybe something that helped with your kids, Kels. Soothing." With each forward motion, we pushed straight into the sightless souls.

Ugh.

I could hear Kelly groan too, so I wasn't alone. She couldn't see the souls so had no idea she was passing through chests and heads, but she could clearly feel them.

Right now we needed to put some distance between the jam-packed soul crowds and us. Where had all these people come from? And why were they hanging around? A better question was, how could I get them to disappear?

Not that they were hurting us. At least not physically. But emotionally? That was a different issue.

Each step, each brush, each pass through was like wading deeper and deeper into a cesspool of despair and unhappiness—an ice-cold morass of misery.

We had a neighbor when I was little that everyone called Old Lady Wilson. She probably wasn't that old, maybe late fifties or early sixties, but her face wore the deep furrows and gouges of discontent—her mouth constantly pressed into a solid frown, her only words were complaints, even her eyes squinted constant disapproval. I used to hate it when my dad would take me with him to visit her. Minutes would stretch into hours and sunny days became gray ones around her.

That's what this felt like. A world of Mrs. Wilsons magnified.

Kelly had started humming some catchy song I should have recognized but couldn't put a name to. It helped. My shoulders eased a smidge. So I joined in. Singing I sucked at but humming I could do.

Slide-shuffle-hum. Slide-shuffle-hum.

"We there yet?" Kelly spoke, making me jump. Not because she sounded worried or afraid now, but just the opposite. Her words were so normal, so neutral they made me smile. Movement must be helping her, knowing we were doing something.

A breath of clean cool air seemed to waft around us even though I hadn't noticed any breeze or tickle of air before. And the spirits? Were some looking away?

"They're zombies, aren't they." Mandy said out of the blue, not making it a question.

Damn.

I heard Kelly's quick intake of breath, felt the falter of her step.

"Smile," I whispered to Mandy, knowing Kelly could hear me. "Laugh if you can."

"Are you crazy?" came Mandy's whiplash response.

Instead of answering directly, I explained in as terse a way as I could. "Emotion. They're feeding off our negative emotions. Fear. Frustration. Anger. We've got to starve them to get them to clear away."

"What—"

"Just do it." Wrong response, or vibration to my response, as the murmuring increased again.

I cleared my throat, raised my head and threw back my shoulders. Yup, just walking through a park. "Lovely day, don't you think?"

The look Mandy gave me as I glanced over my shoulder was priceless. It was Kelly's response, though, that helped turn the tide. "Are we in a park now?"

"Yup." Why not? If she couldn't see how would she know. "Over there a couple of kids are playing on the swings. And an older man is walking his dog. Something small and all brown except for its paws." Crap, what else happened at a park? It'd been so long, I'd forgotten. "Oh, and there, Mandy, is that someone flying a kite?"

I'm sure she rolled her eyes, not that I blamed her. I'd have given anything right then to be in a park, any park, anywhere.

"It's a dragon kite," Mandy said, easing the tenseness in my jaw. "And there're a couple of *comemierdas* passing a joint."

So Mandy's idea of a park wasn't mine. Go figure.

"What's a *comemierda?*" Kelly asked.

I jumped in. "I think it means old men." Not really. More along the lines of assholes, but we were supposed to be aiming for light and happy. Technically, the word wasn't one Kelly would use anyway, and now wasn't the time to teach it to her.

Good news was that the zombie crowd was beginning to disperse, swinging back by ones and twos into their monotonous movement, ebbing around us.

"At last," Mandy sighed.

"What's happening?" Kelly asked from behind us.

Instead of telling the truth, I lied. Why not? We were in Hell anyway.

"We've reached the end of the park." I kept my voice as neutral as possible. Which wasn't easy given what had just opened in front of us. Not more endless flat gray space. A few minutes ago I was wishing for a break in this monotony, but now? Not so much.

"There are two escalators." Which made sense with the whole terminal theme, but there was something about them that gave me the shivers. "They're both heading down."

I think that was the problem. Given both escalators disappeared into the shadows the deeper they went, which one should we take?

"Pick one," Mandy said, knowing in another minute we'd either have to stop or be forced to make a choice—one that could be wrong. "Anything's better than zombies."

Good point.

"Let's take the left one. It's going in the right direction." Both were but we were almost on top of the left one. Taking it meant leaving the zombie crowds behind as there wasn't one zombie on it. It could also mean we'd end up someplace worse than where we were. But isn't that where we were supposed to go? Where the Horned One resided?

Besides, if it was wrong, we could try and walk back up it. Not that it'd be easy with Kelly being blind, but we'd get to that hurdle when we had to face it.

We didn't have time for a vote as I stepped forward, grabbing the moving handrail and calling back to Kelly. "Watch that first step."

Since the zombies were not surrounding us as thickly now, Mandy turned and guided Kelly until the three of us were slowly, but surely, descending.

None of us spoke. Nothing like heading deeper and deeper into darkness to dry the mouth.

"This is better." Kelly broke the strain, until she added, "Isn't it?"

I cleared my throat. "Yup. Headed in the right direction. No spirits to hassle Mandy. What's not to like?"

Plenty. Especially as the escalator slowed and spilled us out into a sandy flat space. It wasn't like the desert we'd been in, more like a sandy beach.

Mandy and I both stopped, which caused Kelly to stumble into Mandy's back.

"What is it?" she demanded. "I can't hear anything."

Neither could I, but I didn't need to hear to want to turn around and run away. I did pivot, looking for the escalator, or a way back up, but there was nothing. Really nothing. Not the escalator we came down on. Not the second one. A big fat donut hole.

My stomach slammed into my throat as my muscles froze, but panic wouldn't help.

"Looks like we've reached a second level," I hedged, swallowing deeply.

We stood in the middle of an island. All around us the sand gave way to what looked like a river—a rolling, seething river of fire. I'd seen pictures of magma but they paled in comparison to this. Easily two hundred yards wide on all sides, the fire oozed along—oranges and reds and yellows twisting and tumbling together.

But that wasn't the worst part. Within the river were body parts—heads and arms and hands—all twisting and straining.

But no sound. Open mouths caught in mid-scream, but nothing audible was there.

"Look at the edges," Mandy whispered next to me, chewing her lower lip.

I wanted to ask what edges. Instead I followed the direction of her gaze. Like a sand castle built too close to an ocean's brutal waves, the island silently, relentlessly eroded as the river ate away the fragile sand.

Soon it'd sink into that river. . .

CHAPTER 21

"Kelly, could you try and reach Aini again?" I asked, more to keep her busy than anything else while I grappled with the task before me. I had no idea how we were going to get across this river. All I knew was we had to do something. Quickly.

Kelly now stood slightly behind Mandy and me where we could keep an eye on her as we tried to figure out what to do next.

"Any great ideas, now?" Mandy asked, looking on either side of us to see if there was any alternative to standing, waiting to slide into the fire.

Nada.

"Fresh out." Every direction I gazed there was just sand, river and far away on the opposite side of the blood-red sludge, what might be more flat land.

Kelly sighed, jerking me back to the present. "Nothing from Aini. Absolutely nothing." She shook her head, her sightless eyes cast down.

"That's not good." Mandy echoed my thoughts.

I expected a why-bother attitude from Mandy but if Kelly was getting worried too, we were sunk.

The only good news was I could still hear the faint drumbeat that indicated we were still alive and connected to the Real Realm. So we weren't cut off. Yet.

"You still haven't told me where we are," Kelly said, walking forward until she brushed my shoulder. "What are you seeing?"

Mandy jumped in before I could. "A wide river with no way to get on the other side."

A good description. Leave out all the bad parts, and that's basically what we had.

"I'm assuming there's no obvious way to cross it." Kelly was doing that head tilting movement as if seeking knowledge from listening. I only hoped she couldn't hear sand eroding.

"No means to cross that we can see."

"Is your brother around?" Kelly asked, looking where Mandy stood.

"No." The word was so sad, there wasn't a lot more to say. Not that I particularly wanted to follow the directions of Mandy's dead brother—a brother none of us even knew she'd had until now.

"Can't you do a spell to fly us to the other side?" Kelly's expression was suddenly hopeful.

I wished it were that easy. Now if I were Sabina, the young witch I'd found and befriended in Paris a few missions ago, flying across the river would be a piece of cake. But I wasn't her.

I squared my shoulders to share the not-so-good news. "Earlier, when we were separated, I tried to cast a spell and couldn't do it." I hated every single word I uttered.

"Was it a flying spell?" That was so like Kelly—keep it positive while looking for the silver lining.

"No, but—"

"Then why not try one." She paused, then added, "You do know one, don't you?"

"Yes. . . and no."

Mandy glared at me. "Either you do or don't. Which is it?"

"Flying spells aren't like scrying or casting a shadow to hide behind. They backfire more easily and take a lot more energy to create. Even then, so many things can go wrong with them."

"Meaning?" she demanded.

"One second you're on terra firma, or whatever the equivalent is here, the next you're soaring in the air."

"Sounds like fun," Kelly said.

"Not if you can't get back down." Sure I was playing Nanny-nay-sayer but magic wasn't all sparkles and love charms. "Besides, I could only move one of us at a time. If the spell worked, and that is a big if, too much magic could send one of us out of orbit. Too little magic and—" I glanced at the flow of dismembered corpses.

"We hit the river." Mandy's words sounded more resigned than angry.

"Exactly." I nodded toward the other side. "Plus we don't have any idea of what's over there. Quicksand? Something worse than where we are now? Who knows?"

"I know what's over there." Kelly stepped forward, raising her chin. "Aini is. Somewhere. And she's running out of time."

A burn started low in my gut. She was right but didn't know what we really faced—do nothing and crumble with the sand into the river.

"I'll go first," she offered, her voice calm and determined.

"No way." I shook my head though she couldn't see me. "There's no way to tell where you're landing without sight." I inhaled deeply. "I'll go."

"That's the stupidest idea yet." Mandy muscled her way between Kelly and me. "If you go and use up all your magic, we're stuck on this side."

"Then I'd go on alone to get Aini." I glanced around. "There aren't any spirits or zombies here to get you. It's as safe as any place we've been so far."

"There's also no way to return to our world without you." She jabbed a finger at the ground. "And we're running out of time."

I ignored the *duh* in her voice because I deserved it. She nailed the problem. Leaving them here was a definite no-win. And since I was the shaman who brought her and Kelly over with me, I had to return with them. If we got to return.

"It looks like I get to do a test flight." Mandy didn't sound too happy about the possibility.

Crap and double crap. Trying a risky spell, one I didn't have a lot of experience with in the best of situations, wasn't easy. Here? No way could I live with myself if I sent Mandy careening into that molten river. Or into an unknown threat on the other side.

Mandy turned toward me, her gaze spearing mine. "There is

no other way. Not with the time we have." She shrugged one shoulder toward the closest shore that was disappearing second by second.

I threw my hands out. "If I screw up this spell, then you'll die."

Yes, I was getting heated. Bite me. Mandy was the one risking her life if she went first, but I was the one who was going to have to live with what happened if I screwed up.

"Then don't screw up," Mandy shot back, as if it was that easy.

"Listen." Kelly spoke up, stepping closer to the river. Close enough I nabbed her arm just in case she got too close.

"What?" Mandy asked.

"I hear her—Aini. Her heartbeat."

"You sure it's not the drums tethering us to our Real Realm?"

"I'm sure."

Crap, I was afraid of that.

"Where?" I braced myself for the answer.

Sure enough she raised her hand like that painting in the Sistine Chapel, the one with one finger pointing. Wouldn't you know it aimed for the other side of the bloody stupid river.

"How can you be sure?" I asked.

"Yeah." Mandy backed me up. "How many heartbeats might be around here?"

That's when the sinking feeling in my stomach hit bottom. "There should only be one other than us. Aini's." I straightened my shoulders, knowing our decision had been made.

"Because?"

"We're the only ones alive, that's why."

I was testy, but for good reasons. I so didn't want to try a spell and fail, try this particular spell. I didn't want to risk my teammates' lives on the iffy chance I could make the spell work. And I really, really didn't want to head in the direction Kelly showed us.

It wasn't that I was afraid, because I was, soul deep rattling in my boots kind of afraid. But because, after facing that

Yggdrasil tree, where I felt centered and sure in a way I hadn't since I'd killed the Were attacking my brother, I knew even as I chose life, that what I faced ahead was death.

My death.

CHAPTER 22

"Well?" Mandy's single word slapped against me. "We're running out of time."

Like I didn't know that. But taking Mandy's head off, metaphorically, before I risked it, literally, wasn't going to change what I had to do right here and now.

"Fine." Nothing was fine, but bitching about it wasn't helping either, so I stepped forward and pulled Kelly far enough back from the river's edge that I didn't have to worry about her while I tried to do what I'd attempted only once before.

I had been about fourteen, standing on the roof of my dad's barn, determined to fly.

Less than five minutes later I was writhing on the ground with my arm broken in two places. Not a story I'd be sharing with Mandy any time soon.

"What should I be doing?" Mandy asked, shaking her arms out like a prizefighter does before entering the ring. A good analogy.

"Stand over there." I motioned toward a sandy area, clear of any debris. "Face the direction you want to go and I'll face away from you."

I didn't know if that was necessary but it couldn't hurt. Plus it meant I didn't have to look too closely at the river and all those body parts floating past, which meant I could focus on the spell and not on all the ways the spell could implode.

"Since I won't be looking at your trajectory—" I steeled my voice so it sounded like I knew what the heck I was doing— "you'll have to let me know if I need to send you higher, or lower, and when to let you down once you arrive on the other side."

If you arrive on the other side.

"How am I supposed to do that?" she asked, her eyes widening. "It's not like we have our comm sets."

"Shout at me."

I got a WTF look. "And if I'm too high or far away? What then?"

Then you're so sorry out of luck.

What I said was, "We'll figure out the small details as we go along." In other words, keep quiet.

"Why can't you just watch me to make sure?"

I nodded toward the river. "I have to keep one hundred percent of my concentration on holding the spell. If you want me to have my attention divided, then—"

"Forget it."

Kelly must have known what I was thinking as she spoke up. "You'll be fine, Mandy. Alex knows what she's doing."

Want to bet?

I spread my feet to create a strong base beneath me and lowered my hands beside me. This had better work.

Then I remembered, "What color of wings do you want?"

"What?"

"Wings? You get a choice of colors."

"*Me lo paso por la cabeza de la pinga,*" she muttered. I didn't ask for a translation as I could guess what she meant and none of it was pleasant.

"Fine. I'll choose the color."

"Can't you just . . . I don't know. . . just levitate me across?"

"Trust me, flying is easier." *If it worked.*

I centered myself, slowing my breathing, easing the tension out of my shoulders, my neck, my arms, and closed my eyes before I started speaking.

"Wings I seek, here and now.
Feel them, touch them.
Wings of light, wings of power.
Bring them forth."

I peeped open one eye, aware Mandy still stood behind me. I cast a glance over my shoulder and caught her head cocked as if taunting me to bring it on.

Fine, Chiquita. I will.

Squeezing my eyes shut once again, I inhaled so deeply my ribcage bowed.

"Powers that be, here and far
I call upon thee.
Lift up the unbeliever. Send her aloft.
Champagne. Lace. Piggy. Rosa.
Unfurl her wings, high and wide.
Rise from the earth, bound no more.
Fly now, fast and free.
So mote it be!"

I heard Mandy cry out, *"Maldito,"* but couldn't look.

"I'm—oh hell."

I took her to mean she was airborne.

"Shit. They're pink."

"What are?" Kelly asked.

"My freaking wings. Noziak, you're an ass."

Since I already knew it, her words didn't scrape my hide.

"Wow!" Kelly whispered, "you did it."

I don't know how she could sound so sure, given she couldn't see.

"Mandy," I shouted, "Where are you? Direct me."

"Oh, yeah." Her voice sounded fainter, which scared the crap out of me. Then she started doing what I needed to know.

"Higher. Not a lot. Whoa. Not that high."

This was harder than steering an ostrich across a Rwandan mine field on an earlier mission, and that was no piece of cake. Using her voice as a guide, I fought to control the magic coursing through me.

"Kelly, keep her talking."

"Mandy?" Kelly shouted. "Directions. Alex needs directions!"

I needed a lobotomy is what I needed.

Mandy kept shouting, sometimes in Cuban Spanish, mostly in English. I know I didn't start breathing fully until I heard her yell, "Down." Then. "Hell, not that hard."

Since I felt like a washrag wrung one too many times, I ignored her. I'd gotten her across in one piece, hadn't I?

By the time I turned to look across to the other side of the river, where Mandy was standing up and waving one hand, I wanted to slide to my knees and hang my head. Magic drains a person. Fighting the Horned One last night and now this? I was scraping bottom, and I still had Kelly and myself to get across.

The fun never stopped.

Yeah, right.

"You ready for me?" Kelly's voice sounded a whole lot too perky for me.

"In a sec."

"Are you okay?" she asked, stepping closer.

Since I could hear the exhaustion in my own voice, no sense in lying to her. "I just need to breathe a moment."

It was true, but so was the force field Kels was sending off. The one yelling 'time's running out'.

Staggering to my feet, I replicated the stance I'd used for Mandy. This time it helped me anchor quaking legs. Even my shifter blood wasn't helping. On the other hand, it might be the only thing keeping me functioning.

"You ready?" I asked Kelly, even as I was asking myself.

"Yup." She straightened up like a little kid heading off to do battle on the playground.

Right then my heart turned over. If I hurt her, in any way, Van would never forgive me. I'd never forgive myself. She was too good, too damn good, to be in this place at all, and here I was, sending her across a river of death and she had no idea what she was facing. Still she trusted me.

I felt like I'd taken a body blow.

But she was waiting and so was Aini.

"Mandy," I called to the other side, "you'll have to direct me because Kelly can't."

Stupid. Stupid. Stupid. I was going to get her killed.

Mandy gave us a thumbs-up signal from across the way.

"I'm ready," Kelly announced, a big smile across her face. "Can I have blue wings?"

"Sure. Why not." Didn't blue make a nice shroud color?

Damn it, Noziak, get your head in the game—focus on what you can do, not what might happen.

I closed my eyes and willed energy to flow through me. By not looking, I wouldn't get distracted, but it was a whole lot harder keeping them shut and trusting that Mandy would be able to direct Kelly to the other side.

No choice though. Standing here like a ninny ate up valuable time.

When I thought my energy was as good as it was going to get I started the chant.

"Powers that be, here and far
I call upon thee."

I cleared my throat, feeling an obstruction.

"Lift up this one. Send her aloft.
Powder. Baby. Periwinkle. Azur.
Unfurl her wings, high and wide."

Someone had hands around my throat, squeezing.

"Rise from the earth, bound no more.
Fly now, fast and free.
So mote it be!"

With a whoosh I heard Kelly lift off. "Wheeeeeee! This is amazing!"

Then Mandy screamed. "Up Noziak. Higher."

But I couldn't do a thing as I tore at invisible hands crushing me.

CHAPTER 23

I was on my knees in the sand, my hands clawing my own throat, being squeezed, squeezed, squeezed.

Mandy screamed from far away, the sounds muting as my airflow decreased.

Then Kelly shouted.

River of fire. Dismembered corpses. Sure death.

Kels. Had to help Kels.

My eyes open, I released my neck, stretching hands and arms outwards, looking towards the river. Kelly skimming the surface.

"Rise from the earth, bound no more.
Fly now, fast and free.
So mote it be!"

The chant was more thought than words but all I had. Pinpricks of light danced in my vision.

This was it. Here. Alone. Kels and Mandy would have to get Aini.

But they couldn't get back without me.

Help. Mother Goddess above. Help me.

I fell forward, face-planting in the sand, keeping my arms before me, my wrists alone elevating my hands, my gaze raised enough to keep sight of Kels. Barely. She lurched in jerky movements, dangling above the fire—her legs curled upward.

"Rise, rise from where thee be.
Fly high, fast and free.

So mote it be!"

She didn't look like a soaring bird, but more like a cowering egg, corkscrewed in on herself, moving in fitful spirals.

Please. Help.

"Link!" a voice shouted, far, far away. A male voice.

"Damnit it, Alex. Link. Now."

Bran?

"Don't be so pig-headed. Link!"

Had to be Bran. Always expecting the impossible. Always wanting something more. Something I couldn't do.

"Now. Or you die."

Always right, too. Damn him.

"Kelly. Needs—"

Not enough air. Time.

"Freeze time. Link. We'll do it together."

Yeah, right.

"Alex, please. Do it for me."

He never played fair.

You'll watch the Guardian die. Then the warlock will watch you die.

A different voice slapped against me. Rough. Raw. Laughing.

The Horned One.

I have the girl. She's mine. Soon she'll give me what I want. Puny witch, you are powerless against me.

Then he laughed. A rolling, chalkboard grating sound. Smug and full of himself.

Wrong words to wave before a Noziak. I might be puny, but I was also desperate. And pissed.

I called every ounce of raw energy I possessed, scraping the bottom of my barrel, and pulsed Kelly higher. High enough I could shift my attention to the linking spell. Seconds only.

I'd take them.

Croaking out the words I promised I'd never use again.

"Adeo. Adeo. Agero. Adepto.
Come. Come. Increase. Acquire.
Suscipio. Solvo.

Receive. Break free."

Then dissolved into a hacking gurgle. I couldn't do this. Not this time.

"Just a little more, babe. Please."

Bran never called me babe. And used the *please* word even less than I did.

More whisper and plea, I uttered the final words.

"As thou be, so now change.
Thought to image.
Image to bind."

Needed blood. Damn. Biting the inside of my lip as hard as I could, I tasted the metallic drops. The demon's laugh increased, a roaring wall of sound surrounding me.

Asshole.

"Bind to blood let.
Continere. Continere. Continere."

My hands dropped. Nothing left.
Sorry, Kels. Forgive me.

CHAPTER 24

Air came first. Seeping into my lungs like the first warm breeze after a brutally cold winter. Teaspoon droplets.

Grit stained my eyes. The wind. I'd forgotten. Not wind as much as a funnel of power swirling around me. Obscuring the river, Kelly, Mandy on the other side.

Damn. I'd lost Kelly.

I rose on my elbows as far as I could get. There, between the waves of fire, Kelly hung suspended, held inches above the river.

Bran's voice roared through me.

"Hemma, hanna, druia.
Hemma, druia, sanctum."

Ancient words, calling forth time. Stopping its flow.

But it didn't still, it slammed to a hard, jerky halt. If I'd had enough air, I'd have screamed against the thunder roaring through me. Fighting time was a PITP, pain in the patootie. You'd think I'd have learned that lesson by now.

The Horned One's laugh tore apart, morphing into a strangled scream.

Take that, jackass.

"Get up, Alex. Can't. Hold. This. For. Long."

Bran. Of course he couldn't. This spell was mine, not his. My bane to endure. He stopped time. My task was to use what he'd done to get Kelly across the river.

"And you," his words whispered across me. "Finish what you came to do. Come back to me."

I clawed to my knees, focusing on Kelly. Using Bran's intensity, his magic joined with mine, I called forth energy and air and hope. The hope created by Bran's words.

"Rise, rise from where thee be
Find the Spirit Walker, the soulless one
Fly high. Fly fast. Fly free.
So mote it be!"

As if I'd released a catapult, Kelly rose upward and snapped forward. She uttered a short, pithy oath I didn't think she knew, but before I could blink she'd landed beside Mandy.

Thank the Great Spirits.

"Now you." Bran's s tone told me he'd hang on until I did what he said, or until the connection drained him dry.

I tottered to my feet. Not steady. Not whole, but I stood. A huge win. Plus I could breathe again.

"Don't know if I can call forth wings." I spoke as if Bran stood beside me, leaning against his strength. What I wouldn't give for that to be true.

"Idiot. Manipulate a Seeking spell."

Of course. How stupid could I be?

"Now. Alex."

Got it. Had to go.

Sucking in one more lungful of blessed, sweet air, even if tainted with smoke and what? Brimstone maybe?

"Alex!"

I'd only used the spell to send others away from me. But if I reversed it then it should work.

Should being the key word.

"To mine own.
Thee I seek.
To go. To go. To go.
Far and fast.
Move me. Move me now."

With a crack of rolling thunder, like heat lightning slashing across a bone-dry summer prairie, time compressed. One second I stood in sand. The next I was doubled over, knee deep in brilliant purple grasses.

Purple? Where the heck was I?

I looked around, half expecting to see Bran, or maybe I so badly wanted to see him that I'd be okay with him being in this place. But he wasn't and for that I could say a silent thank you and release the breath I hadn't realized I'd held.

"Took your freakin' time getting here." Mandy's tone could have sliced petrified rock.

"I'm here, aren't I?"

"Alex?" It was Kels, sitting in the grass, the lower parts of her jeans in tatters. Burned away.

"Ah crap, Kels, I'm so sorry."

"Don't think we should use that word so close to you know what." She glanced over her shoulders toward what looked like a forest. Not an Idaho one of Ponderosa pine with a carpet of yellow cheat grasses and snow berries. No, this looked more like a jungle forest with creeping vines, weeping palm fronds and hulking trees reaching so high their tops blocked the sky. Only everything was the wrong color—neon oranges and vibrant reds. I guess the purple grass didn't look so odd in comparison.

Kelly was still speaking though, ". . . soon."

"What's soon?" I asked, still getting my bearings and my breath back.

"Aini. She's fading."

"You're speaking with her?" Mandy asked.

Kelly shook her head, a sad, tired motion as she stared at the horizon, or where there might be a horizon if not for all the trees. "Not talking as much as hearing her thoughts. Some of them."

"What's she saying?" Johnny-on-the-spot Mandy again. At least her tone wasn't belligerent.

"Pain. Darkness. Hurry."

My insides twisted. Aini was still a kid. Okay, almost sixteen, but no one deserved what she was going through. What she'd already endured.

I straightened from spine to shoulders. "Guess that means we better get hoofing it." I looked closely at Kelly, who looked even more battered and wrung out than I felt. Then I realized something different, beyond the burn marks on her clothes. I'd missed it before what with focusing on the fact I hadn't killed her. "You can see now?"

She gave a rippling shrug. "Better than I could. Not as well as I want."

"That's good news, isn't it?" Mandy looked between the two of us. "Doesn't that mean the blindness is wearing off?"

Here I thought Kelly was the half-full optimist in the group. One look at Kels expression told me I didn't want to be the one to burst her bubble. "Guess so," I offered, already marching toward the jungle, in the direction Kelly had been gazing earlier.

"This way?" I looked at Kelly who was brushing her hands against her jeans—a nervous gesture? It wasn't like she needed to clean purple grasses from her pants.

"That's the direction I hear Aini's voice the strongest," she murmured after moving close to me and staring at where I pointed.

"You still need to hold on to one of us." Mandy said it as a statement.

"I'd like to go on my own as much as—"

"Forget it. We've got to move fast."

Kelly's brows raised but she didn't say anything. Instead she reached for my shoulder.

Mandy did have a point but I also understood Kelly's need for independence. Blind, or sort-of-blind, she was still a liability.

"Don't worry," I whispered to her, "you'll be seeing fine here real soon."

"And if I don't?" a thread of anger laced her words.

I heard the subtext beneath her anger—worry, exhaustion, doubt. But since my job was to get us to the Horned One's domain and out in one piece, I decided to nip her emotions in the bud.

"Suck it up, Kels. It is what it is."

She looked liked I'd slapped her. Okay, maybe I could have been a little gentler.

"We'll find Aini." I didn't need to force determination into my tone. It was there already, in spades. "We'll find her and get her out. But to do that we need to keep focused on what *is* working."

"Got it." She bit out the words. "No more whining."

Way to make a mess of things. Since we were just entering beneath the glaring canopy of hallucinogenic colors, I decided to talk later.

"This is freaky mind-blowing," Mandy said, closing the gap between the three of us.

I couldn't agree more. It was more than just the colors, it was the eerie quiet, as if the place held its breath.

"We get lost in here, we'll be in a world of hurt," I murmured, very aware of how alone we really were. Since landing on this side of the river I hadn't heard a peep out of Bran. I'd sent him a mental thank you which was hardly enough for what he'd done. He'd found me. Saved me and saved Kelly.

Yup, I owed him. Big time.

"Which way?" Mandy's voice sounded like she was screaming in the noiseless jungle. Which she wasn't, but up against quiet this thick, it came across that way.

Kelly pointed but said nothing.

I didn't either as I stepped forward, waiting for the boogie-man to pop out from behind every over-sized leaf, every thick trunk, every twisted, splayed fern.

My mistake was I wasn't looking behind us.

CHAPTER 25

"*Mierda*," Mandy screamed, jacking my heart into overdrive as I spun and pushed Kelly behind me.

It wasn't going to help, as we were suddenly surrounded by what looked like horned tree men. These guys were brutes—tall, with green-masked faces, and massive horns, like elk horns, several feet across. They were draped in fur across their shoulders, clumps of leaves around their waists and carried staves of horn.

"What?" Kelly asked, peering past me with a pronounced squint. If she couldn't see these guys, her blindness was more than she'd let on.

One more freaking nightmare. Instead, I voiced what seemed to be a recurring theme in this realm. "We mean you no harm." I raised my hands in the Universal sign of no-threat-here, bearing no ill will. It also meant we were victims waiting to happen. The kind who didn't bring weapons—of any kind. Yeah, I had my magic, but who knew how much I could summon without Bran's help.

As Mandy, Kelly and I inched closer to one another, one of the men, if they were men, stepped forward, reaching for Kelly's hair.

"Don't panic," I hissed, but Kels had more *cojones* than I'd given her credit for as she managed a wobbly crescent-sized smile while the man ran thick, stubby fingers through her ponytail.

Ugh.

So far, though, no sharp, lethal jabbing implements pointed toward us.

Until a trio of the creatures closest to Mandy took a step back, the better to level their spears.

Great.

Stubby fingered guy shouted something then everyone turned as if yanked on puppet strings and started marching forward, forcing us in the same direction.

"Any idea what he said?" Mandy whispered, so close she nipped my heels.

"March? This way? You're screwed?"

"Thought so." She stepped back, but no more than a hand's width.

"We still heading toward Aini?" I asked of Kelly, earning a grunt from the nearest tree man.

She nodded.

"We veer off let me know."

She nodded again.

Best we could do for now. It wasn't as if we had a lot of options. They were bigger, meaner-looking and held weapons. The longer we moved forward, the better a chance I had of pulling forth some magic—like a battery charger storing needed energy. At least I hoped that was the case.

And if we kept going in the general direction we needed to go, we should be okay.

Then they started double timing it.

CHAPTER 26

By the time the green men halted, the three of us chugged breath like we'd never get enough. That and we were sweating like pigs over a slow cooker. Bending to prop my hands against my knees, I wiped my stinging eyes with one arm. At this rate, we'd be so dehydrated we couldn't protect ourselves, much less do battle with the Horned One. We might not get thirsty, but that didn't mean our bodies weren't being depleted just as they would be in the Real Realm.

One of the green guys pointed to a patch of jungle floor that looked trampled on.

"I think he's trying to tell us to sit," Kelly said, stepping in the direction he indicated.

"Wait." I grabbed her arm. "You can see him? Clearly?"

"Yeah." Her smile wobbled a little. "Extreme exercise seemed to do the trick."

Go figure. I was just happy it'd happened.

The guy grunted again. This time more empathetic.

"Let me go first—" I moved toward the flat patch— "in case it's a trap."

"Like we're not already in one."

Leave it to Mandy to spell out the bad news. Still there were traps and then there was being strung high into one of these trees because someone put their foot in a snare. I learned that the hard way. Being the youngest with four brothers, I made such an easy target.

Swallowing without a lick of spit to wet my throat, I inched forward. Once, or several times, being burned made me twitchy.

By the time I reached the area of flattened grasses my heart thudded against my chest so hard it surprised me no one else could hear it.

"Looks okay," I mumbled, not a rousing endorsement. Then I saw the hole. One with a width wider than my hips, a darker shadow beneath a ferny orange bush. "Wait!"

We all froze.

Gophers? Prairie dogs? Heck, I'd be happy if it was a badger, though they were mean suckers. That hole was huge though, which meant whatever lived in it had to be, too.

The twisting of my gut told me something inhabited that hole. Something I didn't want to see. Plus a stench wafted from within it—the smell of death.

"What is it?" Kelly asked, gazing between the hole and the nearest green man, one I could swear grinned.

"Don't know." Didn't want to know.

Maybe it was my imagination on steroids, but I could have sworn the ground beneath me started moving. A ripple movement. Slow. Undulating. Like a creeping, crawling heave.

"Feel that?" My words sounded more squeak than a question.

"WTF?" Mandy pressed closer.

"I don't have a good feeling about this." Kelly stepped closer, too. Then, without a word, we all edged backwards, away from that hole, only to be immediately met by a wall of testosterone brandishing spears.

I was getting more than a little fed up with this scenario; first green boys, now green men. Who knew green could be so aggressive and lethal.

The ground beneath our feet continued to swell and abate. The three of us crowded closer together.

"Any ideas?" Mandy asked.

What I wouldn't have given for a handy Glock about then. Or better yet, an Uzi.

"I don't think pretty please is going to help," I said, not that I even considered that approach.

"Can you whip us up a few wings?" Mandy's eyes grew larger with more and more white showing.

"No." Not for three of us at once. Trust me, I'd thought about it. "But that gives me an idea."

A desperate one, but whatever was beneath us, and no doubt slithering toward that hole at our backs, called for desperate measures.

"I need some blood," I murmured, stepping closer to the hole to give me some maneuvering room.

Mandy eyed me then shook her head. Who knew what an open cut in this Realm meant. Kelly, bless her, stepped up to the nearest spear and slid the inside of her arm along the curved edge of one.

She sucked in a deep breath to keep from calling out then jumped back, cupping her wound with her other hand. "This enough?"

Man, I hoped she didn't get something nasty from that crude metal. But there she was, doing what had to be done regardless of the personal cost.

I nodded. "Thanks. Perfect."

It had to be.

The green freaks were not happy with her action. They started mumbling among themselves. I couldn't get the words but the tone was loud and clear—obviously pissed off males sound the same everywhere.

"Squeeze as many blood drops as you can here." I pointed to the ground in front of her and Mandy, which would cover me too as I was behind them. I knew blood magic meant dark magic and using it was a big no-no in the Underworld. There was too much darkness and evil here to risk stirring their attention, but I was running out of quick fixes.

Kelly and Mandy faced the green men as I looked toward their backs with the hole behind me. I stilled myself and raised my hands. Not high enough to set off the green men but enough to spread my fingers as wide as possible. Last time I'd done this particular chant, Mandy and I had both ended up in the IR Compound's infirmary.

Let's hope we were luckier this time.

"Here in this place and before the eyes of the unbelievers, come forth.

I call the creatures of the elements.
The seekers of release who wish to walk amongst the humans.
I bid you to destroy the binds holding you in thrall.
Come. Show your power.
Revel in your might. "

The stubby-fingered green guy started jabbing his index finger at me.

Piss off, big guy. Fingers didn't scare me. Sharp pointed spears did.

I kept my voice calm and deep as I raised my hands higher and began chanting again.

"Here in this place and before the eyes of the unknown, come forth.
I call the creatures of the elements.
The seekers of release who wish to walk amongst the humans.
I bid you to destroy the binds holding you in thrall.
Now. Rise and be alive. "

The stir of a sulfur and briny wind crept across my skin. A desert breeze—hot and dry. Here's crossing fingers that I called what I intended, and didn't unleash a whole new world of hurt.

So far so good.

"*Mierde*," Mandy croaked next to me, her gaze fixed on something behind me. "Look!"

I cast a glance over my shoulder then regretted it. A head was emerging from the dark hole.

I squeezed my eyes shut and kept chanting, stretching my arms higher at my sides, deepening my voice, ignoring the frisson of warning along my skin.

"There is a reason for being.
Journey here. Now.
May your masters honor and bow before you.
Sending you on your way.

You who laugh at the mortals.
Come close.
Echo Demon, I summon thee!"

The wind swooped and spiraled around us. Several of the green men edged backwards, eyeing us as they started grumbling among themselves. Good, that meant the spell was working. I swore grit and sand abraded my skin.

"We welcome you demon of the deep.
Come play with us.
Show us your might.
Now! Echo Demon.
Close nearby as light dissolves into night.
Show us your—"

Kelly screamed.
Then all hell broke loose.

CHAPTER 27

The ranks of the green men splintered, some disappearing back into the jungle, others jabbing their spears high above their heads—celebration style.

No Echo Demon had appeared. It should have, but that was the problem with my gift. It was iffy, which downright sucked.

Then I glanced at Kelly who was turned away from Mandy and faced me, staring frozen-like at whatever appeared behind us. I pivoted so fast I was damn lucky I didn't upend myself.

Sweet Mother Goddess.

"What—" The words dried in my throat.

"Snake," Kelly whimpered. "Sssssssnake."

No way. That was like saying a Humvee was the same as a Mini-Cooper. No comparison.

Its head looked snake-like—pointed, triangular flat with golden beady eyes and a tongue as long as my arm sliding in and out of a near-closed mouth. It made a grating, scratching hiss with each slide in and out. But it was the body that chilled my blood. Thick and ropey. Think anaconda times a hundred.

A hand grabbed my arm. Mandy, tugging me away with one hand, Kelly with the other, toward the nearest brush.

The green guys had other plans.

Like corralling terrified greased piglets, the spear guys kept poking at us, pushing us back toward that snake. Prod. Step. Poke. Stumble.

Spear or snake?

No way.

Only good thing about the massive reptile was it seemed sluggish. Like it hadn't regurgitated its last meal so was in no big hurry to chow down again.

And I thought Kels was the queen of illusions.

A quick glance in her direction warned me that she was in deeper panic mode than I was. Her muscles were locked rigid, eyes wide, mouth opened in a soundless scream, face blanched.

"Mandy, take care of Kels."

The Latina took one glance and swallowed whatever she was going to say.

Good.

Bad? An Echo Demon wasn't going to stop that snake.

Just then a pointed spear knicked my shoulder.

None of this made sense. We were supposed to be in a realm of spirits. I got that. So how could they wield weapons, ones sharp enough to slice and dice?

First problems first. Get rid of the green guys.

No longer worried I'd draw their attention, I made sure the blood droplets Kels sacrificed still threaded through the grass then I threw my hands wide.

"Come. Come now.
I summon thee.
I welcome you demon of the deep.
Come play with me.
Show me your might.
Now! Echo Demon.
Close nearby as light dissolves into night.
Prove yourself. So mote it be!"

A crash of lightning lit up the neon reds and oranges of the jungle. The green men danced around, eyes as wide and terrified as Kelly's.

Served them right.

A skin-raising roar washed against us.

I wanted to pump my hand in my own high five as I twisted around. Where was—there. On the other side of the green guys.

One Echo Demon. A large one, over fourteen feet tall, his mottled greenish-brown scales standing out against the foliage.

I wasn't sure who was more dazed—the demon or the green guys. With panicked cries, green men raced in several directions, one toward and past us, right into the writhing mass of the snake.

It took seconds, at most, for that huge reptile head to slap against the man, crushing his skull with a sickening thud.

Mandy started retching.

But we weren't out of trouble yet.

One guy gone, most high-tailing it away as fast as they could run, but a few remained. Warrior trained and either braver or more foolish than the others, they turned on the demon, creating a half-circle of containment around it.

If I were a nicer person, I'd have told them it'd do no good. But I wasn't. Besides I had to get Kelly and Mandy out of here as soon as possible.

"This way." I jerked my head at Mandy to show the direction we needed to go to escape.

She hesitated. The direction I indicated took us closer to the snake.

"That way's suicide," she hissed as if afraid to even speak too loud and attract the snake's attention.

"Walk slow. No abrupt movement. We can do it."

In theory. And it wasn't like we had a lot of options. The second that Echo Demon finished annihilating the remaining green men, it'd come after us. Slipping into the jungle was our only hope.

"Come on, Kels." I tightened my hand around her arm, but she wasn't budging. Her feet seemed cemented into the soil. "We've got to go. Now!"

Still nothing.

Mandy raced up behind her, wrapping one arm around Kelly's shoulders. "We've got to, Kelly. Or we all die." She paused, then added, "You don't want that. Do you? Us dying because we won't leave you?"

Smart move. What Kelly was willing to do for others was always more than she'd do for herself. All she managed now was to shake her head back and forth and start to whisper.

I leaned toward her to catch the jerky, near-silent words. "Can't. Can't. Afraid. Snakes."

More like terrified.

I glanced at where the snake hinged open its jaw, a yawning pit of darkness, to swallow the dead green guy.

On the edge of panic myself I focused on the man's mask and its pointed horns. I hoped they choked the reptile.

We were running out of time.

"Kels, you've got to move." I stood so close I could see the triple time beat of the vein along her forehead. My intention was to block out the sight of the snake. "Please."

That had her looking at me, her blue eyes unfocused but at least they were on me and not the reptile of death.

"That's it, Kels. Take my hand. Just look at me."

Mandy caught on to what I was doing and edged behind me, to steer me walking backwards toward the snake. I aimed for a gap in the trees between where we were and where the snake swallowed with a vacuuming, icky, slushy sucking sound.

Sweet Peter and Paul, I wanted to vomit.

Instead I kept talking, kept my voice low and soothing, kept my eyes lasered onto Kelly's. "That's it. Just a few more feet. We'll be out of here. On our way to Aini."

"Aini?"

"That's right. Next stop, you'll see."

Yes, I lied through my teeth but she at least moved. Small, tentative steps. At the rate we inched forward, the snake would be ready for its next snack, the green guys would be mincemeat and there'd be one hyped up Echo Demon ready to rumble before we were even close to disappearing.

"A little faster, Kels."

"A whole lot faster," Mandy muttered, steering me one direction and then another. I stumbled, more than I wanted to, each missed step a reminder how fragile my link with Kelly was.

That's when three things happened at once.

The Echo Demon screamed its high-pitched howl of victory.

The snake drug itself closer with a rasping, earth rattling vibration.

And I tripped, sprawling backwards on my butt.

CHAPTER 28

With me splayed at Kelly's feet, our contact broke. As if jolted with a fully-charged cattle prod, she reared back, spreading her hands before her as a shield. Helpless.

Then she turned to run. Back toward the remaining green guys and the Echo Demon.

"Nooooo!" I scrambled to my knees and lurched forward, snagging her ankle and pulling backwards.

She slammed into the ground then twisted until almost on top of me.

Better than dying.

Hustling to wiggle out from beneath her while gripping her arm, I shouted at Mandy, "Grab her other arm. Gotta go. Now. Now. Now."

Adrenaline spiked through me, adding strength to what shifter blood I carried. Catapulting to a crouching run, I wrenched Kelly to her feet so hard I almost threw her directly into the path of the snake. It undulated so close I gagged on its stench, a putrid smell of rotting bodies deep in its gullet.

Thank the Spirits that Mandy held on to Kelly's other arm, keeping her anchored even as the two of us turned up the speed and hotfooted it, dragging Kelly between us like a half-empty sack of wheat.

I didn't care where we went as long as it was away from here.

The Echo Demon released another wail as we plunged deeper and deeper into the jungle, fronds slapping us, vines tangling our feet, the shadows growing darker and darker.

"How far?" Mandy gasped as we tripped over what seemed like the hundredth root.

I'd forgotten she didn't have shifter blood to give her endurance. On the other hand,. . . "A little further. Until I can't hear them anymore."

Since shifters also possessed enhanced hearing abilities, as long as I couldn't hear the threat, that meant we should be out of immediate harm's way.

Like that would last for long.

Something wasn't right. Besides the whole traipsing through the Underworld bit. Maybe, if we caught our breath for more than a second, I could figure out what disturbed me—that 'pay attention it might save your life' voice that wouldn't let go.

After a quick glance at Mandy told me she was on her last legs, I gave a quick chin nod. "Here."

She hadn't said anything. Not that I expected her to. When push came to shove, she took her punches and kept going. I could actually admire that about her. Not that I'd ever share. Probably give her a heart attack right then and there, getting an atta-girl comment from me.

We tugged Kelly toward a humongous sky-reaching tree with no leaves, just spiky finger-like branches. First I made sure there were no scary burrows anywhere nearby.

Easing her down until she could lean against the trunk, we plopped onto the ground beside her, breathing hard, our heads and shoulders bowed, looking like marathon runners having given their all.

"What happened back there?" Mandy asked the second she could speak.

I cut her a quick glance. I'd have thought a tribe of green men wearing masks and horns, a gigantic prehistoric snake, and an Echo Demon spoke for themselves.

She waved her hand half-heartedly from the wrist as if she didn't have enough energy to do more. "I know what I saw but. . . something's not right. Something about this place."

So she sensed it too. "You mean like spirits capable of wielding spears? Spears that could have skewered us?"

"Yeah, but more than that." She shook her head. "It's as if. . . I don't know."

Instead of answering her directly, I asked a question that had been bothering me. "What scares you?"

She shot me a sharp look from beneath lowered eyes. "You mean other than you?"

For a second there I thought we were back to our usual shove-and-shove-back opposition, getting nowhere. Then I snorted. Her words were actually a backhanded compliment.

"Seriously," I pushed, changing approaches and offering an olive branch so she knew I wasn't asking just to have something to hold against her. "It's obvious one of Kelly's biggest fears is snakes."

"So?"

I rubbed a hand across the back of my neck where tension still torqued every muscle. "I'm wondering if there's a reason we've dealt with what we've faced since being here."

Sometimes throwing out stupid ideas makes something stick.

Mandy held her tongue, but I wasn't sure why until she murmured, "Zombies."

In a world filled with preternatural threats, I knew there could be zombies even outside of the Underworld. Why not? The walking dead threaded through dozens of fairy tales. Not the kind kids heard these days, but the old ones—the teaching ones. Okay, more warning than teaching, bigger, scarier and darker tales than fairy princesses.

Besides, that could explain more than the one encounter we'd had so far.

"You mean zombies like where we met up earlier, at the airport terminal?"

"No idea what terminal you're talking about but yeah, where Kelly was blind and we found you. Exactly like those zombies." She raised her chin and speared me with a hard as glass look. One I recognized. When afraid, when most afraid, and vulnerable, it was a whole lot easier to posture, to play the kick-ass-nothing-fazes-me response, than it was to give into the uneasiness and fear and admit that it existed.

Time to give her a little maneuvering space. "I've got a theory, but it's pretty off base."

"What's new about that?"

Ignore the dig, Noziak.

"You want to hear it or snipe instead?"

So I sucked at ignoring pointed jabs.

"Go ahead." That limp-wrist movement again, waving me on.

I glanced around, aware of the stillness, the eeriness of this place. Only our rasping breaths broke the silence.

"We're in the Spirit World," I stated, catching her *duh* expression but rushing on even as I grappled to make sense of my jumbled thoughts. "So nothing should be corporeal."

"You mean none of these people or creatures we've been meeting should have bodies? Bodies that we can see as clear as we are?"

"Yeah. Exactly."

"So?"

"But they are three-dimensional forms and not merely shapes. If they didn't have solid bodies, we wouldn't feel the spears or the brush of them against us."

Mandy opened her mouth but didn't say anything. A bloody miracle. Even Kelly raised her head, still looking beat, but focusing in on the conversation.

"Should any of what's around us have substance?" she asked, casting a quick glance toward the trees as she hugged her arms around her knees. "It's not just the beings that appear real, it's the places." With a glance at Mandy, she added, "Like that castle or Great Hall we were in. And the ice in the tunnels. Should we have felt that terrible cold?"

Lucky them. I got blistering desert and miles and miles of hot sand to wade through. But that wasn't the point.

"Look around. What do you see?" I asked.

Mandy shook her head. "Looks like the Tanama Jungle. Hated that place. Hated, hated, hated." Her tone said she'd humor me but only up to a point.

"Be more specific," I nudged. "I don't even have an idea what or where the Tanama Jungle is."

"Dominican Republic."

A small smile bloomed on Kelly's face. Must be a teacher thing, learning something new.

"So what's in this Tanama Jungle?" Then, before Mandy could snap, I raised my hands up, palms outward. "What about here reminds you of there?"

"Fine." She exhaled a breath deep enough to set her thick black hair dancing, those few strands not slicked down with sweat. Looking up she spoke to the trees, more than us. "I don't know what all the plants are called but there were banana trees, ginger plants, and lots of big-trunked trees. The parrots and monkeys always screamed high overhead in the canopy. And crap, the tarantulas were huge, so were the boa constrictors. Just like here. Not as big as that last one. *Que viene el Coco y te comerá.*"

Not going to help if I didn't have a clue what she just said. "Which means what?"

Mandy's smile was not pleasant. "Something the old ones said to us growing up. *Behave or else the Coco will come and eat you.* A dragon. A ghost monster that eats kids and never leaves a trace."

Goose bumps danced up my arms. A quick glance at Kels showed her face paling, so I broke in. "What about the color of the plants there? And the vegetation? Lots of vines and bushes?"

"What the hell are you talking about?" Mandy shot back. "The color was green—acid green, neon green, dark and mid and light green. Everything was so green it made my eyes ache and no, in the real jungles, the trees were so thick overhead that no sun and little rain actually reaches the ground. It was a breeze walking around, like here."

Kelly cast me a quick look then glanced away. But I wasn't going to let her ignore this conversation. "Is that what you see?"

"Not really." We both had to lean forward to hear Kelly's words.

I raised a hand to cut off whatever Mandy was about to say as I pushed. "So what's different than Mandy's description?"

Kelly swallowed and looked around. "Most of the plants are barely taller than we are, with wide, broad leaves. Like corn crops but bigger with flatter stalks. It makes it impossible to see where we're going. . . "

"Any sounds?"

"Yeah." A shudder rattled her but she wasn't a lightweight—too nice, but solid when the going got tough. "I hear lions and hyenas. Some very close. Hiding in all that foliage."

"What colors?"

She glanced at Mandy who sat there with brows furrowed, mouth open, before looking back at me. "Yellows and blues. It's actually pretty now that I'm used to it, but it is very different, sort of scary exotic."

Bingo.

"What are you talking about?" Mandy jumped in before I could hold her back. By the rapid flexing of her fists, I could tell she didn't like what she heard. Not one bit.

I cleared my throat. "I see lush, thick vegetation, everywhere, with trees so tall you can't see their tops, in colors of neon orange and reds. And there are no sounds. None at all."

Mandy clambered to her feet. "I don't know what you two have been smoking but—"

"Listen." I remained sitting as I waved her down. "I think we're each seeing, and experiencing, not what *is* really around us, but what we expect to see."

"I didn't expect to see a snake that size," Kelly said, her voice stronger than it had been.

"No. But we all saw it. Didn't we?"

Mandy folded herself back into a sitting position, still not looking happy as she gave a jerky head nod. Kelly followed suit.

"So what are you saying? We're all going crazy?" Mandy snarled.

"No, not crazy, but I have a theory."

"Which is?" Kelly tilted her head, listening.

"I don't have everything nailed down," I started, aware I was hedging what I was about to say because I feared I was right. "I think the environment depends on what we assume is here. Mandy's been in a real jungle, so her perceptions are based on that experience."

"I have, too. In Sierra Leone," Kelly said.

"And didn't that influence what you're seeing around us here?" I leaned forward, willing them to listen, not to believe. Yet. But to remain open to the possibility I laid out. "From what I know, much of the Sierra Leone 'jungle'—" My fingers made air quotes to bring home my point. "—their jungles have been cut down then have grown back. Original jungles were decimated to create more farmland, then, when years and years of civil war allowed vegetation to grow back, it created the lush, head-high scenario you associate with jungles."

"And you?" Mandy snorted. "Who heard of neon red and yellow jungles?"

"You're right." That made the smug smile slide off her face. "But when I was really little my dad used to read me a book every night before bed."

Kelly smiled while Mandy gave me a get-on-with-it look.

"My favorite book, the one I made him read the most was called *If I Made The World*."

"Oh, I loved that book." Kelly actually grinned. "Ice cream snow and trees like popsicles."

"And jungles of reds and yellows so quiet. . ."

"That you could hear the sounds of your eyelashes opening and closing," she finished.

We both looked at Mandy, who rolled her eyes. "So I see a Dominican jungle, Kelly a twisted Sierra Leone version and you a kid's book. Then why did we all see that gross monster snake?"

Kelly's brows crept so high on her forehead, they almost disappeared beneath her bangs.

This time I was the one who swallowed deep, my mouth was bone-dry. "Because whatever is happening here—" I jerked my hands toward the jungle. "—is not only based on our perceptions but our fears."

"Shit." Mandy added a low whistle. "No way."

I glanced at Kelly to see how she was taking the not-so-good news.

"That's why the snake appeared then." She strangled her knees with both arms, so tight her knuckles bleached. "Because I hate them so much."

"Because you're afraid of them." Terrorized would be a better word, but no need to hit her over the head.

"And that river of molten fire?" Mandy's tone took on that prove-it tone unbelievers used. A lot.

We both glanced at Kelly's burned jeans.

"What river of fire?" Kels demanded. "I thought I smelled campfires but nothing more."

I gave Mandy a now-you've-done-it eye roll. "Not important." I sped on. "I don't know about you two, but I remember Sunday school classes with all those pictures of what Hell looked like," I said.

"Weeping and wailing. The gnashing of teeth. Rivers of fire that are never quenched." Kelly's voice sounded like she'd gotten the same images I did loud and clear.

"This is bullshit." Mandy jumped back to her feet, rubbing her palms against her thighs, no doubt trying to discharge some of the roiling emotion steamrolling through her. "You're just trying to scare us."

"Why would I want to do that?" I wrestled with the anger bubbling beneath my own words. "I'm trying to figure out what the hell—"

"Alex." Kelly shook her head at me.

"Okay, what the heck is going on so we can stop running from crisis to crisis."

"And how exactly are we supposed to do that? Think of bunnies and rainbows?"

Like that would happen, not with the temper juicing her. Any second now I expected to see man-eating rabbits or psychedelic rainbows dripping acid rain pop up all around us.

I rose to my feet, my movements slow and deliberate. I even managed to keep my voice on an even keel, even though I wanted to throttle Mandy. "At least I'm trying." I stepped into her space, almost head butting her. "What are you doing? Running off like a pissed off hausfrau. What good is that?"

Kelly was suddenly between the two of us, her arms creating a physical barrier. "Enough," she said it with more steel than I'd heard in a long time. "Think about it. You're feeding into whatever is happening here."

When Mandy threw her a glance that could peel skin, Kelly actually pushed against us, hard, sending Mandy and me rocking backwards.

"Get your head into the game," Kelly all but snapped. "Emotion creates energy, and not the good kind. The more you snipe and shout at each other, the more likely we draw more negative energy toward us."

"What the—"

I cut off Mandy. "Like the zombies back at the airport, or wherever we joined up. They fed off our emotions." I shot Mandy a take-that glare but turned away the second I realized I'd done it. "Which may explain why the people and everything else are real here. Spears that can kill us. Bodies that are just as alive as anything back in our Realm. Heat and cold and everything. This Realm is using our own vulnerabilities against us."

Kelly gave a slow nod. "This makes a weird kind of sense."

"In what universe?" Mandy huffed, but quietly.

Kelly looked at me. "Go on."

"It's as if something is pushing us to explode. Notice how easy it's been to go from okay to ballistic since we've been here?" I didn't look at Mandy, though it sure tempted me. "And then when we get destabilized, because that's what combining anger or strong emotion does, it rocks our foundations."

"Which makes us vulnerable to our fears," Kelly finished, saying it better than I could.

"Yeah, exactly." I glanced around, raising my voice. "Like some butt-wipe is getting his jollies by manipulating us."

"Rats in a maze." Kelly's hushed voice held trepidation that chilled my skin.

"Why?" Mandy asked, quieter than she had been.

I shrugged. "If we're chewing on each other—"

"Or too scared to act," Kelly admitted, not afraid to voice her own shortcomings.

"Or too scared to act," I repeated, "then it's easier to divide and conquer."

"Or lose time in getting to Aini." Mandy hit the nail on the head.

"So what do we do now?" Kelly asked. "How do we keep our fears buried?"

This time I was sure of my answer, and my tone said as much. "There are three of us. We use each other as a barometer."

Mandy's gaze hop-scotched between us. "A what?"

"A barometer acts as a pressure gauge." Kelly explained in her way that didn't make a person feel stupid for asking. "They usually measure air or atmospheric conditions."

"And that means what here?"

I looked at Mandy. "We watch one another for signs of pressure building, tension getting to us, and, if we see that happening, we help each other defuse the pressure. Make a comment. Talk about something to change our focus."

For a second, I thought she was going to make a half-assed remark, but she surprised me by nodding instead. "Okay. I'm game."

"Good." It was Kelly who answered, stepping back and straightening her shoulders. "Maybe, if we can think of as many positive thoughts as possible, we might even stave off who or whatever is doing this to us."

"Or piss it off." I was back to Noziak style, finally finding a real smile.

"I'm down with that," Mandy piped up.

"And we need to find Aini. Pronto." I added.

As if on cue, Kelly spun a half-circle and pointed toward a deep thicket of those red and orange plants—or a clear path if Mandy's vision was right.

"I'll lead," Mandy said as if aware of the train of my thoughts. The ones along the lines of you-go-first-and-if-you-don't-get-lost-in-a-jungle-I'll-believe-you.

I gave a simple nod and stepped around Kelly so she stood in front of me. When she raised one brow I said, "In my view, there is no path in that direction, but you're my teammates, and I trust you. I'll have your six." I knew it was an old Navy expression meaning to guard their backs, but it worked. I finished with, "You get us to Aini."

She gave a tired smile and stepped behind Mandy who was already strolling along like we were at a mall and not in a jungle from H-Hades. Oops. There, that should keep Kelly happy.

What would keep me happy? Getting out of here. More than that, though, keeping the fear I buried deep inside me a secret. What I didn't share with my teammates was what my greatest fear was—more than heights, more than wraiths or battles I couldn't win. I didn't even want to think about it.

Something told me if I let that genie out of the box, I'd not survive.

CHAPTER 29

The jungle slog didn't seem as hard following Mandy's lead, and gradually the scenery changed from humid lushness to bone dryness and shades of khaki and dried mud.

"Are we in a different environment?" I asked once I was sure I could keep my tone calm and casual. *Tone down the emotions. Don't think about fears.*

"Red brick buildings with all the windows boarded up," Kelly murmured, looking around.

"A barrio. Graffiti, mostly in Spanish. Metal and cardboard shanties and shacks."

So not digging Mandy's view.

I kept talking, like whistling in the dark through a graveyard. "Anybody see live bodies hanging around?"

"Not yet," Kelly said.

"That's a good thing as far as I'm concerned." Mandy kicked at something that went rattling down the twisted, dirt path.

"Mud houses, very old or just crumbling dead ahead, getting closer together," I contributed, brushing against one wall that left pale snuff-colored dust on my shoulder. Or I thought it did. Not knowing what was real and what was an illusion was downright creepy.

"I wouldn't use the dead word either." Kelly's voice had quieted, as all of ours had, walking deeper and deeper into this new landscape. "These buildings squeeze together any closer and we'll be toothpaste."

Nice image. *Not.*

"You sure we're still headed in the right direction?" I asked, mostly to take our focus off the feeling of being swallowed.

Kelly gave a jerky nod. "Yes. But I haven't heard Aini for a while."

"That good or bad?" Mandy's shoulders tightened. I could see them from where I followed, each step weighted.

Before Kelly could answer, I said, "Remember? Positive thoughts create positive energy."

"Bullshit," came Mandy's whiplash retort. Not that I didn't agree with her, but even as the thought slipped through my head, both my shoulders brushed walls.

Noted—bad vibes here meant we might be squeezed to death.

"Tell me something that makes you happy, Kelly," I called out even though she was right in front of me. If anyone could get a happy groove going, it was Kels.

"Van makes me happy."

Great. Van being my brother who'd been so burned by love years ago I cringed at the thought of Kelly hurting him now. Not my happy thought for sure. On the other hand, she might be just what he needed. He'd had one of those sappy grins on his face first thing this morning. It disappeared when Kelly announced she was going on this mission, but for the space of a heartbeat he'd seemed contented in a way I hadn't seen since high school. Back when that psycho bitch did such a number on him.

More crumbling dirt skittered against me as open, gaping dark holes of doors and windows increased. Who knew what could jump out of any of those black holes. The scent of dust choking me grew stronger.

But maybe I was wrong. Squaring my shoulders, I pasted a fake-it-till-I-make-it grin on my face. "I like. . ." Crap, what did I like?

Kelly saved me. "Puppy dogs and kitten kisses." She glanced over her shoulder and tossed me a grin. "And orange sherbet sunsets, summer rains and the first snowfall of winter."

Okay, I could see how to do this. Put myself in a memory, a good one and go from there. "Bran's kisses and dark, rich, sinful chocolate." They were the same to me, anyway.

"Guava *pasteles*, deep fried *croquetas* and a *medianoche* sandwich eaten at midnight."

I had no idea what Mandy was talking about but food always made me smile. "Smores over an open fire, cotton candy at the State Fair—the pink kind not the blue crap—and fry bread they make at the Red River Powwow."

"German chocolate cake with lots of coconut." The tone in Kelly's voice made me hungry. It also created an easing in my neck.

"Did you get to pick the kind of cake you wanted for your birthday?" I asked, adding, "My dad never baked, except for our birthday cakes." Man, there were some epic fails, but I rarely remembered them. Instead I remembered that warm, fuzzy feeling that came with knowing no matter how long a day or what he was doing, there'd always be that special cake sitting in the center of the dining room table for dinner. Most of them lopsided, and some with only a lick of frosting because he'd run out of steam before he could whip some up, but they were there, year after year, five times a year—one for each of my four brothers and myself.

Kelly picked up the thread. "My mom, I mean my foster mom, always made vanilla cake, but she let me pick out the frosting color and, sometimes, an image."

"Like what?" I thought dad was okay with just getting frosting on the cake.

"One year was a princess and another a dragon, with green and blue scales." Kelly laughed. "Mom had taken a cake decorating class that year at the local YMCA."

I smiled with her. My dad had apparently gotten off too easy. I'd never even thought of specially decorated cakes. "What about you?" I called to Mandy who'd gone quiet.

When she didn't answer, Kelly glanced back at me, her brows raised. Just as I was going to ask again, figuring Mandy hadn't heard me, she spoke. "My parents died when I was eleven. No cakes for me."

Crap.

"I'm so sorry," Kelly said, stepping forward to place a hand on Mandy's shoulder. "Was it a car accident?"

Mandy shrugged off the touch and turned, her mouth a straight line as if afraid to release the words she really wanted to say. Instead she bit out a harsh, "No!" Then her voice flat-lined as she added, "They were murdered. Along with my twin brother."

Ah, double crap. I swallowed against the sudden hard lump in my throat. So much for happy thoughts.

That must have been Alejándro. The one she'd mentioned as being here, as leading her. Murdered? How did a person survive that? Especially being a kid when it happened.

All of us fell silent until, without being aware of it, we'd put the cramped cityscape behind us, so we didn't have to continue being jolly. Especially Mandy, not that I blamed her. My mom may have disappeared but I'd always assumed she'd run off to get rid of responsibilities, like my brothers and me. It was her choice. To be killed? Taken away without a choice? Talk about gouging a big, empty hole inside a person.

We continued to move, keeping our thoughts close even as the path became rockier, more uphill. Then Kelly suddenly stopped. "What's that?"

Since she and Mandy were both in front of me, and the path had twisted and narrowed, all I could see was jutting weathered rock hanging over the trail, partially obscured by mist.

"I don't see anything." I stepped up until I stood shoulder to shoulder with Kelly, which wasn't easy given the width of the path, but I still couldn't see beyond Mandy. "Can you move a little to your left?" I asked.

Mandy did, and I saw it. It looked like an open doorway made of wood so aged it was more bleached white than brown. Along the top, two cross beams ended in a slightly upward tilt.

"Looks sort of oriental," Kelly said.

"You're right."

"The Japanese call it a *torii*." Mandy's gaze focused on the gate as she placed an emphasis on the second syllable—making it sound like *toh-ree*. Which blew my mind. Not her pronunciation but because she knew what the opening was called. Kelly looked at me and I shrugged. There wasn't even a Chinese restaurant in Mud Lake where I grew up. Sure my mentor witch had been Chinese but that was a long, long time ago and didn't last long.

Mandy continued, "It's named that because it's supposed to look like a bird perch."

Feeling like a country hick for not knowing any of this, I was curious. "How'd you know that?"

She shrugged. "I worked as a receptionist for a Shinto shrine in Miami for a while. A traditional *torii,* or Japanese gate, is usually found at the entrance of a Shinto shrine. It's supposed to mark the transition from the profane to the sacred beyond."

That had the skin along the nape of my neck prickling.

"You can only find *torii* gates at Shinto shrines because their purpose is to divide our world from the spirit world." She glanced back at us, but I could tell her thoughts were far, far away. "Shinto shrines supposedly don't actually exist in this world. They do, but they don't, because they are always located in a place that overlaps with the spirit world."

The bottom of my stomach twisted. Finding a dividing gate here, in the Spirit Realm, must mean we were getting closer to where the Horned One existed.

"Look!" Kelly pointed at something beyond the gate. "Doesn't that look like a building or something?"

"Where?"

Damn, I hoped this was not one of the fear-conjured images. Except Kelly's tone didn't sound afraid, more hopeful.

"Up there, at the top of that crag." She stared ahead of us. "Follow the path, and at the very top there's something there."

"You see anything, Mandy?"

All I got was a silent shake of her head.

"It's there." Kelly's voice sounded more empathetic. "And if it is a building, it'd mean we can get out of this damp chill."

She was right. While we'd been talking, the mist thickened, now surrounding us, nipping at my exposed hands and face.

"Is it wet and cold for everyone?" I asked, even though I'd already guessed the answer as Mandy rubbed her hands along her arms and Kelly's lips were turning blue.

"Yup."

"Sure is."

"Fine. We'll head toward that building then, but before we do, is anyone really afraid of rocks or high places or anything like that?"

Mandy snorted as Kelly shook her head.

"Just checking."

Since we were all on the same page as far as what we were experiencing, even if I couldn't see the building Kelly saw, maybe it was time to switch positions again. Last thing we needed was a spirit, or host of spirits, to come winging around one of these corners with Mandy front and center. Especially since this gate meant we were crossing into an area where it looked like spirits dwelled. Spirits and who knew what else.

"Mandy, I'll take point for a while. Why don't you pull up the rear and watch for possible attack from behind."

She mumbled something but did as I said. Progress.

Marching forward wasn't easy, as the rock under our feet appeared to be thin-sliced shale, slick with moisture. One wrong step could mean a turned ankle or careening off the side of the path. A quick peek warned me it'd be a long drop. Somewhere along the way, the trail had changed, becoming more a goat track than a path, and the sheer drop down one side was enough to make my head spin. When had that happened? I hadn't even noticed.

Head back in the game, Noziak. All of our lives depended on it.

"Path getting very narrow again." I stated, but also to alert my teammates as to what I was experiencing.

"Copy that," Mandy called from the rear.

"I'm not liking this." Kelly's voice was low, determined, but with that pitch you hear in horror movies right before the killer jumped out of a closet with a chainsaw.

I agreed. The closer we came to that yawning opening, the more I wanted to turn tail and run.

Instead, I took a deep breath, broadened my shoulders and slowed my steps so I could focus all of my attention on the *torii*.

About three feet from the structure, with muscles tensile tight from tension, the mist whirled and swooped like white smoke around the opening. A faint band of yellow joined with the ashen colors. What the heck was going on?

I raised a hand to stop Kelly and Mandy's forward movement. Only idiots went blindly through an opening, especially one associated with passing from one state of being—the profane—to another—the sacred. From what I knew of Realm traversing, there was usually a Guardian hovering somewhere near a gate. The Billy Goats Gruff were guardians of a bridge in fairy tales. In older stories, guardians kept interlopers from entering where they were not allowed, and the penalty was death if caught.

When the smoke dissipated a bit, I thanked the Great Spirits that I'd listened to my hunch. Like a ghost taking shape, a tall man stepped forward, wrapped in white and gold with a bandolier of some sort across his massive chest. He stood in a power stance, legs solidly anchored and spread wide, arms akimbo and loose, shoulders thrust backward. Everything about him indicated an immovable obstacle.

He loomed there, both ethereal and very, very real, while I got enough spit in my mouth to call out, "Who are you?"

"I'm called Yamabushi," he said, an ageless, formal cadence to his words. "And who might you be?"

I knew better than to give beings in this Realm our real names, as knowing what one was called gave power to another. Instead I said, "We're travelers."

The twist to his lips told me he understood exactly what I was doing.

"What is it you seek?" He looked down his nose. If we were side by side, I don't think he'd be that much taller than I was, but he stood slightly higher on the slope, and I had no doubt he was all sinew and muscle. Not an easy opponent to take down. Like I was stupid enough to even consider that option.

No way was I going to tell him we hunted the Horned One. For all I knew, this was one of his minions. "We seek a friend, taken against her will, to the lower levels."

I held my breath as his gaze probed us, one by one, long enough that chills that had nothing to do with the mist, pinched my nerve endings.

"And what do you bring to the Guardian of the Gate for your passage?"

Should have known. It wasn't going to get easier the closer we got to the Horned One so why was I surprised?

"What fee do you require?" I asked as if I gambled with our lives every day.

The warrior demon, because that's what I guessed the Guardian of the Gate was, paused as if considering options. The longer he weighed his toll choices and remained silent, the higher the final cost. That's the way it always worked.

When he spoke at last, his voice rumbled, echoing among the stone and cold. "You must give that which you value most."

Of course. It couldn't be something easy, something we could actually do. No, always suck and suckier.

"What's he mean?" Kelly asked over my shoulder as she pressed closer.

"He means it's time to negotiate," I murmured out of the side of my mouth.

I was a Noziak: I wasn't about to give up at the first sign of rough times, so I raised my chin and steeled my tone. "And if we don't have what we value most, what then?"

"Oh, but you do shaman witch." He glanced at Kelly. "Or the Clavis, or Spirit Walker does."

How'd he—? I swear the guy smugly chuckled under his breath.

Kelly looked from me to Mandy.

"Let's head down the path and consider our choices." No, it wasn't a solution, but I needed to talk to Kels and Mandy without this daunting obstacle breathing down on us.

Like a mother duckling, I shooed a hesitant Kelly and a grumbling Mandy back down the way we'd just come until we turned a bend on the trail and couldn't see that damn Spirit World gate or its Guardian.

"You want to tell us what the—what's going on?" Mandy demanded as I leaned against a rock slab, catching my breath as if I'd just jogged a dozen miles, uphill, with a weighted pack instead of walked downhill thirty feet or so.

"What is it, Alex?" Kelly asked, her voice concerned.

I shook my head, trying to gather a stronger sense of certainty, of what to do next even as I realized my hands were fisted at my side, sweat stained my lower back in spite of the cold and my heart pounded hard against my chest.

"She can't answer. She's afraid."

The male voice came out of nowhere, making us all jump, me the highest.

CHAPTER 30

All of us glanced up, but Mandy recovered first. "Wha—?"

Above where we stood a small slab of rock jutted out, so small I wouldn't expect a full-grown man lounging against it. He looked casual, as if sitting in someone's living room, one arm flung over a crooked knee, the other resting beside him.

That insolent pose was the only thing that didn't have me blasting him with a freeze spell even as my hands were raised to do just that if needed. Nothing in his body language screamed poised to fight, so my first response couldn't be to blow him to smithereens for startling us.

Not that it wasn't tempting.

"No worries, little witch," he said, his voice like a sliver of ice against heated skin. "I mean you and your companions no harm."

I just bet. And how'd he know I was a witch?

He looked naked, or mostly naked, it was hard to tell with him sitting above us. Late twenties, maybe early thirties as his shoulders had a man's breadth, his muscles lean and lethal. His hair swept below his chin and could have been a dark blond or light brown in better light.

The cold didn't seem to bother him any as he leaned against the rock, his muscles relaxed, his smile smug. The most striking thing about him, apart from being naked, was a wide swath of black painted across his forehead from side to side, beginning above his brow to below his eyes and another swath of equal width running from forehead down his face and chest until it disappeared.

His skin shone pale, ghost-like, making his black striping stand out even more. It was hard to see the expression in his eyes because the dark band obscured and hooded them. Very lethal looking—a tattooed mask.

Another reason wariness skittered across my skin.

He remained statue still as I examined him, seeming to expect no less. There was no tensing of muscles, no overt threatening movement, or any other signal. But then a panther didn't warn its prey before it pounced either.

A small inner voice warned me to be wary, very, very wary.

"Who are you? What do you want?" I stepped up the path a few feet, as I noticed Mandy and Kelly doing the same, but in the other direction. Good. If he lunged, he couldn't take out all of us at once.

He smiled, his teeth a flash of ivory against that black face paint. Or was it a tattoo? It looked very much a part of him as opposed to a mask donned.

"They call me Malik. I'm an Ater Angelus." The last word sounded like *Ahn ghe loos*. The first name was easier. He rolled the name across his tongue as if it meant more than I realized. *Ah-tar. Ah-tar Ahn ghe loos*. Who the heck was he and why was he here?

"Isn't Angelus the Latin word for angel?" Kelly asked.

I glanced at her. Of anyone, *I* should have known that. Many spells were based on Latin terms. So why didn't I? Because I sucked at Latin. That and my brain, as well as my body, were so locked into flee-or-fight response I could barely suck in a breath. That's why.

The stranger smiled in Kelly's direction, a grin so sensual and seductive I expected her to sigh. I wanted to and I only caught a glimpse of those slightly upturned, beckoning lips. Damn, this guy had high wattage.

"Very astute," he said it in a way that made it sound like either a come-hither promise or a veiled insult. "As I expect from the Clavis of Dryghtyn."

There he went again. How'd he know about the Clavis? Was he sent by the Horned One?

Mandy stepped closer to Kelly. I wasn't sure if it was to protect her or stop her in case she attacked this guy. Probably fifty-fifty.

Time to shift his focus. "So you're an angel." Like I believed that for a heartbeat. Not that I'd met any angels before, but he so did not fit my definition of a benign, godly being, unless it was a sex god. Weren't angels supposed to be sort of sexless? Wrong issue to focus on, Noziak, get back to the important point.

I'd forced as much derision into my words as possible, which was good. The whole believe-what-you-want-to-believe-it-doesn't-matter-to-us approach. Which was true, but only up to that razor edge between pissing off whoever, or whatever, he was and getting enough intel to know if we should scatter as fast as possible in any direction.

His gaze slid to me. He made no other movement, and yet I found myself bracing, my hands raising—the better to cast a freeze-in-place incantation.

"It is not *I* you should fear." He spoke to my thoughts and not my words. With a slight shrug and chin nod he pointed toward the *torii* gate. "That is where the danger lies."

Duh!

His smile ratcheted up as if I'd shouted the word out loud.

"Very ferocious." No hint of mockery in his tone, though I heard it loud and clear.

"What do you know about the gate? About getting around it?" When push came to shove, Noziaks could do demanding and sarcastic in the same breath. I wasn't even trying.

"There is no way around. Only through."

He sounded like that Star Wars character: Yoda. Made me want to smack him. Not Yoda, no one would want to be mean to that little guy.

"How can we get through it?" Kelly stepped closer to the rock face, obviously keeping her focus on the task at hand. I wanted to yell at her to stay away, far away, but her whole attention was on the Ater guy.

"You heard Yamabushi." He'd gentled his voice, from steel to iron—not a huge improvement in my opinion, but Kelly didn't seem to mind. "One of you must sacrifice that which you value most."

Yeah, we already knew that. Not helping.

"Like what?" she asked, as if they were discussing the price of tickets to a local community center play and not entry into the deepest Underworld.

"A gift you possess." He smiled at her. Then looked at me. "One you love and fear to lose." Another skipping glance, this time to Mandy. "Your life."

If fear locked muscles, anger galvanized them. Before I knew it, I was beside Kelly, pushing her back toward Mandy and shouting at this A-hole. "Whoever, or whatever you are, you can leave. Not helping. Vamoose."

No need to amp up the fear already roaring through us. No way was anyone going to lose their life, or their gifts, if I had a say, and I did. This was my mission. My call.

His brow furrowed, then his head reared back and he released a rolling laugh. A deep-chested, unexpected sound careening off the rocky path and rumbling through me.

Way to really torque a Noziak.

I swiveled to face Kelly and Mandy. "Let's head down the path. This guy's clearly an idiot."

Before I could blink, he was on the path in front of me— between where I stood and Kelly—and this close he was a lot taller, a lot more muscled and a whole lot scarier. Breath backing down the windpipe and choking me kind of scary.

"We Angelli are not known for our patience," he said, frowning beneath that veiling black line, his tone low and lethal. "You are rash."

That had a fist-sized lump closing my throat.

"But I have need of you, so *this time*," he placed emphasis on the last two words, "this time, I shall forgive you."

How magnanimous. *Jerk.*

Fortunately I had enough common sense to pick up on his most telling comment—he needed something from us. That could be good. As long as he needed something, he needed us. Plus, I might have something to bargain with.

I eyed him closely. "What do you want from us?"

"Not from all of you." His lips canted upwards. "Only from you."

CHAPTER 31

Ever notice how some combinations of words can make your blood freeze? Yeah, this was one of those combinations.

He wanted something from me. So had the Ghost Guy, so why was this new request fraught with shadows and hidden dangers?

Adrenaline powered through me with little room to maneuver.

If he wanted me, that meant Kels and Mandy were safe. Weren't they? Or expendable.

Sweet Goddess above, what now?

Behind him, Kelly suddenly cried out, as if something had struck her, her hands clutching at her temples.

I bulldozed by this Malik person, angel or not, brushing him aside to get to her and grab her shoulders, looking for blood or a wound, something. "What?"

She just shook her head, her face scrunched in pain, her fists pressing into her temples. I glanced behind her, at Mandy. "Did you see something? Anything?"

"No. What's going on?"

I flashed a look over my shoulder, glaring at the stranger, noting that he wasn't totally naked—some sort of black loincloth covered his hips.

Sharpening my tone, I demanded, "Did you do this?" When he didn't answer immediately, I deepened my voice, putting my do-it-or-die tone into play. Only it wasn't a game. "Whatever you're doing, stop it. Stop it now!"

He tilted his head as if I'd impinged on his honor. "Not my doing."

"Can you halt it?" Stupid question, I know. Desperation, and a friend in pain, made me riskier than usual.

He shook his head, then took a hard look at my expression and added, "By The One who sits below and The One who sits above, *this* is not of my doing."

No idea what he was talking about, but deep in my gut, I believed him. He seemed as taken aback as I was by what was happening. I pivoted back to Kels, tightening my grip and raising my voice, like that ever made anyone feel better. "What's going on? You've gotta tell me. Say something!"

"He's hurting her." The words tumbled over one another, each one wrenched from deep inside her. "Please. We have to help her."

"Aini?" Of course she meant Aini, and the look Mandy shot me over Kels' shoulder told me I was an idiot. So bite me. "What's he doing?"

Another stupid question, and Kels let me know that as she simply shook her head. A movement that brought tears to her eyes.

"Please," she whispered, curling in on herself. If I hadn't been bracing her, she'd have slipped to her knees.

Sweet Mercy, I had to stop her pain.

No point in spouting useless phrases—she'll be okay, we'll get there in time, hold on—when all were a lie. I had only a faint idea what was happening to Aini, why the Horned One would torture her, or if we'd make it in time to save her. All I could do was try to get to Aini, and knowing if we were close to where she was hidden might help. Like a teaspoon of water to a man dying of dehydration, knowing something was better than knowing nothing. Doing would be even better, but knowledge came first.

"How far away are we from Aini?" I asked, hoping Kels had the answer.

Instead she slumped against me, suddenly deflated, her skin blanched, her shoulders caved.

"What? What's happening now?"

"She's gone." The two words sounded so broken I wanted to wrap Kels in my arms and hug all the hurt away.

"Gone as in dead?"

Another negative head shake. That much was good if it meant Aini lived. If she did, we might still be able to help her. Even I couldn't bring her back from the dead. Bran could, in the right situation, but since he wasn't here it was a non-issue.

What now? We were where hope wasn't, and if that wasn't bad enough, the clock on rescuing Aini was ticking.

I nodded at Mandy to grab Kelly and help prop her against the rock face. Something to support her as I whirled on the being behind me and marched up to him as if he was one of the testosterone-fueled cowboys I'd grown up around in cattle and ranch country.

"You say you're willing to help us. For what? And what can you do?" Then, so we didn't spend a lot of time negotiating and wasting time, I added, "Be specific, and tell me now."

His lips slid upward in a half-moon smile. Not that there was a damn thing funny about this situation. Stepping so close I could smell the scent of his skin—like sunlight in an ancient forest—I jabbed a finger into his chest. "There's a young girl's life at stake here, and we're running out of time. Talk now or get out of our way. Got it?"

He nodded, saying nothing to my useless threats. Smart man. Last thing I needed was a bunch of BS or mumbo jumbo.

"So how do we get beyond the guy at the gate?"

"Pay his price."

"That the only way?"

He nodded, a very solemn, very clear affirmative.

Shit.

My heart took a high dive from a fifty-story building. I knew what the Guardian at the gate wanted—at least from me. One I loved and feared to lose. There was a very small list of people on such a list—my family, Kelly, the teen witch Sabina whom I'd taken under my wing and one more—the one who mattered most.

Why did I know what was being asked meant Bran?

Fear twisted and writhed deep inside me, leaving a cold, empty hole even as I raced through the alternatives.

There weren't any.

I'd faced this fear once before, when my brother was being held by a demented, power-hungry druid. The IR team had come to my, and his, rescue, saving his life. And now?

The dark emptiness yawned wider. *Not Bran, please not Bran.*

But as if an invisible clock ticked inside me, my certainty grew, strangling me until every inhalation of breath was less than the last. To get to Aini, we had to pass that gate. To pass that gate, we had to pay the toll.

I had to pay that toll. No way was I going to let Kelly lose her gift, one she thought she'd lost just recently. I'd watched daily as that knowledge tore her apart. Never again.

Almost all of us agents possessed an ability that set us apart—made us different. We might have fought against or ignored our gifts, but that didn't mean they weren't as much a part of us as any other vital organ—lungs, brain or heart. Amputation of our abilities would destroy the whole—it would kill a large part of what made us who we were. No, Kelly needed her gift, not only to survive once we returned to our normal Realm, but to find Aini and help the girl escape. No gift, no saving Aini.

As for Mandy? We might butt heads like two bull elks in rutting season, but I wasn't going to let her die. Not if I had a choice. And I did.

Past parched lips, I demanded, "When you say I must lose one I love, does that mean that they will be hurt?"

That's where I drew the line. My making a choice that hurt another. Especially if that hurt meant. . . *to Bran.*

The last thought sliced through me, drawing blood and a gasp, too painful to even speak.

"There are many degrees of pain."

"Stop the double-speak," I shouted. Anger was easier than fear. Anger I could use. "Will he die, or be torn apart, if I agree?"

"Physically, no."

Crap times twenty, what did that mean? Losing him. . . I inhaled, so deep the front of my ribs nicked my spine. I *could* survive, I had to, but not if my choice destroyed him. I could live in a world without him, not easily, but I could do that to save Aini, but not if I destroyed him by my choice. "Will he live? Will he be able to move on?"

"Yes." He spoke the word so slowly I knew there was a *but* coming.

"Spit it out," I snarled.

"I am not a soothsayer," he snapped back. So Angelli, or whatever he was, could get pissy. Good to know. Made him seem more human.

The look in his gaze said otherwise.

He leaned closer, looming over me like a vulture, with eyes the color of winter storm clouds—ice-cold and threatening. "The sacrifice is yours alone to make and bear, but nothing we do is done without a ripple. Others will be impacted."

Impacted was better than dying. Wasn't it?

It was my turn to want to shout the *duh* word. Bran would understand. Wouldn't he? If I had to give him up—the hole inside of me gaped, a raw, searing twist of pain that made the river of fire a nice alternative. With a silent sob, I realized I couldn't wave my hands and fly, or cast a protection spell to avoid this.

What choice did I have? Bran, the most secure, self-contained adult I knew, or a vulnerable young girl who had her whole life before her?

Another breath, this one released slowly, buying me seconds before the inevitable.

No brainer. There was no choice. Only the right thing to do now.

I eyed Malik, a look my brothers said I'd perfected in the cradle. A stare that screamed mess-with-me-and-you-die. "If I give up—"

Don't say his name. Don't.

"—if I do this, we can pass through the gate?"

"So says the Guardian of the Gate."

Bullshit.

Ticking clock. No choice. A girl with no options.

I speared Mandy with a look. "Help Kelly. We're going through that gate."

CHAPTER 32

Like a death knell, each step of hard sole against rocky ground reverberated though me.

He'll understand. He'll understand. Please Mary, Jesus and Joseph let him understand.

Like hell he would.

No choice.

Besides, the likelihood that we'd all die before we were able to return to our Realm was so high as to make the issue a moot point. As far as he knew, I was already dead. So it wasn't like he could lose me twice. Right?

Don't think. Don't think. Don't feel.

Gouging out my beating heart and pulverizing it would hurt less.

Tears I refused to let fall blinded me, making the gate wave in and out of focus.

I can do this. I can do this. I can. No matter what.

Kelly followed behind me, Mandy pulling up the rear, both silent. Who knew where Malik disappeared to. Didn't matter. He wasn't part of the team. Only our breathing and the whip of the mist swirling around us disturbed the air.

This wasn't about Bran. Or me. It was about Aini.

By the time we reached the gate, bile threatened to choke me. Some leader I was. Decision made. Follow through. Pay the price.

My voice sounded as thin as the vapor chilling my skin. "Guardian? You here?"

Yamabushi materialized before us, looking larger and more threatening than previously—a warrior and a roadblock, through and through. He said nothing.

How like a male—make the woman do all the work—the emotionally devastating I-may-not-survive work. Beg him to murder the best part of me? Is that what he wanted? To feel what I'd only realized myself? I was casting aside my heart, the part that made me whole, the light no matter what darkness surrounded me. Bran.

Strangling back the grief roaring through me, I raised my chin—a bluff, a useless gesture, a spit-in-your-face look that meant nothing. Not when I was about to hand him what mattered most—my world. I eyed the Guardian and steeled my tone. "We seek passage. Now."

"You are prepared to forfeit the fee?"

Screw you is what I wanted to snarl, but instead I gave a jerky head nod, bit my lip until blood dripped drop-by-drop down my throat, and managed a ragged whisper. "Yes. I'll pay the toll."

As if a cable that bound me to Bran snapped under too much force, I felt the whiplash slash through me. Slicing open a wound, one that would never heal. Not for me.

"No!" A voice called. A male's voice.

Bran's.

I'd made my choice.

If we lived, I'd track him to the ends of the earth and beg forgiveness.

A huge if.

Yamabushi stepped aside, a self-satisfied smirk dancing around his lips. If there were any emotion left within me I'd have struck him right then and there. Not because I could or because he deserved it, but because he knew, as I did, the full cost of what I'd just done.

Giving into regret wouldn't help me to find Aini. Only determination. The only thing I had left.

"Come on," I said, mostly to myself as the three of us marched forward, accepting that there was no going back.

CHAPTER 33

I don't know how far we'd hiked, what the scenery looked like around us, if my teammates were with me or if I was alone. No, I knew the answer to that last one, I was alone—emptily, achingly, totally alone. I stumbled forward on autopilot—find Aini, save her, kill the Horned One.

Don't think about. . .don't think about. . .oh, Great Spirits, what have I done?

So lost in the mud and muck of my own dark thoughts it took me a few seconds to realize Mandy was calling me.

"Noziak? Damn it. Stop."

What? I turned, surprised we weren't on the rocky trail anymore. Instead, we were on some mega-city street—a downtown one, filled with taxi cars blaring horns, thousands of people brushing past, glass skyscrapers bouncing mirror images of themselves off one another. Everything was in black and white and shades of gray. Or maybe that was just me—the murky, no color, no life, guilt-drenched emptiness.

Where were we?

"Get your ass back here," Mandy called again. She hovered near Kelly, who looked like I felt—kicked from the inside out.

"What's wrong?" My tone more demand than question as I walked back to join them. It wasn't impatience as much as my own misery lashing out—there wasn't anything left for understanding or kindness. Not even for Kels.

She wasn't clutching her head like before, but even an idiot could see she wasn't well—pale, sluggish, her hands wrapped around her arms as if to hold herself together.

I could relate.

Once broken, never mended.

I don't know where I'd heard that phrase before. Probably some well-meaning neighbor talking about my dad after my mother had abandoned him, left us all. For years dad was one of the walking wounded. The rest of us, my brothers and I, took to tip-toeing around the house as if afraid our noises—the simple ones like opening the refrigerator, closing a door, or scuffing across worn wood floors—might scatter what remained of him.

"What's going on?" My voice sounded harsh, raspy.

"Not all of us are robots," Mandy snapped, wrapping one arm around Kels. "Share some of your shifter blood or cut us some slack."

That's why they'd stopped? They were tired? Well, kiss my fanny.

Kelly shook her head, not looking at either of us. "We're too late. I know we're too late."

What? It wasn't exhaustion, which at least I could understand—nope, it was feel sorry time. If we stopped, we lost and I'd have thrown away my heart for nothing.

Anger from deep within my soul roared forth. Bad enough to lose Bran, but for no reason? I couldn't handle that. Not and survive.

I grabbed Kelly's arms, no warm and fuzzies here as my fingers bit into her flesh. "Are you saying it's hopeless because you know it? Is Aini dead?"

Her eyes widened, as if looking at a stranger, a stark-raving crazed stranger.

"Tell me!" I shouted, rattling her. "She dead or not?"

Mandy pushed into my face, breaking my hold on Kelly. "Back off, Noziak. You're hurting her."

"No, I'm going to hurt her if she doesn't spit it out." I nearly butted Mandy's forehead to make my point. "Either Aini's alive and we keep moving or she's dead and. . ." Oh, shit—if she was dead, we were too late. We'd already lost. I'd lost, but the world had lost, too. Whatever the Horned One wanted, his threat against humanity, was already unleashed. This whole screwed-up mission was a complete waste.

"She's alive." Kelly's soft-spoken words washed against me, hesitant and trembling.

I looked at her, but didn't see her. No, I saw red.

"You want a breather, fine. Grow up and say so." She looked like I'd slapped her, but I wasn't finished. Not by a long shot—all the anger, the grief, the futility rolling through me spewed forth. "As long as she's alive, we move. We don't sit here and whine." I swept my hand in an imperial, dismissive gesture, way out of proportion to what Kelly had said, but only a tip of the iceberg slamming through me. I pivoted and stormed away toward a small open plaza, throwing words like shrapnel over my shoulder. "You're an agent. Start acting like one. If Aini's alive, we keep going."

The crash against my back threw me forward—forward and down. Hard. Scraping against rough concrete.

What the—

"Asshole!" Mandy straddled my back, her fists pummeling me. "Freakin' asshole."

Oh no, she didn't.

Like a rattlesnake whipping around, I twisted and thrashed until the two of us became a flurry of flailing arms, ramming knees and oaths in English, Shoshone and Spanish.

She punched. I bit. Somewhere Kelly shouted.

Mandy snagged my hair and pulled. I scratched at her eyes. No Robert's Rules of Order here. Far from it. This had been building for a long time.

My elbow slammed into her nose, spewing blood over both of us. Point to me.

Her knee jammed into my ribcage, swooshing my breath out in a big humph. Point to her.

"Stop it!" Kelly screamed, then released a piercing whistle so loud and so close, she finally broke through. That and the fact the two of us were huffing and writhing on the ground like playground bullies. "Enough."

Kelly was pissed as she pulled me backwards, away from Mandy. Like I'd started the fight. My face ached, my cheek abraded by the rough paving, I was doubled over sucking in small breaths so my ribs didn't have to move much.

"Look around us," she whispered, suddenly squatting down in between the two of us, her tone urgent. "No, don't make it obvious."

I'd only moved my neck, about the only thing I could move without setting off a rumba of pain. How the heck was I supposed to—oh!

Since we were all at sidewalk level, at first I'd only seen the legs of the people around us. Then I'd noticed those legs weren't moving.

Probably lookie-loos, gawking at a catfight between two women, but then I became aware, too aware, of the absolute stillness of those legs. The lack of any motion—no fidgeting, no turning to talk to another, nothing. Nothing except a low, quiet murmur, one that didn't sound like talking, but like a low frequency rustle. The sound of a rattler creeping across rocks, a cougar sneaking through dry cheat grass, a rapist hiding behind a door. A sound that scraped along my nerve endings and made my muscles clench.

Keeping my head bowed, as if still recovering from Mandy's lucky punch, which I was, I managed to look upwards from out of the corner of my eye.

I wished I hadn't.

They weren't people. Shades of gray, murky shadows, and not all there. They were more like those damn zombies we'd run into once before, only these had glowing red-yellow eyes.

This might be Mandy's worst fear but they were quickly becoming mine.

"Your fighting brought them," Kelly whispered, just one of three friends chatting away while two sprawled across the sidewalk sporting blood and bruises. Yup, an average day in the life of an IR Agent.

"There a way out?" I asked, wiping a trickle of blood from my swelling lower lip. Guess Mandy had gotten more than a few lucky licks in.

"Possibly." Kelly stood, slowly, not a care in the world, and extended her hand to me.

Ouch. The first tug was a doozie.

We'd only been fighting for what seemed like seconds, not much more, but man, every muscle screamed.

Once on my feet, I reached for Mandy. She looked as pummeled as I felt, but it didn't make me feel like a winner, more like a fool. We needed all of our wits about us and I'd tossed that away. Mandy was more than hurting if the whiteness of her eyes and the difficulty she had swallowing were any indication. She was scared out of her gourd.

So was I. This might be her nightmare come to life, but all three of us were trapped in it.

As she straightened next to me, I murmured in her ear, "I've got your back. Get Kelly out of here."

"Not without you."

That was us—one second trying to smash one another into oblivion then bring on the freaky zombies and we were back to being a team.

Brushing off my jeans, with feigned nonchalance, I scanned as much of the area as possible. The small plaza I'd entered prior to Mandy's tackle looked wall-to-wall zombie people— shades of gray with laser red eyes and expressions that ratcheted up the scare factor—a lot.

"Start walking toward that doorway." I nodded to the only exit I could see from where I stood. Heading down the sidewalk wasn't an option, as that scraping humming sound had increased, so did the press of bodies. Another few minutes and there'd be no door to duck behind.

Bless Kelly and Mandy, they didn't hesitate, but plastered smiles on their faces and started chatting about mall shopping. They actually made it sound fun, which amazed me as I'd rather have a lobotomy than go shopping. One of the things Bran used to tease me about.

Quick stabbing emotional pain overwhelmed all physical aches and bruises. Plus the humming increased, as if the hive got tasered.

"Move a little faster," I murmured, almost stepping on Mandy's heels. I didn't have to say more as they'd picked up their tempo.

Our escape route was still about twenty feet away.

The door we aimed for looked like any office entrance— double-wide glazed glass, a shadowed recess and huge gold letters written in Chinese or some similar language branding the building above the entryway. I hoped it didn't say *this way to more trouble*.

Ten feet now.

"You sure it goes anywhere?" Kelly didn't even turn around as she murmured, "Excuse me. Sorry. Pardon me," jostling through the crowd.

That actually made me smile, her being nice to the creepy dead, which helped take my mind off the fact I had no idea if the building was real or an illusion.

Five feet.

Show time.

Mandy reached the glass doors first, managing to edge between a couple of demon zombies blocking her way without ever touching them.

Go Chiquita!

She jerked open the door with such force I was surprised it didn't shatter, then disappeared inside.

So far so good—if she hadn't stepped off into an abyss or slammed into more zombies inside.

Think positive, Noziak. *Or die.*

Incentive was good.

I all but pushed Kelly through the door, following so closely we probably looked like one person instead of two. With one hand on the door behind me, I slammed it shut, ignoring the clawing arms and hands caught in the opening.

Not real. Not real. Not—oh crap I was going to upchuck.

Then they vaporized. Not poof, they were gone, but more like smoke fading away, leaving an inky residue.

Worked for me.

I turned my attention to the lobby. Not out of the wicked woods yet as a dozen demon zombies were inside and, as if pulled by a puppeteer, they turned toward us.

Hive mentality all right, and I had no doubt who drove them.

"Elevator?" Kelly asked even though Mandy was already headed in that direction.

"No!" Yeah, I shouted too loud, which was dumb, but we had seconds max. "Might be zombies in it." No way did I want to be trapped inside a steel box with no way out, especially if these creatures were inside that same box or waiting for us once the doors opened elsewhere. "Stairs."

I had no idea if the sign on the door I slammed through said *stairs*, but it was close and we had no other options.

Thank the Great Spirits I was right.

We took the first level two steps at a time, my heart racing, sweat dampening my back.

By the second level I could hear the zombies following us— a faint shuffle compounded by lots of feet scraping against the concrete stairs.

"Keep going," I called over my shoulder, hoping I wasn't leading my teammates into a dead-end trap. Third floor, fourth, we hit the fifth. Sounds still echoed behind us but not as loud. "We get far enough ahead. . . *huff*. . . we can . . . *huff, huff*. . . duck down . . . a floor."

What was going on? Had my oxygen supply been cut off?

Grasping the handrail as a lever, I kept going, Kelly and Mandy wheezed behind me. No shifter blood. Had. To. Remember.

By the seventh floor, I was sure my heart would escape my chest it thudded so hard.

"Here," I panted, pulling the door leading to a hallway open though I could have sworn it weighed a good ton.

The second it snicked closed behind us, all three of us stopped, bent double, chugging breath.

"What's—" Kelly couldn't finish her sentence.

I shook my head. No idea. Unless all of this was a fabrication. If those zombies expected their Hell to be a cityscape, complete with the trappings, that might explain the surroundings. And the air? They didn't need it so guess what, it wasn't here. Or maybe it just thinned the higher into a building we went.

Not that the demon zombies would notice.

"Find a room." I pointed down the hall that looked like a million other hallways in professional buildings I'd been in. Not in Mud Lake. Our tallest structures were the grain silos.

Fluorescent lighting, linoleum floors polished into submission, closed doors, all with Chinese writing on them, a few had English, too.

We staggered forward, weaving down the hallway, punch drunk with no air, all of us straining to catch any murmuring sound from the stairwell.

I paused in front of Wang, Lee and LeRoux. That last name struck an odd note, not being oriental at all. But odd worked for me.

"Here." I had no idea what I'd find as I twisted the knob and poked my head in, sighing when I realized it was empty. That was good. Empty meant it held no zombies, until they found us. "It's safe."

Safe being a very iffy word.

A lawyer's office maybe with the traditional waiting room, over-creased magazines scattered on tables, an abandoned receptionist area.

I aimed for a short hallway to the right, the primordial part of my brain screaming—hide, hide, hide.

At some point though, we were going to run out of doors.

CHAPTER 34

We ended up in a corner office that looked out over the small plaza we'd escaped from—no doubt some huge cosmic joke. One big fat circle.

"What now?" Mandy asked, hanging near the door, listening.

"Now we hope those zombies can't smell us, or hear us, or find us."

"And if they can?" Her brows climbed her forehead.

I was tempted to tell her then that we were screwed. That was the problem with plans made on the fly—there wasn't enough time to think through the ramifications. Minutes ago we were all thrilled to be away from that undead mob still hanging out on the streets. Now? Now it wasn't good enough.

"If you want to lead, be my guest." I'd had it up to my eyeballs with this whole you-lead-so-I-can-bitch attitude.

"This isn't getting us anywhere." Kelly glared at the two of us. "I'm ashamed of you both."

Geez Louise, I didn't start it. Nodding toward Mandy I said, "She hit me—"

"You sound like a two-year old," Kelly snapped. "And you!" She whirled on Mandy. "There was no call for literally jumping on Alex outside. She was right. There's no time for lightweights if we're to save Aini."

Nah, na nah na na.

Mandy mumbled something, and Kelly was verbally all over her. "She's trying her best." I almost gave a pump of my fist into the air, when Kelly cut her glance back at me. "Mandy didn't have to come with us, but she did. She's here to help us and if you two can't grow up, I'm going on without either of you."

She stood there, hands on her hips, her legs wide, mentally shaking a finger at us. Teacher-mode all the way.

That's when we heard the sounds. We all froze.

The zombies had reached the outer waiting room.

"Mandy and Kelly, get that desk in front of the door."

"Then we can't get out." Mandy eyed the door.

"Yeah, but it'll buy us a few more seconds."

Kelly already had her butt scooching the desk toward the door. "Bitch later. Help now!" she ordered.

Way to go, Kels!

No time for high fives. I stepped up to the window. Seven stories up, no place to land, no fire escapes. Options?

The murmuring intensified. Coming down the hall. Beating a tempo with my screaming heartbeat.

No weapons. No tools.

Magic. And only one spell I knew might, with a very slim chance, *might* get us out of here.

Running to where the desk had been, I grabbed the chair. Thank heavens someone's imagination created one with heavy rollers on the bottom of it. Hefting it with strength given me by my shifter blood, I swung it toward the window.

The crash muted the first hammering on the other side of the door.

"Gotta—" Mandy eyed me.

"I know, we're getting out of here. Come here." I didn't have time to explain a lot of the fine details. Wasn't sure I knew them anyway. "The flying spell."

"Don't have time." Mandy pointed toward the door. "That's not going to hold for long. Sending us one at a time out the window won't help."

"I know that." Glass crunched under my shoes as I moved close enough to the jagged opening to feel a cool breeze washing against me. "Kelly, you stand here." I positioned her about a foot away from the window, facing it. "Mandy, right behind her."

The banging on the door made us all jump as the desk began dancing in place.

I stepped up and positioned myself facing Kelly with my back to the window, my heels right on the edge of oblivion. "When I tell you to, grab my hands. Mandy will grab your feet."

"I don't think—"

"Good, it's not that kind of a plan."

"What?" Mandy all but squealed. Didn't blame her, but I only had two hands and no way could I hold on to them one-handed each.

I didn't even glance her way. Couldn't afford to, because her fear was my fear—my winging my way out the window was one thing, carrying the weight of my teammates was a whole other issue. There were so many ways this plan could go wrong and only one way it'd work. A bloody miracle.

No time to still or center myself. Instead I reached to my side and sliced my hand against the edge of the open window. Damn, that hurt, but it brought forth blood.

White magic worked for sweet, simple charms. Dark magic, the dangerous, powerful, punch-to-the-gut kind, needed blood. Human blood being the best.

Flicking my hand before me, I splayed bright red drops on the glass, the floor, myself.

Now or never.

"Powers that be, here and far
I call upon thee."

I raised my hands, calling upon the winds, praying to the Spirits of my ancestors that I didn't stir anything else to life.

"Never going to work, Noziak," Mandy called out.

"Lift me up. Send me aloft.
Wings of power, wings of strength."

"You're going to kill us all."

"Unfurl my wings, high and wide.
Rise from the earth, bound no more.
Fly now, fast and free.

So mote it be!"

A crack of lightning lit up the room. I closed my eyes, grabbed hold of Kelly's hands and launched myself backwards out the window.

CHAPTER 35

There are stupid plans and then there are downright suicidal ones. Guess which kind I'd hatched.

Yup.

My wings erupted. That was good. It went downhill from there. Fast.

Kelly held tight, so tight the jerk when her whole weight suspended from me almost popped my arms from my shoulder sockets.

Someone screamed. Mandy? Me?

Kelly's weight acted like an anchor, pulling both of us down. Then Mandy joined the fun and we started to plummet. Not a slow, lazy spiral to the hard sidewalk below but a speeding bullet on a downward trajectory.

We all screamed. Loud. The sky, building, demon zombies below—everything blurred.

"Rise from the earth, bound no more.
Fly now. Fly high. Fly free."

I chanted as fast and hard as we fell, then squeezed my eyes closed.

This was it.

Then something grabbed me from behind, around my waist, cutting my breath in half. Oomph!

Arms encircled me as someone uttered an oath. Our free fall slowed, then stopped.

I could have sworn I heard Mandy's boots scraping the pavement, we were that close.

A quick glance up didn't reassure me as we climbed higher and higher into the sky. Inky black wings blocked everything except below and directly in front of me.

But they weren't my wings. That guy—Malik—the Ater Angelus—they were his, and he wielded them with a vengeance.

Faster and faster, we catapulted through the air. The pressure of Kelly's grip increased, but I didn't know if it was enough. Fear slickened my hands, dried my mouth.

"Hang on," I prayed out loud. "Please hang on."

"Don't. Know. How. Long."

"Long as it takes, McAllister." My words sounded like an oath. "You fall and I'll. . . I'll come after you and kill you again."

She may have snorted. Or released a desperate cry.

Who was this guy and where was he taking us? More importantly, how long could Kels and Mandy hang on?

"Gotta put us down," I shouted, looking over my shoulder, up into the feathered blackness surrounding me. "Can't—"

He didn't answer, unless increasing his speed was his response.

Great! Death by demon zombies might have been the quicker, less painful option. If Mandy fell, Kelly wouldn't be able to live with herself. If my grip on Kelly lessened, I'd never be able to face Van. Or myself.

Please hang on.

Kelly's hold on my bloodied hand slipped. I windmilled my freed arm, straining for her. Both her hands banded around the wrist she still clung to.

Stop!" I screamed to the dark-winged one. "Stop or they die."

"Only need you," came his response, vibrating through me.

Oh, no, he did not just say that.

I yelled up at him. "They fall and I'll jettison myself after them."

Silence. Did he hear me?

"Not a bluff," I snarled. "One of us dies, we all die."

Either he believed me or decided we weren't worth the effort.

Without warning, one second we were in the air, the next we were cartwheeling, head over heels, downward.

CHAPTER 36

When I was about ten, my older brother Jake dared me to jump off the high dive at the YMCA pool. Being a Noziak, there wasn't a dare I hadn't met head on, no matter how stupid it was. Diving from a minuscule slab of fiberglass into a pool that looked smaller and smaller as I climbed was no different, except what Jake hadn't told me was how to land in the water—not in a belly flop.

I learned that lesson all over again when in quick succession—one, two, three—and no time to realize we hit liquid and not solid ground—I face-planted into a hard-as-metal body of water.

Splat.

Sink.

It was damn lucky Kelly had enough sense to grab my shirt and haul me upwards, otherwise I'd have remained rolled into a breathless puddle of misery long enough to drown myself. Instead, we all broke the surface sputtering and gulping for air.

"*Hijo de puta!*" Mandy muttered, dog paddling while glancing around. "That asshole."

I agreed a thousand percent but couldn't say anything, not until my diaphragm started working again and my chest quit screaming. Didn't think that was happening any time soon.

"That way." Kelly wiped her hair from her face and nodded in the direction over my shoulder. Then she looked at me. "You need me to pull you ashore?"

I shook my head, amazed I could do that much. As soon as I got enough air, I started stroking in the direction both Kels and Mandy headed—my shifter blood pumping enough energy through me to swim in their wake. Not at turbo-speed, but my heart kaboomed as fast as it could, my brain sluggish in comparison. The temporary wings I'd sported, and still had, acted like dead weight dragging me down. Down. Down.

Should get rid of them.

What was that spell? Why'd it matter?

My head slipped beneath the surface before I knew it. Between one breath and another.

Come this far to drown.

At least Kelly and Mandy lived.

Should fight. Should . . .

Why? I'd lost Bran. Threw him away. He didn't even know it.

Right before my lungs burst from holding my breath, or I just gave up, a hard jerk shot me upwards, breaking the surface with a loud whoosh.

Someone had a fist in my shirt collar tight enough I started choking. The fun wasn't over yet. Skimming the water like a wakeboard on steroids, I surged forward until, with a heave sucking a trail of water behind me, I was tossed onto dry land with a solid plop.

As if I needed a few more bruises and banged up muscles.

Death by falling, drowning and then strangulation. This so wasn't my day.

Curling into a ball of misery, I coughed up water until I had the dry heaves. Only then could I spread sopping wet arms and legs among the grass, waiting to see if I hadn't really died and just didn't know it yet.

"You okay, Mandy?" I heard Kelly nearby. Not on top of me but near enough.

That was good. It was better when I heard Mandy cough out a Spanish reply. Must still be pissed. Nothing new there.

I don't know how long it took me to roll from my stomach to my back and sit up, with a whole lot of groaning.

"You're alive, aren't you," said a deep male voice right beside me.

At another time, I might have jumped. Scaring the willies out of me resulted in that kind of reaction. But today? I barely managed an eye roll in his direction. He sat just opposite me,

looking like a well-satiated panther, lazing in the grass—
indolent, arrogant, without a worry in the world.

"I really hate you," I muttered, probably not the smartest of
comments. Bite me. I hurt too much to be sweet and nice. Hell,
I hurt so much I barely managed snark.

"That's a witch's way of saying thank you?" He actually
looked at his nails, like he'd gotten them dirty thanks to
helping my friends and me.

"You could have killed us," I pointed out. "Tried to in
several ways."

"I saved your lives." He glanced on the other side of me
where Mandy still cussed in Spanish. "Even the two I do not
need."

If I'd had enough whomp left in me, I might have reached
across and cuffed him. But I didn't, which gave me enough
time to realize he spoke the truth, even if I didn't want to hear
it. He had saved us. From out of nowhere. If he hadn't sprouted
wings and found us exactly when he did, we'd be icky goo on
the sidewalk for zombies to walk on.

That didn't mean I was feeling really thankful right then.
Not with a thousand questions zipping through me. Starting
with, "Why did you?"

He arched a brow as he stopped perusing his nails and cut
me a quick sideways glance. "Why did I what? Save you?"

I nodded.

"I told you. I need your help."

"To do what?"

"When the time comes, I'll let you know."

As if I'd have no choice if and when that happened. No
point arguing that right now. Not when I had other things to
learn.

I angled my chin toward his back, which looked like a
perfectly ordinary back. Now. "What's with the wings?"

"All Angelli have them." He shrugged as if the answer
should have been obvious. "It's one of our perks."

"They're permanent?" As opposed to magic-conjured ones
like I'd created. Which, thankfully seemed to have
disappeared. I hoped it was because I'd stopped using them and

not because there was a time sensitive detail about the spell I didn't know.

"As long as I'm an Angelli, the wings are part of me."

For a second I thought his voice sounded tired, a weary kind of waiting for something just outside his reach. Then I heard Kelly call out, "You want to ask where we are?"

I glanced in her direction. She and Mandy were about thirteen feet on the other side of Malik.

Heck, I hadn't even thought of that detail. Guess too many near-death experiences in a row knocked the important things right out of my head. A quick look around didn't help me either. The body of water we'd been tossed into looked like a small lake, its surface a still, rose-colored hue. Except for the matted grass we sat on, the rest of the area looked craggy with rough, volcanic rock I recognized from growing up in Southern Idaho. Pillow-shaped, black chunks that looked spewed from the deepest levels of earth, which was exactly what they were.

I started with the easy question first. More of a comment than a question just in case asking anything of him might be construed as seeking a favor. I knew better than that, not that I'd remembered it when I needed it. "I never knew there were lakes in this Realm."

"There aren't."

Sure buddy, sell me some more crap. But damn if he wasn't right. The second I glanced back toward the lake it'd disappeared, becoming a bed of orange-looking sand.

"What the—"

"You conjured a soft place to land."

Obviously not soft enough, my body still screamed.

"So all of this is my imagination?"

"We all have our illusions. Especially here. The one with the strongest illusions creates a reality for herself and her companions."

It was a good thing I thought water instead of rock or concrete. "What if my illusion killed us?"

"Then you'd be like me. Only spirit, not an Angelli."

He didn't have to sound like I could never be on the same level as he was. As if I even wanted the position. It wasn't important. I'd gotten off track.

"Where are we?" I echoed Kelly's words. Yeah, it was a question but it was time to get this show on the road.

"Just over that hill there," Malik glanced to my left and a low ridge of jagged mountains marching off into a gray-blue shadowy distance, "lie the Gates of Hell."

As if the day hadn't been rough enough already.

CHAPTER 37

I waved Kelly and Mandy over to where I still sat, not quite ready to get up and face what I knew had to be faced. Yes, time was ticking past, but right then the weight of the world pressed against me. The sheer enormity of the task we'd undertaken slapped against me with the same force as slamming into the water.

What naïve stupidity drove us—three clueless humans—to beard the Horned One in his place of power? And to think, even for a second, that we stood a chance of rescuing Aini and escaping?

Idiots.

"You look sick," Kelly murmured as she crossed over and sat down beside me. "Why? Did he do something to you?"

"No." The single word said everything and nothing.

Mandy eyed Malik like he was the devil himself, and who knew, he could be.

Which had me asking, "Are you. . ." I didn't even know how to say what I wanted to say.

"Am I a servant of the Dark One?" he said, doing that creepy mind reading thing.

That had me pausing as I untangled his words. "Is the Dark One the same as the Horned One?"

His lips inched upward. "No. The Horned One is to the Dark One as I am to the Horned One."

Like that meant anything. I glanced at Kelly who held her attention one hundred percent on Mr. Cryptic.

"So there's a greater evil than the Horned One?" she asked. Which was a very good question, and one I should have thought of if my brain cells were clicking.

"Yes."

"So who exactly is this Horned Guy?" Mandy asked as if we hadn't just gone head to head with him a short while ago.

"He is a bottomless well of desire."

Not how I'd have thought to describe the threat we'd faced yesterday. In fact, desire would be the last word I'd use. Puking, bottom-feeding, evil maybe, but not desire.

"Explain." I, too, could do one word cryptic.

"His tools are fear, scarcity and envy. He wields them in ways to undermine hope, joy and security."

Actually, some of that started making sense. I didn't like it, but it did make sense.

"So what does he want?" If I could get a handle on that, maybe I could figure out a way to undermine him. A big maybe.

"He seeks power."

"To go up against the Dark One?" Why else did powerful beings seek more of what they already had? There was always someone bigger, badder and ready-to-be-toppled. Guess the Underworld was very much like the Real Realm we came from in that regard.

"He has other plans." Malik looked at me as if I should have already known that.

Which I did, as the light bulb clicked on for me. "He wants to escape here for good."

"And return to where we came from," Kels whispered, making it a statement of fact.

Malik nodded, and now Kelly looked ill, as if hit too hard where she was most vulnerable. She'd been the one who killed the human vessel the Horned One had used to get to Aini. She knew what it took to accomplish that, how hard that had been. She also knew, more than the rest of us, what could be unleashed if the Horned One found a way to not only return to our world, but remain there.

She was supposed to be Aini's Guardian, the one who protected her. Which sucked as a job so far. It wasn't as if

Kelly had been given a choice to take on this impossible task, but she stepped up to her role when it would have been far easier to turn tail and run.

We'd understood, or guessed, that The Horned One wanted Aini's powers, but had been hazy on the details. If she turned sixteen, it seemed she could fight him off, but if he could tap into her abilities, or coerce her to give him what he wanted before then, it looked like not only would he connect with the Seekers, but also score a Get-out-of-Hell-Free pass.

This kept getting worse and worse.

Seekers evidently once ruled on Earth, back in the time of myths and fairytales. Then they screwed up, their own arrogance and self-indulgence finally caught up with them, and were booted out—that was my abridged version, anyway. The Horned One wanted the Seekers back—the theory being if he scratched their demi-gods' backs, they'd elevate him to a higher position of power plus let him leave the Underworld.

No wonder the egomaniac had kidnapped Aini. If he could get her to wake from her coma, the one she'd been in when he kidnapped her, or maybe he didn't even have to do that, he'd have won and humanity lost. Especially since the Seekers seemed to think humans were best used as playthings or food.

The shudder jolting through me had nothing to do with my damp clothes or exhaustion and everything to do with pure, unadulterated fear.

"So what's your angle in this?" I demanded, feeling very much like we were being used here. Why had Malik helped us? He had to have an agenda.

Malik gave a one-shoulder shrug before answering. "It's simple."

"Explain simple."

"You have your quest, which involves the Horned One. When you are finished, if you survive, you will be returning to your Realm. Correct?"

Kelly nodded before I could warn her not to give Malik too much information.

"And what's any of this have to do with you?" I braced myself for the answer.

"I'm the one who can get you into the Horned One's Realm."

"And?"

Kelly looked at me like I was crazy, after all this was the first clear indication we were heading in the right direction. Something other than the sound of Aini inside Kelly's brain.

But I didn't trust this guy, regardless if he saved our lives or not. Trust had to be earned. Another Noziak rule.

"And?" I repeated when he hesitated. Noziaks were nothing if not pugnacious.

"And. . ." He lasered me straight on with those cold, silver eyes of his. "And when you return to your world, you take me with you."

CHAPTER 38

"Not going to happen," I barked, making sure everyone understood this was not open for debate. I scrambled to my feet, glaring down at Malik, only he was no longer sprawled on the grass but standing right in front of me, glaring down at me.

How'd—

Just proved how sneaky and conniving a spirit could be. No way was I going to be responsible for letting one out of the Spirit Realm. No way!

Kelly's hand tugged on my sleeve. "Wait. Let's hear him out."

I turned on her like a striking cobra. "There's nothing to hear. He belongs here. We don't. And no way in H—"

"Don't say it." Her brows arched.

Fine. I wouldn't say the H E double L word but that didn't mean I changed my mind. "He stays. End of story."

"But what if he can help us get to Aini?" Kelly asked, sounding reasonable and adult. I hated when she did that, mostly because it was at times I couldn't. Like now.

"He can't get us to Aini." Technically he might be able to, but if I opened this door an inch, Kelly, and Malik, would slam it all the way open so fast my head would spin.

"Alex." Kelly's tone shaded entreaty with determination—a powerful combination. "Aini. . . I can't hear her all the time. Her voice grows fainter and fainter." She paused and swallowed deeply. "If I can't hear her, we won't find her in time."

Damn, damn, damn, damn.

Kels had a point, a good one, but that didn't mean I was willing to give this Malik a one-way voucher out of the Underworld.

I turned on him, hands curled into hot fists at my side. "I don't even know if I can release you from here." After all, he had no body waiting in the Real Realm.

"I do." He sounded so smug.

Time to take a different tact. "Exactly how are you going to help us?"

I could have sworn Kelly released a long held breath.

Malik nodded toward those smudged hills. "I know a back way into where you want to go. One that can get you there sooner and without as many obstacles."

I noticed he didn't say with *no* obstacles. "And you know this route because?"

"It's the way I escaped the Horned One."

Talk about sucking all the air from the Realm. His words held a bitterness that scalded, but they also carried hope for us. If he could do the impossible, why couldn't we?

Kelly recovered first. "You were a prisoner of him? Of it?"

"Yes."

We were back to being cryptic.

"Why were you a prisoner?" I asked, aware of a tremble that started low in my nerves and tingled throughout my body.

"My business. Not yours."

Which didn't tell me a bloody thing. Escape or was released? If released, it could be to do exactly what he was doing—heading us off at the pass.

"Why should we trust you?" Mandy pushed.

Go, Chiquita.

"Because you have no choice."

Not feeling the love.

"How long ago was it that you escaped?" My turn to prod. "And how many obstacles exactly?"

"Not long and enough challenges to scare most creatures from even considering escape."

"And yet you did." My tone could have slashed through him but he didn't seem to mind as his mouth kicked up into one of those wouldn't-you-like-to-know smiles.

"How long will it take us to get through this better, shorter route?" Kelly jumped in, clearly having made up her mind.

"If you follow my instructions, about two hours."

She looked at her watch. Thank the Spirits she'd brought it because I had no idea how much time had passed since we'd entered the Spirit Realm. One lifetime? It sure felt like more.

Her eyes, when she looked back up at me, were bleak. "Aini will turn sixteen in three hours. If we can get to her before that, and that bastard hasn't found a way to break her, we might . . ."

I knew why she trailed off. The odds were not in our favor.

Mandy scuffed one boot along the ground. "That's cutting it fine."

"Sixteen?" Malik suddenly looked wide-awake. "You're not trying to reach the Horned One but the Seer?"

"What do you know about Aini . . . I mean the Seer?" I demanded. The Underworld might not have cell phones but clearly the ability to know everything that was going on and keep up on the most recent news put AT&T to shame.

"He'll never let her go." Malik's words sounded like a chisel striking hard stone.

In other words, don't bother. Turn around. Go home. Saving Aini wasn't going to happen.

Scarlet flag waving to a Noziak.

"Good thing we don't really care what the Horned One wants."

He looked at me, that black stripe across his face making his expression intense, and threatening. "Your chances of returning went from about twenty percent to less than five." He glanced then at Kelly and Mandy. "Even one of you surviving at five percent, makes the chances of all of you escaping. . . " He simply shook his head.

Kill joy.

"You got out."

"But I'm an Angelli. You're not."

Wasting time on a pissing contest wasn't getting us anywhere. We all knew the mission was a long shot. Nothing had changed. If Malik's promise to show us a secondary route in could buy us some time, we might still be able to reach Aini.

Might not be able to save her, but she wouldn't die alone. We'd be able to die with her.

CHAPTER 39

Malik kept his own council as he led us up to a ridge that overlooked, at first glance, a lovely valley with a meandering dirt path through patches of trees and wildflowers. In the distance, a rocky crag ended in a fairy tale castle with tall turrets, crenelated towers and the expectation that at any moment Tinker Bell would fly past sprinkling fairy dust.

Except in this Realm, Tinker Bell would probably drop acid rain or incendiary devices.

We lowered ourselves to the ground, lying prone, keeping a low profile until all four of us could scan the horizon. No one said a word.

"That doesn't look too bad," I murmured, shocked that such evil could lurk amongst such beauty.

Malik and Kelly both shot me a WTH look. Mandy didn't bother.

"What?" I nodded toward the vista. "Looks doable."

Kelly shook her head as if dealing with a clueless child. Malik ignored her by raising one hand and waving it in front of him as if erasing the sky.

Damn. That's just what he did. Now what lay before us was a desolate valley reeking of smoke and pain.

My stomach took a high dive into an empty pool.

Think of every painting from the Middle Ages and Renaissance, the ones showing souls in torment and misery, and that's what spread out in front of us. Even from here, high about the tumult below, we could hear the cries, the gnashing of teeth, the screams of torment. Pain and despair rolled like a thick fog off the land with the people in misery packed shoulder to shoulder. No one seemed to be aware there were others beside them, and maybe that was the hardest punishment to endure—being forever alone and forsaken.

An image of Bran flashed in my thoughts, and I ruthlessly shoved it away. This was not the place to allow any self-pity or doubt. Focus on the mission, and how to find Aini.

"Where's your route?" I demanded of Malik, not looking at him, but very much aware of him to my left.

"South of here." He nodded his chin in that direction. "Through the land of the Lost Children. That's your route."

Kelly rose to her elbows. "What? No child deserves—"

"I did not create this place and do not determine who is here." Malik bit each word off.

Got the message—not his fault. That said, it still didn't mean crossing an area of children in pain was going to be a stroll down the street, especially for Kels.

"Is there any way to save the children?" Kelly asked before I could ease us away from what we couldn't do and back to what we could.

"How do we reach this place and get through it?" I was back on task, even as I dreaded that I wasn't any better equipped than Kelly to do what needed doing.

"The Horned One captured the souls of these children, that's why they are lost—cut off from ever being with those they loved." Malik spoke as if I'd asked. "The only difference between them and your Seer is she's still alive and stands a chance." He glanced at Kelly before he added, "If you stop the Horned One—if you kill him—only then can the Lost Children return to where they belong."

I eyed him, surprised. It wasn't a perspective I expected from him.

"Kels," I gentled my voice, hating to have to be the voice of reason here, "we've got to think about Aini first. About *all* the children who won't survive if we don't free her and get her away from here."

"But—"

"I know." I glanced at Mandy who shrugged and looked away. Not that I expected a lot of support there, but the last thing we needed was to have Kelly fall apart before we could even get to Aini. I turned away from Kelly and steeled my voice. "Time to put your big girl panties on," I said, expecting her to tell me where to take my platitude and stuff it.

But this was Kels. She'd do the hard thing when it needed to be done. No matter what the personal cost.

If we got through this, I'd tell her. Now I bit my tongue and turned back to Malik. "Okay, Big Guy, give us the low down."

"Big Guy?" His brow furrowed. "Low down?"

"The scoop. We need the details."

He nodded before spreading his palm across the ground between where he and I lay.

"We're here." He thrust a finger into the ground. "The most likely place your girl is being held is here." It looked a fair distance in the dirt. "The children are here." A triangular area about equidistant between the two indents he'd already made.

"How far apart between the children and here?" I pointed to the second divot.

"A few miles in your terms."

That didn't sound bad. Fifteen minutes to a mile, we were talking about six miles. If we hustled we could cut down on that time.

He continued as if I'd spoken out loud. "It's not the distance, it's what's awaiting you along the way."

He really did have to work on his doom-and-gloom attitude.

"Such as?"

"Marshy land where one step off the path means being sucked in and disappearing in seconds." He indicated an area even before we reached the children. "And here, the carrions lie in wait to pick off any morsel they can find."

This was getting better and better. *Not.*

"Anything else?"

"The Ghosts of Love Lost are through here." Another line across his map. "Murder victims here." He glanced up at me. "They'll want justice. Prepare yourself for them."

I looked at Mandy out of the corner of my eyes, hoping she wasn't thinking of her family when we passed this particular obstacle. If she did, we'd deal with it then.

"That about it?" A prickling beneath my skin warned me that we were losing precious time.

"When you reach the Horned One, know that he cannot be killed." He paused. "Only by one of his own."

"And what the h—heck does that mean? You mean a demon? Or someone dead?"

His shoulders rippled in that non-response shrug.

"You want out of here, you listen up." I pointed to my eyes but didn't speak until he looked at me and focused. "Tell me what I need to know on how to kill *you know who*. We don't do that, you don't escape this Realm."

"I think he means that if we're not dead by then, we'll probably be shortly thereafter," Mandy broke in, keeping Malik from answering. As if he would.

"You're just a fount of cheer, aren't you?" I threw out to my teammate, when what I wanted to do was kick her. Instead I scooted away from the edge of the cliff facing before I stood up and brushed off blood red dust from my pants.

Malik stood up next to me and lowered his voice. "I will not be able to help you once you pass through the Cave of Madness."

"What?" Kelly drew near me. "What kind of place is that?"

"It's the first stage. Hold your hands over your ears, don't speak and don't stop, and you might get through."

And this was the route he said was easier?

I looked out toward that fairy tale castle that still remained, even if everything else had been revealed as only an illusion. How were we going to keep an eye on it if we were wandering around some spooky cave?

"How will we know we're on the right path?" I asked, hoping for something like a yellow brick road or maybe even gingerbread crumbs.

"Follow the tears."

Great.

"Like little droplets of water?" What kind of roadmap was that?

"You'll know them when you see them."

Even more vague mumbo jumbo. And I thought Ghost Guy sucked as a guide.

Malik's voice hesitated. "Once you embark on the path, do not, for any reason, leave it."

I didn't even bother asking why because, deep down, in the empty darkness of my fears, I already knew his answer.

Leave the path and we'd never be able to get back on it. End of mission, no saving Aini, nothing.

Malik nodded as if I'd spoken out loud, his dark, hooded eyes confirming my fears.

CHAPTER 40

Thirty minutes later Mandy, Kelly and I stood at the opening of a yawning black hole. The Cave of Madness, according to Malik. He'd pointed the way then disappeared in a swoop of his carrion black wings, but not before one final word of warning.

"Do not use your magic until you reach the chamber of the Horned One, and even there, it might not be a wise idea."

"Because?" I wanted all the bad news spelled out loud and clear.

"It can be used against you," came the not-so-reassuring response. "And stay on the path, no matter what."

"Yes, Mom."

I could have sworn he ruffled his feathers a little more than was technically necessary to launch himself. Score, Noziak.

"You up for this?" Kelly asked, standing so close her arm brushed mine, and I could smell her fear.

"I was wondering the same about you."

"If there's any chance to save Aini, we've got to take it."

"Agreed." I looked over at Mandy on my other side. "You ready?"

"No, but I'm coming anyway."

An answer I could respect.

"Remember–" I stared straight ahead, feeling cool air waft from inside the darkness, like a musty disused railroad tunnel. "—hands on ears. Don't stop. No talking. Any questions?"

Mandy shifted in place, a nervous don't-want-to-be-doing-this shuffle. "Who takes point?"

"I will." Didn't want to, not with the heavy weight of fear burning through my gut, but I also didn't want Kelly to face what I wasn't willing to face myself. And Mandy? Her turn would come, I had no doubts.

Right before we started, I offered my last advice. "Remember, we'll be facing our fears. Doesn't mean they won't be real, but they will be harder to fight because we'll be fighting ourselves." I sucked in a deep breath. "Don't let them stop you."

Yeah, right.

The first step down a path you don't want to travel is always the hardest. Before I took it, I glanced again at Kelly. "Can you hear her?"

She knew who I was talking about. Aini.

Kels closed her eyes for a second, bracing herself, which made me realize what a heavy burden she'd been carrying since we entered this Realm. To listen to Aini's voice, her entreaties, her whimpers of pain, without being able to do a thing about them until we got close enough, would have broken most people. But not soft-hearted, strong-willed Kels.

Maybe she was the right one for my brother. Someone as loyal and determined as he was and who cared as deeply.

When she shook her head, a single tear escaping beneath her closed eyelids, I knew it was time to get going.

Tears? That's what Malik said we had to follow. So how did one see tears inside a cave?

I guess we were about to find out.

"Stay close," I whispered to Kelly, worried that if I spoke louder, I might stir something or someone awake. It was that kind of place.

I waited until she nodded before I strode forward, part of the fake-it-until-you-make-it approach. Let's hope it helped. With a deep breath as I passed beneath the overhanging lip of the opening, I clapped both hands over my ears and entered a world of silence and darkness.

There was no need to follow tears, yet, as there were no tunnel spurs. A greenish-yellow phosphorescent glow held the thick darkness at bay, barely, as we inched forward, together but isolated. Maybe that was the real test of this part of the path? Divide and conquer.

The quiet got to me first. I never realized how much I navigated by sound until I moved in a muted world. Not totally quiet, though, as a low hum started growing around me, like listening to ocean waves that became louder and louder.

Then the other noise threaded in, a shrieking wind building to a crescendo. Every horror movie mimicked that sound and by the chilling of my skin, I knew why.

I pressed my hands harder against my head but they did little to stem the pressure, an invisible heartbeat thrumming, thrumming, thrumming—my heartbeat, kick-started into overdrive with each step. Part of me wanted to shout against it. I went as far as to open my mouth then remembered Malik's words—no speaking.

What was that other sound? The scalding wind noise? Desperation. Fear. Remorse. All and more. Souls in unrelenting, never-ending torment.

If Malik hadn't warned us to keep our ears covered, it'd be easy to go crazy in minutes. On the other hand, even now there was no telling how long we could last with that madness swirling around us. If we were lucky, the cave would be a quick through and through.

Yeah, right, as if anything about this mission had been easy.

Fine. Focus forward. Keep the pace steady. Think of something, anything else.

Like what? Losing Bran? The fight up ahead? The fear coiling deep within me until I could feel its icy chill even as the temperature in the cave became hotter and muggier.

At first the path was wide enough we could stop walking in the shadow of one another and pull together, shoulder-by-shoulder, ignoring the putrid way the light made our skin look. Then the walls began pressing closer together. Soon we were single file, burrowing deeper and deeper as the route angled in a downward slant.

Great. Talk about entering the bowels of desolation. Not only did the tunnel creep downward, but as the air warmed humidity dripped down my forehead and stung my eyes.

What I wouldn't give to wipe one hand across my face. Just one quick swipe. Not possible if I wanted to keep my ears covered.

Water torture. Drip by agonizing drip.

A quick glance behind me showed Kelly and Mandy struggling against the same issues.

I remembered something my dad had said when I was still a little girl. Something about it wasn't the big problems that wore us down, it was the unrelenting small ones—the day-to-day easy steps paving the path to damnation. He meant the white lies, the small unkindnesses we inflicted on one another, the petty thoughts leading to even pettier deeds.

If I didn't know better, I could have sworn he'd learned that wisdom by being in a place like this.

Step after hesitant step, we skidded down a pebbly slope, the whispering wails increasing, the suffocating heat increasing, the annoying sweat rolling out of our pores. By the time the walls squeezed in so close I bruised my arms and elbows every third step, I was sure this place couldn't get worse.

I was wrong.

CHAPTER 41

The path took a hard right into a blind corner. I cut a hard glance over my shoulder to make sure Kelly followed when I stepped into a wall of gelatinous fiber.

First reaction was to rear back, but I couldn't. Whatever snared me stuck like bubblegum on a hot sidewalk glued to a shoe.

What the—

Panic set in, kicking my heartbeat into hyper-drive. I bit on my lower lip to keep from screaming.

Hands on ears. Keep my hands locked. Don't talk.

It was a spider web, a huge, floor to ceiling and side-to-side woven net of death, and I was the foolish fly caught tight.

I could turn my head just enough to see Kelly behind me. Not stuck, thank heavens, but helpless. She thrust one foot forward, trying to help break through the individual strands, but wasn't doing anything more than wrapping goo around her shoe.

As hard as it was to stop spinning and fighting, that made the most sense, except we couldn't stop. Wasn't that Malik's third warning?

Crap. My being trapped meant both Kels and Mandy had halted.

What now?

It wasn't like I knew a handy-dandy-cut-through-a-web spell either. And no spell-casting. Well, according to Malik, but he wasn't some arachnid's lunch.

Then I heard a sound, a new one.

Kelly, whose eyes grew as wide as a Texas-sized dinner plate, was looking at something on the other side of me. The mewling noise she made crossed a squeak with a scream, high-pitched between lips pressed in a tight line.

Great Spirits, we had to move.

Staying here meant I was a sitting duck to whatever used this web to secure a dinner. And I had a feeling it wasn't far—

That's when a long, bony something touched my shoulder.

Don't scream. Don't scream. Holy Mother Mary, don't scream.

Screw Malik's words about not using magic.

An invisibility spell wouldn't help. Maybe a freeze spell? Or a blow something to high smithereens casting would be better.

Since I couldn't speak, I'd have to internally shout the chant and hope to holey moley it worked.

"Eye of newt and tongue of lizard.
Powers that be and future that will.
Blast forward, fast and furious.
Escape the here and now.
So mote it be!"

Two things happened at once. The poke at my shoulder became a jabbing spike of pain and a flash of light threw me against the far wall, where I crumpled into a puddle of pain.

Keep moving. Keep moving.

As if Malik lived in my head, I scrambled to my feet as fast as I could, ignoring my shoulder as I lowered my head and scrambled forward, through the strands of remaining web filaments like a tight end heading for a do-or-die touchdown.

Whatever I'd done, I'd broken the bottleneck and prayed to the Great Spirits the spider was stunned or, better yet, killed.

I knew the spider was only doing its spidery thing but when push came to shove, and one of us had to go, I wasn't grieving that it was dead and not me.

Hands still cemented against my ears, I trusted my teammates would follow close behind.

I really, really wanted to squeeze my eyes shut as I edged past the bloated carcass of a black and orange spider that all but choked the path. Brushing against hairy legs that snatched at my clothes and breathing through my mouth because of the stench, I swore if I ever saw Malik again, I'd wring his neck.

Did he mention huge spiders? No. Did he know about them? Probably. He was just a mean, sadistic bastard and no doubt he had a closed-caption TV screen capturing all the fun.

Once past the spider to end all spiders, I started sprinting. Not a long-limbed easy gait but a hellbent for leather I-want-out-of-here-now burst of speed. The Marshes of Despair had to be better than this.

By the time I burst out from darkness to light, I wanted to weep, only part of that being from relief. The other part was pure pain. Whatever that spider had injected into me had me bent double, knees scraping the ground, hands still pressed against my head.

Mandy pulled my hands away as Kelly knelt before me.

"Let me look," she said, staring at my shoulder, her familiar, caring voice the sweetest sound in the world.

"It'll hurt." Nothing like spider venom to reduce me to a whining toddler.

"Of course it's going to hurt," she said, reaching toward my shoulder. "Remember you're a Noziak."

That was just mean—sneaky, conniving, backdoor mean. Using a person's strength against them just wasn't playing fair and besides—"Ow!"

"Hold her still." Kelly directed Mandy, ignoring me totally.

"Forget this." I went to rise, but Mandy must have been a Sumo wrestler in a past life—I wasn't going anywhere.

"Quit being such a baby," Kelly cooed, as if she was used to appeasing whiny kids. Come to think of it, as a kindergarten teacher she was, but I wasn't.

The more she poked and prodded, the more the pain intensified.

"I'm going to be sick," I warned, but she didn't listen. Instead she spoke to Mandy. "You have that credit card you carry?"

"What credit card?" I tried to turn my head but Kelly grabbed my chin. Who needed a credit card when I was dying?

"You stay still."

"So you can charge something and get me the hell out of here?"

"Don't be silly. The only way to get rid of the poison is to give it a way to escape."

With a credit card?

"Says who?" And no one was poking at me with a dull-edged piece of plastic. No freakin' way.

Yes, I was being a baby but damnit, my shoulder felt like a hot golf club was being rammed through it.

"Now this might hurt a little," Kelly murmured.

I gave her a you-think look just as Mandy sliced open my shoulder with what had to be a machete.

Then I fainted.

CHAPTER 42

"Alex? Alex, wake up." Kelly spoke somewhere nearby, her voice thin and urgent.

"Noziak, get your ass in gear. We're losing time."

Mandy. Which meant I really was in Hell.

Moaning, I opened my eyes to see Kelly's face hovering in front of me.

"What? Where?" Cripes my head hurt, my shoulder hurt, even speaking hurt.

"Remember?" Mandy's mug pushed aside Kelly's. "Spider. Poison. You swooning like a drama queen." She glanced over her shoulder before throwing out her last words. "Don't have all day so if you're through lying around, let's go."

Right, sweet cheeks. Next time she got to be spider bait, and then we'd see who was the bigger baby.

"What kind of credit card do you have?" I demanded, glaring at Mandy.

She flipped out what looked like an innocent chunk of plastic then did a few slick moves and presto, a razor-edged, slice-and-dice, six-inch blade appeared.

"Credit card my hiney." I so was not a happy camper.

"I knew we couldn't transport a weapon here so thought I'd give this a try," Mandy said with a score-one-for-Reyes look.

The logical part of my brain said kudos. Between the three of us, we now had one weapon. Not a big one, or one that would last long, but in a pinch might help.

Thankfully, Kelly helped me stagger to my feet before I had to admit Mandy was brilliant. Kelly stayed close until she was sure I wouldn't topple over. "I was able to get a lot of the poison out, and your shoulder's wrapped with a part of your T-shirt."

What? I liked this shirt that, glancing down at it, now was a good three inches shorter.

"Sorry," Kelly mumbled as if translating my expression. Didn't think it'd be too hard. "I'm sure it'll hurt for a while but. . ."

"Yeah, yeah." Time to move on. Save the girl. Kill the bad demon or demi-god or whatever The Horned One was. Get the hell out of Hell.

And Kelly *had* done the right thing. Saving my shoulder and halting the spread of poison trumped a favorite, now ratty T-shirt every day. I tried to give her a hey-I-get-it smile, but think it was more of a grimace.

Mandy had already started walking. Guess she was point person through the Marsh of Despair.

Best of luck with that, Chiquita.

Actually it didn't seem too bad at first, which should have clued me in right there. Initially there was a sandy path, not real clear but clear enough, like a deer trail to water, but it was a path. That helped because I still wasn't seeing any tears, if that was even possible in a swamp.

Then the sand gave way to clumps of moldy grass with puddles of water lapping on either side, murky, dark pools spreading wider and wider. Pools that stunk of rotting vegetation. Phewwwww!

A damp mist wove in and out around us, looking like every outdoor scene in every horror movie I'd ever watched. My brothers made damn sure I knew all the horrible, creepy, crawly things that could jump out at me from exactly this kind of thick mist.

If I didn't loathe scary swamps before, I did now, with each sucking step I took.

"You see the trail?" Kelly asked from behind me as we blindly trudged after Mandy.

I would have shrugged except that'd move my shoulder too much. Instead I sluice-scooted up behind Mandy to tap her on the shoulder. "You sure this is the right way?"

I didn't think she heard me at first because she didn't flinch, snarl or whip around. Then she spoke. "Of course, I'm sure."

No reason why. No reassurances. No power-packed speech to rally the flagging troops.

So who died and made her Queen?

"Malik said to follow the tears." Which looked darn near impossible with all this muddy water around us, but if Mandy thought I wasn't calling her bluff as much as blaming the guy who wasn't here, she might get off her high horse and communicate.

I should have held my breath.

The little grassy islands became smaller and smaller, more like mini-discs, as we started hopping and then leaping from one to another.

"Alex?" Kelly's quavering voice whispered in my ear. "Did you see that?"

Crap, what now? I glanced in the direction she pointed and my heart stuttered.

Coming from the high desert world of Southern Idaho, I was used to facing rattlers and coyotes and the odd cougar every now and then. I didn't do crocodiles, or alligators or whatever that prehistoric beast with row upon row of ginormous jagged teeth was to our right. I especially didn't do ones a good twenty feet long. What did it eat to get that big?

Better question was how were we going to avoid being on the menu?

Shuddering to a stop, I shouted at Mandy, who was already disappearing into the murky mist about twenty feet in front of us.

"Reyes!"

She didn't slow down.

"Reyes, stop right this second or deal with me!"

That had her pausing and glancing over her shoulder. "What?"

"We're a team, remember." I jerked my thumb at Kelly and myself. "And this part of the team aren't reassured that we're heading in the right direction." Then I jabbed my index finger toward the mammoth crocodile that had been joined by its twin cousin who was at least as long, if not longer, judging by the ripple it caused inches below the water's surface.

Mandy shook her head as she nodded toward Kelly poised one grass clump behind me. "The crocs won't get you unless they're hungry. What you have to worry about is that."

Kelly and I swiveled at the same time to watch a long, thin ribbon of yellow and brown slither through the water, aiming at Kelly's small circle of solidness.

"Oh, fuck," Kelly screamed, launching herself forward to where I stood in a one-shot leap so fast we both about toppled.

"Didn't know you knew that word," I said, swallowing back a laugh and a scream as I grabbed on to her. Just what we didn't need, an impromptu bath in croc-infested waters.

"Don'ttttt likkkkkeeee sssssnnnn—"

"I understand." I squeezed my hands along her upper arms. "I won't let them get to you."

"How—"

"Even snakes are afraid of Noziaks."

That earned a wobbly smile and put a little color in her cheeks. Then her shoulders slumped. "Some agent I am. First sign of. . ." She glanced over her shoulder where the water now looked glassy smooth. I hadn't the heart to tell her that was an illusion. I'd seen where the water moccasin disappeared to and, for a moment, we were safe, but that moment would soon be over. There'd be another snake, another spider, and more fear to batter back into submission before we faced our worst fear of all—failing Aini.

"First sign of you-know-what and I panic," she finished, her voice little more than a hoarse whisper.

I rolled my eyes at her. "Just proves that you're human."

"Mostly human," she mumbled.

Great, I just stepped into a different quagmire. Kels had only recently discovered she'd been adopted, or fostered, and when the parents who raised her realized she knew the truth of not being their biological daughter, —" they'd washed their hands of her. One of these days, when I didn't want to throttle them both, I'd give them a piece of my mind. Not in the near future 'cuz I was still at the throttling stage.

"Look, Kels. So you've got some extra abilities. Doesn't mean you're not human." Then, before she could protest, I rushed on. "Being able to turn invisible is a gift—an extra edge. Being human means you get tired and frustrated and, yes, scared. Deal with it."

"This a pep talk?" she asked with only one small crook of her brow.

"My version of one."

She managed a real smile this time. "So if I get really scared I'm mostly human?"

"Yup." I nodded, glancing to where Mandy waited with crossed arms. "Being human is to admit that at times you'll be scared. Being an IR Agent means you keep going, scared or not."

"You two done with your bonding time?" Mandy asked, already turning to march away.

"You think she's human?" Kelly spoke so only I could hear.

"No. Gotta have some demonic blood to be that pissy all the time."

Kelly fell into step behind me, a true grin on her face as she yelled at our smug leader. "Mandy Reyes, you start talking right this second. How do you know we're going in the right direction?"

I admit it, I had to duck my head and swallow a smile. Kelly chewing out Mandy was like watching a Chihuahua go after a Rottweiler. My money was on the smaller, feistier dog that, once roused, would not back down. A quick glance at Mandy who'd looked at us, rolling her eyes, told me she knew when to fight and when to fold.

"Alejándro's telling me which way to go."

Kelly frowned then asked, ". . .Alejándro, being. . .?"

"My brother. I told you that."

Maybe a million years ago. Besides, wasn't Alejándro dead? And how did he know where to go here? Wouldn't that be like expecting someone who lived in Idaho to give directions to someone maneuvering through Iowa? Sure there were some similarities between the two places, but not enough to assume the same person—alive or dead—would be an expert navigating both areas.

After schooling my voice to a neutrality I wasn't feeling, I decided to ask, "You sure Alejándro knows the way, given this is where *you know who* lives?"

There really wasn't an easy way to ask that question without implying her brother ended up in this area of the Underworld, so I was glad when Kelly nudged me to give me a quiet, "Good call."

I expected Mandy to snap back but she didn't. Her shoulders hardened and her voice lowered as she said, "He's my brother. I trust him with my life."

Bully for you.

I admit it, that wasn't my finest thought. If it was my brother, any of them, I'd think the same way, but from what Mandy said, her brother was just a kid when he died. How many kids would I want guiding me through this swampy mess? Zip zero, that's how many.

Kelly spoke up before I had a chance. "As long as you trust him, we'll trust him." She offered an atta-girl smile and a thumbs up. Then added, "But since Alex and I are not as familiar with the wildlife of swamps, I'd feel a whole lot better if you stuck closer so we don't make a mistake knowing what's bad versus what's deadly. If you know what I mean?"

Yeah, the kind of mistake involving snakes, crocs or anything kin to a reptile.

When Mandy nodded, we started moving again.

I didn't say a word. Just bit my tongue and fell into an uneasy single-file formation close behind Mandy.

I don't know if it was hours, or days later that we finally wended our way out of that mess. Never again would I go swamp bivouacking. This was enough to last several lifetimes.

And then I remembered what was next—the Land of Lost Children.

CHAPTER 43

I grew up in the learned faith of my father, with its rules and regulations. He accepted it as having its own validity as did the faith of his Shoshone forefathers—the shaman side of him. But I never had, and never would, accept a belief system that could doom children in an afterlife of pain and misery.

Made no sense to me. A loving deity did not forsake the most vulnerable of its people, especially little kids.

Malik said the Land of Lost Children was something else though, as if I was going to believe anything he said. This time I hoped he was right. Here were souls the Horned One had captured, just as he'd captured Aini. Seized to feed off their torment, their misery, their helplessness. The rat bastard.

There was something else Malik had said—oh, yeah, there wasn't a darn thing we could do to save them. Not unless we reached the Horned One and took him out.

So the kids were not here because they deserved to be here but because even after death there were victims.

That just sucked, down in the bone, sap the life right out of me kind of sucky. But it was going to be worse for Kelly.

"I'll take lead or sweep," I announced, glaring at Mandy so she'd understand what I wasn't saying—keep Kelly in the middle where one or the other of us could stop her from doing something stupid.

Then I realized something that had been nagging at me since she brought up the subject of her brother and blurted out, "Why does your brother know this place so well?"

Kelly cut a quick look at me, one that took away all points for my earlier handling of this sensitive subject, but if both of my teammates were at risk through this next part of the trail, I wanted to know.

What I really wanted clarified was not what Mandy wanted. Not by the bullish tightness of her jaw, one I recognized from looking at my own reflection in a mirror a time or two.

"That's none of your business," she said, her shoulders rock-hard and pulled back, her feet solidly planted in what looked like sand, an I-dare-you glint in her eye.

Crusin' for a bruisin', Chiquita.

Another place or time, I'd have called her on it. Not now. Ticking clock and more important issues at stake.

I raised my hands, palms forward, and kept my voice as neutral as Switzerland. "You're right. But I don't want to make things hard for you or Kelly. That's all."

When she just stood there, not saying anything, I glanced at Kelly.

"I'll be okay through here," she murmured.

Like I believed that.

Mandy, for all her faults, must have heard what I did when Kels spoke—that sound people can get when it's taking every ounce of determination to face something they don't want to face. Problem with reaching that stage is it also means you're on the razor's edge of snapping.

"Noziak," Mandy said, stepping around Kelly and me, "you take point and get us out of here pronto. Got it?"

Oh, yeah, I got it. In fact, if we jogged, it might help keep Kelly, and all of us, distracted from what we were about to encounter.

So I started double timing it, which made the fire in my shoulder flame higher, but I could deal with that. I couldn't deal with the sounds of weeping children.

My footsteps slowed, then faltered. I, too, was human, which meant I was hardwired to hear heartbreak, and sadness, and longing when uttered by newborns, infants and toddlers. By the Great Goddess, send me back to face the spider or the crocs, but not this.

The sand path contained a thin line of what looked like an oil spill, but it wasn't. It was the tears Malik mentioned, so many tears they etched the ground with their salty pain.

I swallowed, but nothing would clear the fist clogging my throat—the inability to do anything for all the small faces surrounding us.

It wasn't the sounds alone, though they wrung my heart and blinded me with my own acid tears, it was the little ones. So many of them, some so faint they were more impression than substance, with hands extended and eyes too large for their faces, some curled in on themselves and others slumped into tiny heaps of misery.

"Help me."

"Please."

"Mommy. I want Mommy."

If I held any doubts about stopping the Horned One, once and for all, ten minutes, no make that ten seconds, in this place was all I needed to convince me.

I glanced back at Kelly, at the paleness of her face, the tightness of her jaw. She wasn't going to make it. "Give me your hand," I ordered.

She didn't even glance at me as she extended one hand to a little girl curled in a fetal position on the side of the path. Kels was on auto-pilot. If we stepped off the route, we were all goners.

I grabbed her before she could touch the child and jerked her forward.

"But—"

"No buts about it Agent McAllister. Aini is depending on us."

She shuddered—a nightmare-walker pulling herself back from the edge of a cliff.

"Repeat after me." I had to get through to her. "You're Aini's only hope."

"Aini. . ."

"That's right. Say it, Kelly. Say it like you mean it." I tugged her forward, small steps but we were moving again. "Aini. Think of Aini."

"Aini." She wasn't all the way present, but I'd take my wins any way I could get them.

"Aini. Aini. Aini." I kept muttering the words like a mantra, helping to drown out the children's pleas. Hardening my heart.

Vowing that even if we didn't survive what was ahead, the Horned One was going to pay for what he'd done here.

Death was too good for him. I wanted him to suffer. Really, really, really suffer.

CHAPTER 44

By the time we staggered the last yards along that path, we looked rode hard and put away wet—an Idaho expression that seemed very appropriate. Ripped from the inside out was a better description.

A quick glance at Kelly told me she tottered on her last legs. Unfortunately, we had two more sections to make it through before we even reached our adversary.

I glanced at the castle looming closer but still out of reach, now shining as if a million mirrors were built into its walls, tiles of lapis blue coated several shingled roof tops, and mullioned windows stared blankly at us.

How could a place so beautiful contain such evil?

But why not? Who made the rule that beauty meant goodness? Hadn't Bran's cousin been one of the most eye-catching women I'd ever seen? Before I killed her. Yup, evil through and through. Not that Bran ever saw it, even after she shot him.

Talk about a good reality check. Think about the man I gave up and the woman who tried several times to murder me in the same sentence. Ice water couldn't have helped more.

"How much time left?" I asked Kelly, sounding asthmatic. We hadn't run that hard or that far, but there was more than physical exhaustion at work here. There was emotional burnout.

Emotion was not something a Noziak did well, or often, so I was damn near bankrupt. Give me a Fedor demon to fight, or a druid to zap into oblivion over this gut-wrenching emotional crap any day.

Kels glanced at her watch, which is what I'd intended. Take her mind off of those hundreds or thousands of desperate children. The ones we couldn't help as long as The Horned One existed.

That was the part to remember. Eradicate him, save them.

Worked for me.

"About forty minutes," Kels murmured, her gaze bleak as her eyes met mine. "We're not going to make it."

"Sure we are." We were in a worse predicament than I expected if I was the one taking the Pollyanna role. I looked at where the trail wended through a copse of aspen trees. Pretty benign-looking.

"The ghosts of love lost are through there." I nodded with my chin and didn't mention the last section we still had to travel. The one where murder victims were trapped. "Piece of cake."

"Yeah, right." Kelly gave me an eye roll as we started forward again: Mandy leading, Kelly in the middle, me bringing up the rear.

How bad could this be after what we'd already been through?

Me and my stupid illusions. I knew I'd given up Bran. I'd made that choice, but here? The path meandered, between newly leafed trees, beside rustic wood benches, all bucolic and pleasant except for the people who wandered on every side. Many young, teens and early twenties, but not all. Some in their late seventies and eighties, walking, not really seeing, though they all were looking as hard as possible. Dressed in clothing from every generation, all cultures—there a leather and sandal-garbed Roman gladiator, a woman who might have been from an African tribe before Europeans arrived, a Victorian-era sea captain—all aimless and lost.

The one commonality was they all looked as if around the next bend, over the nearest horizon, they'd find what they sought.

But they wouldn't. That was the pain of hope never realized, always just out of reach. I wanted to speak to them, to offer them some comfort, but there wasn't any to offer. Who knew love lost could hurt so much?

I did.

Every second among these mourners, because that's what they were, made my steps heavier, my heart crack and shudder over and over again. Biting my lip so I didn't cry out Bran's name, I wiped my eyes until I rubbed them raw, glad I trudged at the rear where my teammates couldn't see me.

Anger. I could do anger easier than grief.

Anger at Bran. He'd done nothing. Just existed and owned my heart.

Anger at that damn Guardian of the Gate who'd extracted such a high toll.

Anger at myself for agreeing to give—no—throw away something so rare, so valuable.

"You doing all right?" Kelly asked, suddenly beside me.

Instead of squaring my shoulders, choking down the emotions strangling me, I paused and shook my head.

"No." I allowed the single word to escape as I drowned in wave after wave of misery.

She looked around, seeking help and finding none, as if there was any help in this place. When she glanced back she murmured, "Bran?"

I gave a hard, jerky nod, feeling as ripped open and vulnerable as I'd ever been.

She stepped closer, hiding my pain from Mandy. "You've got to believe if he cares for you as much as you care for him, that it'll all work out between you."

She had no idea what she was talking about. Platitudes and lies. *If it's meant to be, it will be. To love and lose is better than never having loved. Love makes the world go round.*

All a pack of soul-searing lies.

I waved my hand to indicate all the lovers stumbling around us. "Isn't that what they believed?"

Anger. At last. Not at Kels, though she was taking the brunt of my wrath. "Every single person here believed in love. Trusted it. Was betrayed by it. So tell me again that *things* will work out."

She stood there, her eyes wide, one hand reaching for me until I stepped out of her reach. She pulled back as if struck.

But I wasn't done yet. Not with so much regret and bitterness burning through me. "If you gave up Van, how would you feel?"

Yup, some teammate I was, lashing out at the only real friend I had, the one who'd lanced my shoulder to save my life, the one who always stuck with me, no matter how petty and small-minded I behaved. But like love, friendship could be destroyed.

Her face paled as she sucked in a deep breath. Held it as if struggling with what she really wanted to verbalize versus what good-girl Kelly had been taught not to say. I braced myself, expecting a blow given for the blow taken.

"Coming here meant I gave Van up." Her words sounded lacerated, dredged up from deep inside, where we bury our deepest hurts. The rawness that we shy away from. "I know exactly how these people feel." She didn't even look at them, only at me. "Exactly how *you* feel."

Way to go, Noziak.

How big an idiot could I be?

I shook my head, a slow, labored let-me-take-it-back gesture. I knew Van. Knew he'd have tried to stop Kels from taking this mission. Would feel betrayed by her choice. And here I was pouring acid in her wounds as if that would ease mine.

She started to turn away, but this time I reached for her, snagging her arm and forcing her to stop. Her gaze wouldn't meet mine though. Not that I blamed her. What I deserved was for her to come around swinging, so her not doing that was my win.

"I'm an ass," I said, as clumsy at apologies as I was at loving. "A selfish, know-nothing, horse's patootie."

When she said nothing, did nothing, I sucked in a deep gulp of air. "Van is an ass, too, but he'll come around. He cares for you more than anyone I've seen since high school. He just doesn't know how to show his feelings except by protecting you. Which he can't."

She didn't move. Guess I hadn't groveled enough. "Being idiots in the emotion department is a Noziak fault."

"Among many," she snapped, but at least she was talking again.

I wasn't finished. "In case you hadn't noticed, we Noziaks have some abandonment issues."

"Some?" Her brow rose.

Okay, she'd earned that one. And I deserved it.

"Yeah." My glance slid away this time. A strained silence hung between us until I cleared my throat and added, "Okay, more than some. But we do have some good qualities."

Obviously being able to ask for forgiveness was not among them.

Kelly must have known, and accepted that, because she leaned forward and wrapped her arms around me.

"I know," she murmured, even if all I could give her was an awkward back pat. Hugs were another Noziak failing.

Damn. It was a bloody miracle anyone had anything to do with us. With me.

"You two done with your warm and fuzzy moment?" Mandy's voice hailed us from farther down the trail.

I was half-tempted to tell her no, but there wasn't time. I might not have Kelly's link with Aini, but even I could sense how close and yet how far away we were.

"Okay now?" Kelly asked before she stepped back. Damn, how I wish I could do that so easily. Just once. Offer forgiveness so readily.

"Yeah." Not really, but enough self-immolation. Time to buck up, move forward and get back to the mission.

Noziaks might suck at the emotional stuff but we could do the hard stuff.

Which was exactly what waited for us ahead.

CHAPTER 45

There was no more speaking. No more group therapy, if two made a group. No more acknowledgements that we might not make it to Aini in time, even though that awareness took on a life of its own.

Too late. Too late. Almost, but still too late.

The mantra dogged every step I took, every jar of my aching shoulder, every swallow of my too-dry throat.

Yet we kept going. Until Mandy came to a jagged stop.

"What is it?" Kelly asked, sliding up beside her.

I stood behind them, waiting.

"I don't know if I can do this," Mandy said into the strained silence.

Kelly glanced at me, looking for clarity.

Unfortunately, I knew exactly what Mandy was talking about. We'd reached the last hurdle before the Horned One's lair—the stretch where Murder Victims resided. Where her family might be.

No might about it.

To love and have lost at least meant you once loved—a balance of sorts. There was no balance for murder victims—those whose lives were cut short because of others. No justice, even if the killer was found and punished. Lives brutally, senselessly ended. Anger, fear, hatred—all the negative emotions rolled into an act so horrific that every culture, since man first walked upright, created rules and laws to punish murder. Even as those same cultures, those same people, knew the killing would continue.

The dark side of humanity—our shadow selves. No wonder the Horned One wanted these individuals to linger closest to him. What better way to roil and wallow in their misery?

Murder victims were the ultimate victims. Death forced upon them. No retribution, no recourse for a second chance, no options. Forever.

"I don't know if anyone can do what we're asking you to do," I said at last, aware that it wasn't pity I felt for Mandy, it was awe.

She turned to look at me, and I met her suspicion head on.

"I'm serious." I stepped closer and looked at the scene spread before us. Gone were the trees, the cave, the desert, instead there was a series of city streets, but not the same city. A suburban cul-de-sac in one direction, an urban high rise in another, a bamboo hut village straight ahead. The closer man lived to another, the easier to allow envy and greed and resentment to foster and grow—the roots of evil that spawned murder.

Enough. I wasn't here to intellectualize what we faced, but to get the three of us through it.

I turned to Mandy. "What happened to your family?"

Kelly kicked my foot, but the words were already out. I gave her a trust-me look, then glanced back to Mandy. "I'm not being grossly insensitive." Even if I was. "I really want to know."

"Why?"

Legitimate question. If she'd asked me to bare my deepest torment, I'd have the same response. Ducking my head so she could feel what she needed to feel without my staring at her, I grappled with the words I wanted, no needed, to speak. "I have no idea what you went through, what it means to have your parents and brother taken the way they were—"

"Damn right."

I raised one shaky finger. That's all I could offer. "I do know what it's like to wake up one day and have no mother." Crud, it wasn't going to help if I couldn't speak because tears clogged my throat. "I do know what it means to be a child and wonder, day after day, what I'd done wrong. If I could have said or done something different? If my actions, my thoughts. . . if *my* very existence made my mother leave."

I'd never shared any of this with anyone before. Not my dad, not my brothers, hell, not with myself. Some things hurt too much to ever face twice. But something told me that Mandy needed to hear that she wasn't alone. That she wasn't crazy. That whatever happened to those she loved was not *her* fault.

She turned away. Kelly moved to step closer, but I held her back. Some wounds could not be healed with a hug. Especially those suffered as a child, when you're too young to understand, to fight back, to do anything. You take the blow and bury it deep.

"I snuck out of my house that night." Mandy's voice startled me—the depth of her pain, laced with regret and what-if doubts. Man, did I know those feelings intimately. "I'd begged my mom to let me see the new Spiderman movie. Promised her the sun and the moon. Anything to let me see it."

She went silent until Kelly asked, "What happened?"

Mandy looked over her shoulder, not really seeing either Kelly or me, and shrugged. "I snuck out without her permission."

Of course she would. I'd probably have done the same thing.

Mandy sucked in a jagged breath before turning away. "If I hadn't, I'd have been there. Died with them."

Survivor's guilt. I recognized it as a close cousin to my abandonment issues. The endless, pointless, useless questions starting with why me? Why not me? Knowing the wrong person survived. That I was an imposter. That nothing seemed right and there wasn't anything I could do about it.

Only one way to deal with what Mandy faced, especially given the time constraints we faced.

I stepped up beside her so she couldn't ignore me and used my best bad-assed tone, which I'd developed early and used a lot. "Sucks to be you."

Kelly inhaled a breath loud enough I could hear it. I ignored her, ignored too the way Mandy braced herself.

I pushed forward. "They died, you lived. You think your mom would have wanted you dead, too?"

"Alex—" Kelly whispered.

"Quiet. Mandy needs to hear this."

Mandy whipped around to face me, her fists hard balls of misery, her body vibrating with coiled tension. "Who the hell asked your opinion?"

"You did, the second you risked jeopardizing this mission." There was tough love and then there was what I was doing— cauterizing a wound so deep I might kill Mandy in the process. "I'm not judging you, really I'm not, no matter what it sounds like."

Please let her hear the truth in my words. Please. Aini needed us, all of us, and we couldn't fail her now.

"You're full of shit, Noziak."

"Yeah, I am, but not about this." She hadn't hit me yet. Which was a good sign.

"You've heard of survivor's guilt?"

"More times than I ever wanted," she bit off.

"Understood." I released a deep breath. "But did anyone ever tell you it never goes away?"

She cut a hot glance my way but remained quiet.

"Yeah, didn't think so." I rubbed one hand across the tension in my neck and kept talking. Just like Kelly and Mandy had done for my shoulder, lancing a wound, any kind of wound, wasn't a painless process, but had to be done in order for the wound to heal. I hoped Mandy would accept that. "Survivor's guilt is a badge of courage not everyone is lucky enough to earn."

Sarcasm intentionally coated my every syllable.

"No one asks to earn this badge. No one in their right mind." I stared straight ahead at the cityscapes before us, and what lay on the other side of it. "But once we get inducted into the select club of survivors, there's no going back, no do-overs and no escape."

Then I fell silent. Yes, time was precious, but there were some processes that couldn't be rushed.

"What are you babbling about?" she bit out, just about the time I thought I'd failed.

"I mean you had no more control, no more choice in being part of the survivor's club than you did in being born with brown eyes and black hair. No more choice than Kels had in being born with the curse, or the gift, of invisibility. We've all

been given certain life cards to deal with, that's reality."

"So life sucks and then we die?" she said.

"No." I glanced at Kelly, including her before I continued. "Life sucks and then we deal with it. That's where we get our choices." Isn't this what I'd learned at that tree, the one the Red Guy brought me to? There I chose life. Learned what life really meant. I wanted the same choice for Mandy. "Bad things happened to you, and me, and to Kelly. That's our pasts. It's what we do next that matters. It's the next choice, and the one after it, that matters. That's the only thing we can control."

Mandy just looked confused. I didn't blame her. This was more of that messy, feel-good stuff that I avoided like the plague.

I cleared my throat to muddle through. "If you want to stop, avoid what we have to deal with next, that's your choice."

And to think it wasn't that long ago that I'd hated that single word—choice.

"You can also choose to keep moving, to make a difference to Aini. That's what life comes down to every day, every hour, sometimes it's down to the minute of making hard choices. Hold a grudge or release it? Tackle a project or let it slide? Take the risk to love someone or remain safe and silent?"

Kelly nodded her head, but said nothing.

I walked around until I stood in front of Mandy. "It's your choice. If you choose to stay, we'll go on without you." I raised my hand to Kelly, who'd started to speak. "We won't like it, but that's our choice—how we react to your decision." Another deep breath. "But if you decide to continue, we'll be right there with you, helping you any way we can."

A profound silence settled on us. No bird song. Nothing except our breathing, our palpable waiting.

Mandy broke eye contact, turning to Kelly. "You'll be there?"

She nodded with a sniff.

Then I got the I-dare-you-look. "You?"

"Yeah." I watched Mandy take a hard swallow and added, "Like it or not."

"Fuck you, Noziak," she muttered, then turned and strode forward.

Yup, awe. Pure awe. It's not often you get to see courage in action, but I was looking at its back marching ahead of me.

Way to go, Chiquita.

CHAPTER 46

I thought we'd escape the Vale of Murder Victims with no more drama. And we almost did. Almost.

Until Mandy stumbled and stopped. *"Mamaíta?"* she whispered, looking in front of us. *"Cómo?"*

I couldn't see anyone. That didn't mean they weren't there, not based on the expression on Mandy's face—longing, want, shame.

Kelly moved up to bracket Mandy on her other side as she gave me a what-now glance. I shrugged. Not much we could do unless Mandy decided to do something stupid. She was sandwiched between us like ham between rye, so if she did move in any direction, we'd be right on top of her.

She seemed to be listening, but I heard nothing. A little ways off there came a faint scratching whisper—the rustle of clothes rubbing together. Then she erupted in a spate of Cuban Spanish I couldn't keep up with—I'd barely understood the words *Momma* and *how*.

When she started shaking her head and made to step in my direction, I got worried.

Not going to happen. Malik had been clear—we leave the path, we were doomed and so was Aini.

I wrapped one hand around Mandy's arm, a preventive measure more than reassuring one. When Mandy tried to shake off my hold, I squeezed tighter. There'd be bruises tomorrow, if there was a tomorrow. I also used the one Cuban phrase I'd learned hanging around her. *"Creo que no.* I don't think so."

The look I got told me she understood completely. Understood and planned to act anyway.

With a quick one-two side-step, she aimed for Kelly, assuming she was the weaker barrier to getting what Mandy wanted.

She was wrong.

Kelly blocked, thrust back and then tackled Mandy with a move that would make an NFL linebacker proud. It took everything I had not to break into a high-five victory dance.

But we'd underestimated Mandy.

Butting Kelly in the face, leaving her cradling a bloody nose, Mandy scampered to her feet, making a beeline for the far side of the path.

Not going to happen.

I body checked her, rolling both of us on the ground until I came out on top. Both our legs sprawled off the trail, but technically we were still on the path. I only hoped the rules about leaving the route were a mite flexible.

"Listen to me," I shouted, my face so close to Mandy's, volume wasn't needed, but insistence was. "Listen!"

She was beyond listening. Like a wild animal with a single goal in mind, reaching whomever she saw beyond the track—talking wasn't going to reach her. Not unless I broke through to her.

With a move I'd learned from my brothers when they wanted me to stop crying, also known as gaining the attention of our father, I opened my palm and slapped her hard across her face, leaving a weal of red behind.

Crap, I was tired of beating on my own teammates.

"Alex," Kelly shouted behind me.

"What? It worked." Well, not all the way. But it was a start. Mandy now fully focused on me. Not in a good way, but I'd take what I could get.

"You think this is what your mother wants?" I knew what *I* wanted—to shake some sense into her—but held back. "You think your dying, which is exactly what's going to happen if you go to her, is going to fix your *not* being killed with your family?"

"You. Don't. Know."

"Course I don't." This time I did rattle her, cupping my hands on her shoulders, not to hold her down, but to hold her.

An action that no one, especially me, expected. "I can't even begin to understand what you're going through. But that doesn't matter."

She stopped thrashing as much, but it held a waiting quality, as if the second she could, she'd cut and run.

I nodded my head toward the side street beyond her, in the direction she'd been running. "That your mom over there?"

"*Si.*"

The fact she didn't speak in English wasn't lost on me. She was more in the past than the present, a child's reaction, a fact I had to change. Or lose her.

"Anyone else?"

"*Papito.*"

Her dad. "And your brother? Is he there?"

She shook her head in the negative.

"Anyone else?"

"No. They're all I have, all I want."

This? This I understood and could counter. "But what do *they* want?"

She shook her head again, a way to not listen, to avoid. Man, did I know that, too.

"You think either one of them want you dead?" My tone scoffed, which I meant. Now was not the time for a warm and fuzzy approach. "Is your dying going to change anything? Is it going to bring them back? Make them feel better? Make them happy?"

Kelly cleared her throat. Not speaking but getting her message across to me. Back off.

I'd only begun.

"Quit being so freakin' selfish," I snapped at Mandy, earning a sharp, "Alex!" from Kelly and a rearing back from Mandy as if I'd slapped her again. Which I had—verbally.

"I'm serious here." I leaned in closer, aware Kelly had reached for me, just in case I meant to hurt Mandy.

That wasn't my intention. For once. All I wanted to do was help her, and to do that, I needed her to listen.

"I know you lost your family." The words came dry and rusty, because they came from my heart, that deep, hidden part I'd locked down and had thrown away the key to years ago.

"Nothing will fix losing your mom, dad and brother, but you've created another family." I nodded my chin at Kelly. "We're your family."

I choked on the words, my eyes stinging because what I said struck me as forcibly as it struck Mandy.

"You've got a choice here, Chiquita." I didn't use the word in derision but with compassion. "I'm going to stand up. And you get to choose."

I shifted, enough so I wasn't pressing her hard into the ground anymore, but not all the way freeing her. My action held risks—lots of them. If Mandy made the wrong choice, wrong for the mission and for Aini, then I'd just helped her commit suicide.

It came down to that simple fact.

"We may not always be the best family for you—" I jabbed my thumb into my chest. "—especially me, but we *are* here for you. Choose us and we might, just might, save Aini. Choose the ghosts and you make an impossible mission that much harder." I swallowed deeply as I threw down my gauntlet. "It's your choice."

CHAPTER 47

Funny how so much came back to that one insidious word—choice. Isn't that what I faced at that Tree? The one that was in the beginning and no doubt would be at the end? I chose to help Benjamin and he chose to leave to be with his family, as he should have. And at the *torii* gate? I chose to give away what I had with Bran for the chance to help Aini. And now?

I chose to stand up, release Mandy and step back.

It hurt. I didn't want to have sacrificed in vain. To fail on my mission. Most of all, I didn't want to lose Mandy—PITP, head-butting,   not-who-I'd-ever-thought-I'd-call-a   friend Mandy. I could imagine the eye-roll and snort I'd receive if I admitted that out loud. Heck, I could hardly believe my own thoughts.

Nine-tenths of me wanted to reach out as she rose to her feet, eyeing me as I'd eye any dangerous, unpredictable threat. I wanted to rationalize, heck, I'd even beg. *Please. Please. Please.*

But this was her choice. I'd given her that, and I meant it.

Facing Kelly and me, Mandy stepped away from us, a hesitant shuffle backwards and toward her birth family, and my heart shuddered.

She was going to do it. Leave us.

Kelly made an abbreviated, gasping noise, which caused me to raise my arm, a useless barrier, but a barrier nonetheless. I didn't even know if Mandy had moved, but if she hadn't, she'd want to soon. It's what I wanted to do—run fast and far.

And Mandy's step off the path would seal all our fates.

"Your call," I repeated to Mandy, already prepping myself for disappointment—for tossing the dice and losing—aware of the sweat dampening my back, the chill sliding down my arms.

Dumb move, Noziak. Bad decision. This huggy-feely emotional crap was so not my thing, and because I'd given it a try we all stood to lose.

Those were not tears making me blink. Tears weren't in Noziak DNA. We fought, and fought hard. I'd go down fighting. I'd not go down hugging.

Squaring my shoulders with each mini-step Mandy took toward her choice, I was already running through and discarding scenarios of how Kelly and I could rescue Aini on our own. There weren't many options. We couldn't even reach her because we'd end our lives here. In a puff of smoke and ash. Or something slower? More painful?

Who was I kidding? The Horned One would want a slow death for us. He'd get his jollies that way.

Then Mandy paused.

You know that breathless second of hope you can have as a child, when you believe in a Santa, or a Tooth Fairy, or even a parent—the wholehearted, raw trust that what you needed and wanted most in the world was going to come true? That's what roared through me. Even as my breath clogged in my throat and my muscles tensed.

Come on, Mandy. Come on. Stay with us. Help Aini. Help us help Aini.

She looked over her shoulder with an expression that broke what remained of my shattered heart. A look I bet my father saw for those weeks and months when my five-year-old self would stand at our farm house window, looking out, thinking that if I could catch a glimpse, just a glimpse of my mom, that she'd come back. That all the betrayal, anger and sorrow would magically disappear. If only I watched hard enough, remained patient long enough, was somehow just *enough*. I'd be whole again.

It didn't work that way, a lesson I grasped only now. One that Mandy would learn in her own fashion, if we survived—and not an easy lesson.

"*¡Carajo*," Mandy muttered under her breath. I didn't know the literal translation but I could guess. She'd made her choice. Wasn't happy with it, or me, but she'd made it. Her voice rasped as she mumbled, "You want to go. Let's go."

I lowered my arm, and Kelly moved forward, wrapping her arm around Mandy's shoulder and making soothing sounds I would probably gag on if I tried.

Each to our own. We were still a team. We still stood a chance. A slim one but a chance.

As Kelly and Mandy walked ahead, Kelly with long strides while wiping blood from her nose, Mandy with stiff-legged, faltering steps, I pulled up the rear.

We'd won a skirmish, but the big battle still lay ahead.

CHAPTER 48

It was only minutes later, but it felt like forever when we finally stepped away from the cityscape and the Vale of Murder Victims. I noticed the change first in Mandy's posture, from world-weary to tense. Then Kelly looked up as if she'd heard a silent cry.

"Aini?" I kept my voice low as I stepped up to stand beside my teammates.

Kelly nodded but said nothing.

I don't know what I expected once we reached the abode of the Horned One—the castle, or huge manor house, or the McMansion—whatever it was called had disappeared, lost in a smoky gray mist. I could feel it, its presence, looming over us, but there was no front door, no gate, no way in.

Instead there were the gnarled roots of an ancient tree stretching toward us. A tree so broad it looked like a building—an old, weathered, time-worn barrier between us and any entry into the castle.

Figured. I started this journey having to face the Tree called Ygdrassil, and here I was again. Someone had a sense of irony. Right now it wasn't me.

"You guys see a tree?" I asked, almost wishing they didn't.

"Yup."

"It's huge," said Kelly, sounding bone-deep tired. "At least there's a door in it."

Where?

I hadn't noticed that, but she was right. Near the base, at a height we'd have to bend to enter, stood a weathered door. It blended so well with the bark I'd missed it.

Or didn't want to see it.

"You think that's our way?" Mandy asked, no longer belligerent and combative as she had been most of the trip. I hoped *all* the fight in her hadn't been snuffed out already.

I pointed to the trail of tears, now simply a faint squiggle amongst the root shadows. "Looks like the yellow-brick road leads right to that door."

Silence wrapped around us—an expectant, waiting stillness.

Guess it was up to me to break it so I stepped forward. "Anyone else feel like a Hobbit right now?"

Mandy marched up beside me. "I wish we had a few dwarves or woodland elves at our back. The sexy kind, not the too-smart-for-their-own-good ones."

We both turned to look at Kelly who'd remained locked in place. Tears now stained her face, mixing with the remnants of wiped blood from her nosebleed there.

I was at her side before I realized it. "What's up? What's happening?"

When she raised her gaze to mine, I knew it was bad.

"Aini?" I prodded in as gentle a voice as I could find.

She nodded, but said nothing.

My imagination jumped into hyper-drive and not of the good kind.

CHAPTER 49

There was bad news and then there was disastrous. A fender bender was bad. Having a semi slam into your compact rated disastrous. That's the impact of Kelly's expression—that crushing, twisting, deadly wallop you had no idea if you could recover from.

"What?" Mandy demanded.

Think, Noziak, think. "Details. We need details. What exactly is happening?"

Kelly shuddered.

"Kels, we need to know what's going on before we barrel through that door." My tone told her we were going in one way or another, but forearmed was the better option.

"She's giving up," Kelly whispered, each word threaded with aching sadness. "She's saying goodbye."

Crapola. If Aini gave up, the Horned One won. We were so close. We were so screwed, if we didn't reach Aini. Right now.

"Oh no, she doesn't." I pivoted away from Kelly, throwing words like hand grenades over my shoulder. "You tell her to hang on. We're almost there. Tell her until you're one-hundred and ten percent positive she's heard you."

I'd reached the door and wrenched it open so hard it shuddered, but stayed on its hinges. Clearly doors that had weathered millenniums were up to one pissed off Noziak.

Ducking through the low opening, I charged ahead, down a tight, winding tunnel, so narrow I angled my shoulders through sideways and so windy at times I didn't know if I headed forward or back.

The sound of my frantic breathing echoed around me. Mandy, at least, had followed, as her footsteps pounded behind me. I hoped Kelly had, too. Or would as soon as she connected with Aini. And if she didn't? Or couldn't?

Didn't matter.

Aini, we're coming! Don't give up.

Maybe she could hear me, maybe not, but the words kept me focused while charging blindly ahead until I ran full speed into a solid wall.

"Ow!" What I wanted to scream was WTF, but I was too busy nursing my shoulder, my already injured shoulder.

"Watch out," I called to Mandy whom I could hear coming up fast in the murky shadows.

She rounded the last corner and careened to a stop. "What's up?"

"Dead end." Yes, I was stating the obvious.

She looked behind her. "But there wasn't any other way."

That's what I was afraid of. Still I had to ask, "You sure? It's dark enough in here. We could have—"

"Not as tight as this tube is. We'd have felt an opening."

Not what I wanted to hear, but she was right.

Maybe I could use a little magic? Blast our way out.

The echo of Malik's words haunted me—don't use magic because it could easily cause more harm than good. With my luck, any spell would back fire and blow all of us up. The tree would become our coffin.

I turned back to the tree, reaching out my palms to press them along it.

"What are you doing?" came Mandy's whisper.

"Looking for a handle, or lock, or—" Bingo! "Found it."

"What?"

My fingers cupped beneath what at first touch seemed like a bump or abnormal growth. But it wasn't. Instead, the ripple in the wood acted as a lever.

"If I can get enough lift and pressure," I mumbled, aware of how cramped the space was and how thin the oxygen had become. "Mandy, help push as I lift."

Last time I'd felt so smashed was during high school when a gang of friends and I decided to see how many people could actually fit in the front seat of a Ford F-150—the kind without an extended cab. I was sure I'd be squished to death before we called a stop to our stupidity.

Today I didn't have that option.

"On the count of three." We weren't going to get a lot of traction because there was no room. My bad shoulder still faced the wall, and I couldn't turn around to use my good one. Mandy squiggled in beside me, two sardines in a tin can, only this can was wooden.

"One." My fingers dug into the wood to lift.

"Two."

I sucked in a deep breath, getting light-headed with the effort.

"Thre—"

I pulled up and we both pressed forward at the same time.

Like a cork held in place under pressure, a doorway exploded open and the two of us flew outwards, landing in a tangle of arms and legs against a hard, compact floor. A very hard, bruise-inducing floor.

Images spun around as I scrambled to my feet. Blood-red veined marble, greedy firelight; huge, grotesquely carved chairs and benches large enough to seat trolls; and a stench that seared my nostrils.

I pulled Mandy to her feet, her free hand clasped over her nose, both of us trying to breathe through our mouths.

"What's that stench?" Mandy gagged.

"Putrid flesh." Living in farm and ranch country, I recognized the odor of slaughtered animals, but my gut told me these carcasses were not animals. I twisted around to see where we were.

We were in a hall, large enough to house two or three basketball courts, with that cavernous echoing feeling such space contained. Candles sputtered everywhere: overhead, on sconces along every wall, in holders placed on every flat surface, including the floor. The light should have been warm and cheery, but it'd take a forest fire to create any warmth here.

I'd just noticed the bizarre furniture when Mandy looked over at me and whispered, "Are those. . ."

I nodded. "They look human."

Grotesquely human, chairs crafted with human arms and legs and a rocking chair that was the lap of an old man, seated, his face caught in an endless scream. Beside it a panel of arms and legs stacked one against the other—gnarled arms, young arms, even the small arms of children.

Don't throw up. Don't. . . no matter how my stomach convulsed. This was evil—pure, unadulterated evil.

There was more, though.

A shiver spiraled down my spine, but not because of the chill. It was because I'd turned full circle and spied two more things.

Three really. A raised dais about twenty feet away, stepped higher than anything else around, and dominated by two carved chairs dwarfing all the other creepy furnishings in the room. And in those chairs were two familiar figures—the Horned One. Not as I'd seen him last, in his guise of a human, but in another image—gigantic, bare chested, with the head of a beast; long snout, sharp teeth and curling ram's horns. An image as old as cave art and nightmares. I'd memorized them in the fairy tale and myth books; dark stains in my memory that would never be erased.

I swallowed, tamping down the need to step back.

Next to him lounged Malik—a smug, gotcha grin creasing his face, his brows raised, examining his nails as if we'd arrived just on cue.

The third thing I saw, and the one locking a scream deep in my throat was Aini, hanging from that huge ceiling, her arms stretched as wide apart as possible with chain so thick I wouldn't be able to wrap my hand around the individual links. Her body sagged, arms tearing from shoulders, wrists bloodied by twisting from her own weight, her head sagging forward.

"Bastards," I spit out, unable to tear my gaze away from the teen and from the evil done to her. Sick, twisted evil.

"Welcome." The Horned One's voice rolled and rolled, echoing from all the corners of the hall and still Aini didn't stir. "We've been expecting you."

CHAPTER 50

Screw you and the mule you rode in on.

I just bet they'd been waiting. Sickos were excellent hunters, willing to be patient. Not glancing at Malik, I didn't want to give him the satisfaction of knowing he'd scored by letting me lead my team down the path he'd devised—I kept my gaze upwards while my thoughts raged and tore through me.

What an easy mark I'd been. Trusting his directions. Blindly believing.

As if to rub salt in the wound he'd created, he spoke. "You surprise me. Not many would have survived that journey."

Yup, one hundred percent pure idiot.

"Yet I see not all your friends have arrived."

I refused to look behind me. I'd assumed Kelly had followed us. Or she was still trying to reach Aini's lifeless-looking body telepathically.

If Kels did follow, I hoped she heard us talking and stayed inside the tree where she'd be safe for a bit. Ultimately there was no safety here. Anywhere. Unless. . . only one win-win outcome—the Horned One had to die.

Mandy was here and so was I. It'd have to be enough.

Game on.

Best approach? We had no weapons so we had to use the enemy's strengths against them. Big bastard looked like some of the Weres I'd battled recently, so I'd use the same approach on him as I did on them. Get him riled, let him act first, use our agility to avoid and deflect until we could take him down.

Not a great plan, but it was a plan.

I whispered to Mandy out of the side of my mouth. "Find a way to release Aini. I've got the two A holes."

She didn't reply, which I took as agreement. Let's hope it didn't mean she didn't hear me.

Squaring my rigid shoulders, I threw my words at the Horned One as if he alone sat on the throne. "Somehow I expected more from you."

The taunting tone I used I'd learned in grade school from Pepper Dillenty, shadow bully extraordinaire. When the teachers were around, she radiated sweetness and smiles. But when they weren't—then her true personality ran rampant. I swore she was pure viper beneath curls and simpers.

Most of the girls just tolerated, avoided, or followed her lead as the only way to survive, but I had a weapon Pepper didn't have. I had older brothers who watched out for me. One taunt too many and little Pepper Pisspot found herself in a mud puddle, cut down to size.

My brothers weren't with me now, so I was on my own, ready to wield any and every weapon I could find, including Pepper's screw-you tone.

"Big, brave bad guy like yourself, can't do better than torture a girl?" I shook my head. "Tsk, tsk, tsk."

"What are you doing?" Mandy mouthed beside me. "Want to get us killed?"

Malik answered, as if he'd been asked. Must have a Shifter's hearing ability or he really could read minds. "You're all dead anyway."

"I don't think so." I ratcheted up my biggest come-and-get-it look, one I had down pat. "Not by the likes of you."

He smiled. A genuine smile crinkling the black tattoo around his lips and, if we'd been closer, no doubt darkening the silver of his eyes. Damn, not what I should be thinking about him. Sadistic, betrayer, psychotic—those were better images.

"I'm actually going to miss you, Witch." He leaned forward on his seat, his grin deepening. "Maybe I should keep you around. I haven't had a plaything for years."

"Poor baby," I cooed, laying it on thick. "What's the matter? Your mommy here not taking good enough care of you?"

Suddenly all of the air in the room sucked out. Even Malik froze.

My attention had never left the Horned One, so I caught his response and braced myself. He might be the Numero Uno power here, but obviously it'd been a while since he'd heard sarcasm, especially describing him. It took him a second or two to figure out what I'd just said. That length of time between one breath and the next.

When he did react, he rose slowly, foot by foot, until he reached at least ten feet tall.

I swallowed a basketball size lump of fear and raised my chin.

He widened his stance, threw back his shoulders and head and released a shout that rattled the chains holding Aini. "You dare. . ."

"Sure do, big guy." My words were all bravado. They had to be as I didn't have any other weapons. "In fact I think you're a blustering bully. Nothing more." I glanced around as if looking for someone to tell me otherwise.

Actually I was scouting out escape routes. None that I could see. What I did notice was how many of those creepy, over-carved furniture pieces I'd noted earlier populated the hall—real people, frozen in painful contortions. By the Great Spirits, how could anyone, anything, do that to another?

Is this what was going to happen to Aini once she was released from her chains? Or to Kelly and Mandy? I had to stop him. Had to. Had to. . .

The Horned One stepped forward on his raised platform, as if towering over everyone around him wasn't enough. Even from this distance, I could feel the heat roil off of him, a tsunami of anger slammed into me, enough to stagger me backwards.

Okay, maybe he had a few abilities I hadn't expected. But I'd learn.

I was so in over my head.

It'd better be a quick study.

"You shall pay," he railed. "Two thousand years, you shall hang before me. Let the carrion birds of death devour your eyes, your tongue, your flesh every night, and then I shall bring you back to life every day, knowing your torment will continue."

I swallowed. Creep could be inventive, but so far we were in a pissing contest only. Time to ramp up the annoyance factor. Weres, when angry, got stupid. Here was hoping demi-god demons acted the same.

"Oh, piddle." I took a step forward even if it was one of the hardest things I'd ever done. Not the hardest. That had been giving up Bran. A small smile curled my lips. Good to remember—I had little left to lose. "You're such a blowhard. Do something risky for a change. See if you've got anything left in you but hot air."

Mandy groaned behind me. I hoped she was smart enough to step away when the fireworks began.

"What exactly do you propose?" It was Malik asking. I doubted he meant to offer me the opportunity his question gave, but I grabbed it anyway.

"Release the girl." I glanced upward, even though seeing Aini like that was like pouring vinegar in an open cut, then I jerked my thumb toward Mandy. "Let my friend here take her away." I paused, as if slowly realizing something, before adding, "On second thought, that's not that risky because without me, they can't return to where they belong."

"So what do you wish?" That's it Malik, let me lay it all out.

"Send them back to their Realm and fight me one-on-one."

Malik's lips twitched upwards until he realized I meant every word I said. "You're a fool," he muttered.

Well, duh. I was here, wasn't I? Didn't that describe idiot with a capital 'I'?

I glanced toward the Horned One. "So, you game? Or you want to keep hurting those who can't fight back."

"And you think you can?" Not sure I liked his tone—one that kicked my heartbeat up a dozen notches until it screamed to escape my chest.

"You fought me once before, in my world, and lost." I laid a lot of emphasis on that last word. "I'm betting I can win here, too."

So, I stretched the truth. The last battle pitted the whole IR team against the soldiers Kincaide allowed to die senseless deaths. And technically, it was Kelly who separated the Horned One from his human host's body, but no need to focus on the pesky details. Especially when those details gave me plenty of reasons to turn tail and run.

"Why don't you take her up on her offer?" Malik sat back in his chair again, all casualness, but a tenseness in his shoulders betraying him. "It's been a while since you've had a chance to really play with one of the live ones."

Who knew being alive could be such an insult? It sure was a liability. On the one hand, Malik played right into my strategy, unless he worked a deadly game of his own. A very real possibility.

One step at a time. Get the Horned One to release Aini. Pray to the Great Spirits that Mandy could escape with the girl back into the hollow tree tunnel while I kept the Horned One occupied. Survive long enough that Mandy, Kelly and Aini got free of his Realm.

They still couldn't return to the Real Realm though, not without me.

Okay, add survive long enough to escape after them to my list.

There. Probably a one in one hundred, no, make that one in one thousand shot at success but as long as I breathed I'd take the risk. It's why I came.

"So big bonzo, you ready to take me on?"

I could have sworn I heard a groan. Maybe my own. How stupid could I be?

Stupid enough to save Aini, if she still lived.

"You puny insect," the Horned One spoke, sounding bored. "You are no threat to me."

Good point. Not that I'd admit it out loud, but he was right. So how did I show him I was worth his attention. Magic. That's how.

I glanced at Malik, watched the steepling of his fingers as if he waited for me to do exactly what he had warned me not to do.

If magic, badly used, could buy us some time, then it'd be worth the cost to me in using it.

I inhaled a deep breath of that rank stench then coughed. Not an auspicious beginning to spell casting. Breathing through my mouth, I tried again, stilling my body, lowering my voice, calling from within me.

"Protector, I call upon you.
Make me a barrier between man and monsters.
Between dark and light.
Between good and evil.
Protect me as I am willing to pay the cost."

I sensed Mandy stepping away, readying herself to act when, and if, I could get her a window of opportunity. The Horned One cocked his overlarge horned head at an angle—the predator-to-useless-prey look.

I got the message. I was going to die. We all were. All the grief, all the misery and fear we'd faced and overcome to get here wasn't going to make a difference. I got it.

But that didn't mean I'd give up. Not yet. Not until the last breath was pummeled from my body.

Fear slickened my skin and tightened my muscles as I raised my chin and continued.

"To the light, better things.
To death, watch over and guide.
To struggle and emerge, advance as I follow.
Going on forever, light shines in the darkness.
Dispel the darkness.
Crush the evil.
Circle round and protect. So mote it be!"

CHAPTER 51

The lights in the hall fluttered. Nothing more.

Malik laughed as the Horned One lowered his head, patience thinning, waiting for something more. So was I.

What did I expect? It was a protection spell, nothing more. A warm-up act. Now for the real show. Time to see if I could tap into The Horned One's own power just long enough.

By the Mother Goddess, and for those who suffered and would continue to suffer at the hands of this monster if I failed, *please* make this work.

The one fluky ability I possessed, a twist on my magic—my personal gift/curse was to be able to pull power from other preternatural beings. Yup, that was me, a psychic vampire.

If I used this spell, it required blood, which made it black magic. Using the dark arts in the abode of the Horned One could be pure suicide. But if I didn't try, I'd lose. We'd all lose.

If Bran had been here, he could help. Once again the loss of him reverberated through me. My choice though. My decision. Now it was time for action.

Here goes nothing. Biting my lip until I tasted coppery liquid, I raised my chin and started the chant.

"Adeo. Adeo. Agero. Adepto.
Come. Come. Increase. Acquire."

"Shit, Noziak, not that!" Mandy cried out from somewhere behind me. I didn't blame her, last time she saw me use this ability, I'd died. Thankfully Bran was near and he used his gift to resurrect life, my life. I wouldn't get such a reprieve here.

Aini to live. Mandy and Kels to live. Stop the Horned One. Was this asking for much? Didn't think so.
I started in again.

"Suscipio. Solvo.
Receive. Break free.
Singluaris. Praesentia presencia
Free the power."

I could feel it, the beginning swell, low inside me, the murmuring rush of power. And what power—ancient, tainted, deadly—answered my call. The power of my mother's Celtic ancestors. Her witch-born blood to mine.

Malik rose to his feet. I ignored him. Riding this whirlpool would take everything I had and then some.

Blood. I needed more blood. This was dark magic, the kind the Horned One knew well. The kind I'd been warned against time and again. The kind that could suck me in like it'd sucked in my mother until she tossed everything else of value away. Including me.

But how?

My shoulder. Pressing one hand to my shoulder until I bit back a scream my cotton t-shirt dampened with fresh blood, my blood. Close, so close.

Thrice called, thrice to contain.

"As thou be, so now change.
Thought to image.
Image to bind.
Bind to blood let."

I raised my hands skyward, aware of the swirl of air from this airless place whirring around me.

Almost there.

But I'd miscalculated. The Horned One wasn't sitting idly by, twiddling his fingers while I proved I was a worthy adversary. You didn't rule a Realm within the Underworld for more than a thousand years by being slow or stupid. And he damn well wasn't waiting for me to suck his power dry.

As if I could.

Before I finished my twitch of magic, he pounced. Flicking his fingers and calling in a language much older than Latin. One I didn't recognize, but he knew, and I could only tremble against.

With a rustle then a roar, the furniture around me started morphing, elongating, screaming in agony as chairs rose to stand on two feet, as chests broke apart and became two, three and more bodies, as trapped souls sprang free—to do their Lord and Master's bidding.

Sweet Goddess above, we were screwed.

CHAPTER 52

"Run!" I shouted to Mandy. The coward's way. We'd regroup. Find another plan.

But Mandy couldn't run. She was surrounded by half a dozen souls heeding the Horned One's command. If they succeeded, if even one of them pushed into her, Mandy was a goner.

Grabbing the nearest weapon, a wicked looking metal candleholder that stood waist-high, I used it as a pike staff, running up behind Mandy's attackers and sweeping them right and left.

"Take that. And that!"

I sounded like a cartoon character but it worked—at least enough for Mandy to jet around behind me. As a soulless one, all it takes was one of these tainted spirits to possess her and she'd stay here for eternity.

One? Heck, the hall was alive with mindless, robotic beings—souls held in thrall and heeding the Horned One's command to annihilate us. We couldn't hold them all off.

"Here!" At the first break, I shoved my weapon into Mandy's hands and barreled forward, thrusting as many souls as I could this way and that, like a human battering ram.

They might be more numerous than we were, and the Horned One more powerful, but I was more desperate.

Worked for me.

Racing toward the dais instead of away from it, I shouted out the last words of my spell.

"Continere. Continere. Continere.

Hemma, hanna, druia.
Hemma, druia, sanctum. "

I pulled forth magic and owned it, amplifying a thousand fold. All non-human abilities near me were mine and I reveled in the power. I'd only begun. The closer I came to the Horned One, the more I tapped into his potency.

Please the Spirits, don't rip me apart.

Mandy called Kelly's name somewhere behind me, but I ignored her. Sometimes the team worked as one and sometimes not. This was one of those all-for-ourselves-and-we'll-pick-up-the-pieces-later times. I wasn't even sure if Kelly was in the hall yet.

Maybe she'd miss the slaughter. Later we could give her a hard time.

If there was a later. Thrice the spell needed to be called so I shouted the second time.

"Continere. Continere. Continere.
Hemma, hanna, druia.
Hemma, druia, sanctum. "

Time was meant to slow, to stop. Instead it increased, fast forward on speed.

What—

I spun in a vortex of power, lifted off my feet, higher and higher into the rafters until I reached out and grabbed with both hands a ring on the chain holding Aini. Now we both rocked through the air, like a carnival game run amuck.

"Puny human, you are no match for me!" roared the Horned One.

I still had to finish the chant by saying the words for the third time. Out of breath, heart stampeding, I rasped out the words,

"Continere. Continere. Continere.
Hemma, hanna, druia.
Hemma, druia, sanctum. "

My head roared, blood pounded behind my eyes, nerve endings jangled as my fingers clawed for a stronger hold.

A flash of jagged, raw light split the cavernous hall.

But I had nothing. No power. No head rush of energy. Nothing.

"I smell her." The Horned One ceased his bellowing and the whirlwind thrusting me upwards winked out. "The Clavis is *here.*"

Double damn. Now I was swinging like a monkey without a limb. Who knew where Mandy was? Same with Kelly. And who the heck was the Clavis? Would they help or be another force to fight?

Wait, wasn't Kelly the Clavis? There'd been some other word to describe her. Malik had used it. The Clavis of Dryghtyn. So did that mean Kelly was here? But where?

What now?

I could drop the twenty or so feet onto the hard marble floor and hope I didn't break my skull, or. . .

Why not? See if a Release spell could free Aini's manacled wrists. I'd worry about the drop if I unbound her.

Spell casting while dangling one-handed while I reached for Aini wasn't easy. But I hadn't signed on to be an IR Agent for the easy things. Plus, I wasn't so sure there was a Release spell that I knew well enough not to tie us both into double knots. Maybe a Reverse Binding spell might work better.

No way to center myself. No runes, herbs, nothing to help. Good thing I hated backing away from a challenge. Speaking low, low enough not to attract the attention of anyone fighting below us, I began the chant.

"Air to wind, earth to dust.
By water and by fire.
Trouble heeded and trouble bound.
Compel. Coerce. Constrain.
Reverse. Release. Reframe.
I thee ask. I thee implore.
Threat be gone. Power be undone."

I now had one hand hooked on a chain loop, which saved us both from dropping, and one wrapped around Aini as her wrist restraints popped off with a puff of rust-colored smoke. Her chains still dangled in the air, but her hands were free.

If I let go, or my hand continued to slip, we'd both plummet. By the screams and cries I heard welling up from below it sounded like Mandy still wrestled with the souls by beating them off. No help there.

Malik shouted. I didn't catch what but it reminded me— wings.

Another spell. At this rate I'd be wrung from the inside out. Magic took energy and I was running on faint fumes. Plus I didn't dare try more black magic. Not here.

Needs must.

"Powers that be, here and far.
I call upon thee.
Lift us up. Send us aloft.
Alabaster. Pearl. Silver. Fair.
Unfurl my wings, high and wide.
Rise from beneath, bound no more.
Fly now, fast and free.
So mote it be!"

Wings erupted from my back.

I wasn't graceful, jerking up and flapping around as I reached for Aini's other hand—which I never did catch. Instead, I whirled and twirled in a counter-clockwise huge spiral, aiming for some place, any place, far enough from the fighting to lower Aini and give her a chance to survive.

At the last moment, I pulled up to lay the girl down as gently as possible on that cold marble floor.

At last something right.

Before I could land fully, and dispose of my wings, something jumped onto my back and began slamming against my head.

What the—

I couldn't see what it was and, short of throwing myself backwards against a wall or floor, I couldn't get the bloody thing off.

Time to go for broke. Maybe a Reverse Binding spell?

"Light come forth.
Clear the darkness. Guide and protect.
Light to dark.
Clear and guide.
Light to dark. Protect.
Dark to dark, seek thy home. "

I expected the threat to fall off. Instead a wall of sound roared around me. The souls! I'd forgotten the hall full of souls, tainted by the darkness of the Horned One.

Like a scythe mowing down ripe grain, a ten-foot swath all around me opened up. I couldn't worry about their damned souls. If I could stop the Horned One, they'd be released from their torment. That I could focus on.

Hot damn, I was good. Plus a little breathing space might help Mandy.

Only problem was whatever was riding my back like a bronc rider still remained.

Fine. It wanted to play nasty, so could I.

With both hands covering my head and neck as much as possible while flapping one wing, because that's all I could work until I rid myself of my nemesis, I aimed for the nearest wall. Kamikaze pilots had nothing on me.

Remembering to turn at the last moment, we both thudded our backs against the wall hard enough to rattle my bones.

Son of a b—it wasn't letting go. The smacking had slowed its hammering on me, probably because it wrapped two arms around my neck to hold on. Choking me to death was no doubt a side benefit.

Only they weren't really arms, they were more like tentacles, spidery type things ending in claws.

Freak out time!

Screaming like one of my mother's Irish banshees had me in its grip, I launched off the wall, then smashed back into it.

Again and again. If I survived, I'd be one solid bruise. Small price to pay for release.

"Get off."

Womp!

"Off."

Womp. Womp.

"Get the frick off, you—"

With a wail sounding like a death knell at rock concert volume, the claws clicked loose and my unwelcome guest plummeted downward.

I didn't even care that it landed with a cracking thud. Better it than me. My luck it landed near Aini, too close, where it continued to twitch. A small, vicious, bug-spider beast.

Wasn't I ever going to get a break?

Floundering to the floor below, I landed as close to Aini as I could. A quick pulse check told me she was still alive. But barely.

In front of me, Mandy was doing a great imitation of the Three Musketeers with her metal candleholder—a thrust here, jab there, deflecting an incoming soul right and left. But she looked like she was flagging.

I couldn't see Kelly anywhere.

Not good.

Staggering to my feet, I pivoted to look toward the dais. Malik was gone. Figured. Rat bastard skipped out.

But the Horned One was still there, legs braced wide, flaming eyes staring right at me.

What would it take to kill the guy?

That wasn't my most pressing problem, though, as the black, creepy spidery clawed thing wasn't dead yet. It continued to twitch and spasm, spitting a greenish goo from where its mouth might be.

The Horned One shouted something and the spider creature multiplied over and over: one into two, two into four. . . they started moving toward us, their bodies making a click-clack sound across the tile floor, like scratching a chalkboard.

Ugh.

I stood by Aini, my legs shaky with fatigue, no weapon at hand, little energy, and no back up. If I did nothing, the creatures would swarm over Aini. If I could get Mandy's knife, the one Kelly used to open my shoulder wound, I might be able to—nah, wouldn't work. No telling if a knife small enough to turn into a credit card could pierce them. Plus, there was that whole getting too near thing.

Think, Noziak, think.

Many of the sick-looking creatures weren't much larger than footballs, with the same shape except for their spidery arms ending in claws. Others were larger, but if I could cut down some of them, I might, just might, handle the rest.

I had an idea. Warped and desperate but it worked for me.

Not waiting for the closest one to get any nearer, I staggered out to them and started kicking with everything left in me.

Kick. Splat.

Kick. High in the air, then hard trip down.

Kick. Yeah, that took out two.

I was on a roll.

Only problem was kicking took a whole lot more energy than simply standing. Each swing of my foot became shorter and smaller and yet they still came with the Horned One cackling in the background.

I'd love to aim just one of these things right into his trap of a mouth. That'd shut him up, at least for a second or two. With an humph, I swung and lofted the nearest insect as high as possible. It missed by a mile as I staggered backwards.

I'd have fallen flat on my backside except someone grabbed my arm and stopped my trajectory.

"Thanks," I said to Mandy as I glanced over my shoulder, only it wasn't her. It was Malik.

In a perfect world, I'd have hauled off and knocked him arse over teakettle, but all I managed was a low throat growl. The sound a mangy junkyard dog makes when leashed and powerless.

"I'm not the enemy." His voice rumbled low and close to my ear. Too close. He still held my arm and I had nothing left to fight with. Only my words.

"You look like an enemy to me." I gave a chin jerk to the dais where the Horned One was no longer focused on me but sniffed around as if scenting something foul. "You and your best friend there."

"I'm as much a prisoner here as your friend was." It wasn't his words but the bitterness beneath them that had me looking at him twice, with a slow bloom of hope whimpering to be released.

But I'd trusted him once and look where it got us.

As if he guessed, or heard, the train of my thoughts, he nodded toward the Horned One. "He smells the Clavis. Blood of his blood, she is the only one who can end his reign."

She who? I didn't see anyone.

I squinted in the direction he stared but didn't see anything. "Where?" My voice sounded hoarse and raw. Which is exactly how I felt.

"There. Lowest step. Left of the dais."

I looked again and still couldn't see anyone. But I did see a small flash as if something cleaved the air. I looked closer.

What was that? A thin, small shape. Not much longer than a hand but skinny. Like a—wait, it was, a knife.

Not any knife but Mandy's knife, only Mandy wasn't holding it. No one was.

Which meant—oh, crap—Kelly.

Her hand must have been shaking as the image winked in and out. She'd turned invisible and was approaching the Horned One. All alone.

No she wasn't. Not if I still lived.

CHAPTER 53

Saying something didn't make it so.

There wasn't anything left in me. I'd burned through more magic than I'd ever used before and, except for some banished souls and one wounded girl, I had nothing to show for it.

I couldn't stop Kelly, so what could I do?

Like a battery refusing to turn over on a cold winter's morning, it took a bit for realization to slap me upside the head. I could distract the Horned One. It was about the only thing left for me.

Give Kelly a chance—slim to none, but still a chance. Not by using black magic—the tool of the Horned One. Evil begot evil. Which left me with white magic. A concept that would never occur to the Horned One.

Fight dark with light; good against evil. And what was better than being willing to sacrifice the only thing I had left— my life—for a chance for my teammates to survive.

"Keep Aini safe," I directed Malik, well aware of the risk I took. If he was truly an ally with the Horned One, then leaving Aini under his protection meant she could die. But if I did nothing, letting Kelly face the danger alone, Kelly would die and then we'd all die.

I was getting freaking tired of impossible choices.

Sucking in a deep breath, I accepted my only truth. The Horned One was going down. For the Lost Children waiting to be reunited with their loved ones, the lovers trapped forever in mourning, and for Mandy's family who didn't deserve to spend eternity anywhere near this evil.

I might not be enough, but I was all that was available.

"Come on, Seeker Wannabe," I taunted. It'd have been a whole lot more effective if I had some lung-power behind my words.

He didn't move an inch.

Okay, if he wouldn't come to me, I'd go to him.

I tottered toward him, looking more drunk than lethal, and wasn't sure what I'd do once I got his attention, but moving forward was better than standing still and waiting for death.

For Kels. For Aini.

That was it. That was the burn igniting my anger. For what he'd done to a helpless girl who couldn't fight back. What he'd do to my friend if I didn't help her.

Shouting louder, I called out. "Hey, Asshole!" When the Horned One glanced my way, I waved my arms. "Yeah, you. You big. . . big bully."

I so scraped the bottom with taunts. But Kelly needed a chance . . . "Yeah, ugly mug. Bring it on!"

He didn't move, but he was focused on me. Good.

Hadn't I done this once before? Taunted a threat? Oh, yeah, two ugly Weres trying to kill me. Seemed like a lifetime ago. I'd used ugly mother jokes then. Might work here. Might not.

"Yo mama's so ugly, her birth certificate is an apology letter from the condom factory."

Nothing. Probably didn't have a clue what a condom was.

"Yo mama's so ugly, they changed Halloween to YoMamaween!"

I was batting zip-zero.

"Yo mama's so butt-ugly that not even CSI could solve *that* mystery."

At least the winking knife was inching closer. Top step. Now all Kelly needed was to edge around behind the Horned One and hope a wicked sharp, but very small, knife could do enough damage.

She had maybe one chance to slide it in, between the ribs, deep enough to hit the demon's heart. If he even had one.

"Big Guy?" I screamed again, staggering a few steps forward. "Ready to quit?"

Instead of responding, he raised one arm, mumbled something in a low, guttural growl and between one breath and the next, I slammed against the floor, face first.

Hurt was an understatement. I could have sworn ten tons of compressed metal smashed against my back. Blood spurted from my nose, gagging me. My ribs screamed in pain, making it hard to breathe in anything but short, wheezing gasps.

So much for helping, Kels. I couldn't even help myself.

My brothers always said my mouth would get me in trouble. Now I was never going to get to tell them they had been right.

CHAPTER 54

Out of one eye I could see the Horned One raise his arms high over his head, cawing that high-volume, nail-scratching laugh of his. He thought he'd won.

He was right.

I couldn't budge, barely breathed and didn't see any sign of Kelly. Who knew where Mandy was, or if she still lived. Aini?

Only Malik to protect her. What a crap shoot.

If I could have shaken my head, I would have. To come all this way, for nothing. Absolutely nothing.

The only saving grace? Bran would never know I gave him up.

A sudden movement on the periphery of my vision snagged my attention. Mandy. Staggering forward, clutching her metal candleholder like a broken blade, she still moved, inching toward the dais. Not fast, but enough to make the Horned One change his tune. From victory glee to a bellow of rage.

No. No. No.

She had nothing to fight him. Nothing to protect herself. Nothing. . . except me.

A Protection spell. Against the Horned One? Like a raincoat holding back a tsunami.

Whispering because there was so little left to even speak, I flicked the fingers of my hand facing Mandy.

"Air, earth, water, all three, I summon thee.
Elements of earth, smite my enemy."

The biggest, baddest enemy here. He couldn't win. Please Mother Goddess and Spirits of my Ancestors, help me.

"Elements of air, surround us and protect us.
Elements of water, rise between us.
Darkness banish. Lightness flare forth.
Thee I call. Thee I seek. So mote it be"

A quiver, so faint it barely touched my awareness, wafted then went out.

CHAPTER 55

My eyes closed before I could see if the spell helped. My ears still worked though as a loud, high bellow ripped through the room. It rolled and rolled like thunder up close, vibrating from within.

The pressure holding me flat eased just enough for a great gulp of air. I didn't even care that it tasted like rotten eggs. Lifting my head, I glanced at Mandy first. She stood as if caught in a time warp, her face now registering shock instead of determination.

Angling my head enough to look at the dais, I caught the Horned One spinning around, his tree-trunk arms like windmills run amuck until he lurched forward, teetered, hit the first step and toppled downwards.

Thud, landing right at Mandy's feet.

The marble splintered and cracked with a jagged scream where he landed and the whole floor rippled, as if a great wave surged from beneath. I was thrown upwards then landed hard again.

Man, that was getting old. I glanced toward Mandy who raised the metal candleholder she clutched in both her hands as high as possible and smashed it with a cry of anguish on the Horned One's head. Over and over. "For Alejándro. And Momma. And *Papito*. For Aini."

I mentally cheered her on. Make sure that rat-bastard was dead, dead, dead.

A murmur, starting low but growing from far, far away. Voices? Maybe. A rumble-roar raising the hair on my skin.

"Get up!" Malik shouted.

Like I was lounging around by choice. Sheesh.

I crawled to my knees and spotted Kelly. She huddled on the steps, visible now, her head bowed, one arm covered with a purple, puke-looking slime up to her shoulder.

"Kels," I cried, reaching toward her until I could get the legs to work.

She lifted her head, but even from here I could tell she couldn't see me, not really. The double-edged sword of using her power: blindness. Exhaustion and grief etched her face. Had she really knifed the Horned One? All by herself?

No time for questions as I spotted what was happening beneath the hulk of the Horned One's carcass. Not blood, thank heaven, but a rupture in the floor, one spreading, expanding, as was that roar I'd been hearing. Closer now.

Like ice breaking beneath a Chinook wind, cracks expanded outward, seams widening. Soon they'd splinter apart and swallow the Horned One. Him, and us.

Oh, crap. Didn't know what the crumbling meant, except for trouble. I wasn't game to find out the details.

Jerking to a standing position, I called to Mandy. "Grab Kelly. Now. Go. Go. Go!"

There wasn't time for more as I reeled toward Aini. She hadn't moved but a quick touch to her throat told me she still breathed.

A small win, but still a win.

That could change any minute if we didn't all get out of here.

I swung toward Aini and hoisted her in a fireman's hold over my wounded shoulder. The sharp spike of pain acted as a cattle prod. I needed it.

Mandy reached Kelly, tugging her to a standing position. "Which way?" she shouted, looking at me.

Hell if I knew.

Where was Malik?

Gone. Just when we could have used him. Not that he'd tell us the truth, but even a lie could help direct us in the other direction. But he hadn't killed Aini when he had a chance, so I'd give him a good-deed-done for that.

Back to the tree tunnel? A quick glance nixed that idea as no door remained in the wall. In fact, most of the wall was missing, crumbling in waves of rust-red dust.

Not good. Really, not good. It was as if the Horned One's evil held his Realm in place. Now that he was gone?

"This way," I shouted, heading north in King Aglaand's direction. His was the name many magic spells called upon. He and his warriors. It was a slim chance that north was right, but I didn't have a quarter to flip.

Hopping over a small fissure, I aimed to intersect Mandy and Kelly. The cracks widened from finger-sized to wrist-sized. Kelly kept tripping so I grabbed her free hand as soon as I reached them. Now bracketed between us, we all hustled as fast as we could go, deeper into the hall, looking for a door, a path, something.

But we weren't fast enough. Not between the weight I carried and Kelly's blindness. The roar nipped our heels. Crashing sounds told me the hall structure was disintegrating.

"This way." Mandy veered us to the left, down a side hallway.

I hesitated, stumbling, then righting with a groan.

"Trust me," she said, tugging Kelly. "My brother says there's a way out."

No time to think through the what-ifs. Sometimes all we had left was trust. This looked like one of those times.

Saying nothing, I struggled just to breathe and move. Mandy had better be right. Or what? Couldn't kill her because we'd all be dead.

The hall narrowed even as the floor buckled and heaved beneath us. I glanced back and swallowed a scream. The floor no longer splintered—it was dissolving, chunk by chunk, dropping away into inky blackness.

"Faster," I urged, as I picked up my pace. "Gotta go faster."

"Leave me behind," Kelly whispered.

"Forget it, McAllister." I all but bit the words out. "You don't get to sit this one out."

Mandy slowed, as if listening, but we didn't have even that luxury.

"Move it, Reyes." I yelled, repositioning Aini on my shoulder so I could use Kelly as a human rope to jerk Mandy forward. What was that game I hated as a kid? Crack the whip or something. I only remembered I usually got to be the last kid

in a line of racing kids—the whip—which meant winging through the air willy nilly. Out of control. Waiting to be flung aside.

A lot like now.

Another sound crept into my awareness. A small niggle that grew as we skittered forward.

What was that—drumming? The CD I'd left behind creating a steady beat to tether us to our world.

Halleluiah! I wanted to shout. The beat that echoed our hearts. Mine pounded so hard right now, it threatened to leap from my chest.

Keep moving.

I had to get us somewhere, anywhere safe enough I could connect to the drum beat tethering us to the Real Realm. Using that as a guide, I might, just might, return us home.

"There!" I pointed dead ahead. Toward a faint light. It beckoned and I lurched toward it. The steady thud, thud, thud came from that direction.

"What is it?" Mandy called, bringing up the rear of our desperate rag-tag team.

"Gotta reach it." I gasped, then added, "It's the way home."

Our pace kicked into high gear, having a goal, a sliver of hope. The word *home* acted as a magical beacon. That and the volume of screams behind us increasing until I could no longer hear my labored breathing, the straining of my heart.

It was as if all the pain, the torment, the tortured souls shouted in one voice.

Faster. Faster. Go fast –

Almost there. The light grew brighter. Glaring after the shadowed darkness of the hall. Blinding.

A door? Window? Something. Didn't matter. The floor beneath me roiled and shifted. Any second and it'd suck us under.

Mandy caught up so we dragged Kelly between us in an uneven run-weave pattern, hampered by Aini's weight counter-balancing my every step.

"I'm not sure," Mandy called out, skidding to a sliding halt. A stop that had her falling backwards.

"No choice," I shouted, launching myself forward, pulling Kelly along with me, and Mandy along with Kelly.

Out.

And down.

CHAPTER 56

Falling is not a quick or painless way to die. It looks easy, watching from afar, but when caught in a free fall there's time, way too much time to think.

Mistakes made. Loved ones I'd never get to say goodbye to. Bran, never knowing what happened to me.

Bran. I'd cut myself off from him and yet the thought of him filled me, even now.

Seconds swept into minutes and stretched. Around and over, like buffeted autumn leaves, we slid through a white blue sky. Down. Down. Down.

I squeezed Kelly's hand tighter. The only reassurance I could give. We'd done the impossible. Killed the Horned One. Saved Aini, only to—at least she wouldn't know we failed her in the end.

We'd saved the world.

That had to be enough.

Even before that last thought escaped, the light changed, became gray, then black.

Then we hit.

CHAPTER 57

"Alex, come back."

The male voice sounded familiar.

"Come on, girl. Come back."

"Dad?" The word came as a croak, past a throat so dry it ached.

"That's it. Open your eyes."

Was my dad dead, too? Last thing I wanted was to see where I was. Once I did, hope would vanish. No chance of ever seeing Bran again. Of explaining to him. Finding out what it'd meant to give him up.

Okay, maybe that last part would be good. Sometimes I could be a coward, especially in matters of the heart. And emotions. And all that touchy-feely, messy stuff. Yeah, I was a big chicken-livered scaredy-cat a lot of the times. I wanted to live yet still hide from feeling. Emotions. If I got a chance. . . maybe. . .

"Alex. Wake up."

Dad actually sounded pissed. Or worried. Which wasn't like him at all. He was as solid as rock, the rock all of us Noziaks depended on. So if he said do something, I didn't have a choice.

With a groan that sounded more like a whimper, I peeled open my eyelids, bracing myself, knowing what I'd see— spirits and souls caught in torment, misery and longing.

Except I didn't.

I lay crumpled on a floor somewhere. A hard one, not marble but wood. The gym floor, in the IR Academy, where we'd left our bodies behind, our human shells, waiting for us.

We were back? We'd made it?

My dad's face hovered into view as he knelt beside me and cupped my head. He looked different. Worry lines scored his face, even his dark eyes held a half-crazed look. A lot like he'd looked when I was seven and broke my arm after trying to get on a bronc I had no business riding.

"Here, drink this," was all he said.

I sat up enough to sip a glass of water. Never, ever tasted anything so good in my life.

"Where?" I murmured, then jackknifed up to a sitting position, one making my head spin, my vision blur. "Kels? Aini?"

"They're safe." He didn't sound like he meant it. "Everyone made it back in one piece."

I leaned forward and did something I hadn't done since I was a child—I hugged him. Wrapped my arms as tight as I could, murmuring, "I love you. I love you so much."

Tears poured down my cheeks as I clung to my dad, inhaling his scent, dampening his worn plaid shirt.

Biggest surprise? He hugged me right back, rocking me like I was still his little girl.

I was home, and home meant being with the ones you love.

Like Bran. If it wasn't too late.

Dad pulled back first, swiping a hand across his eyes and clearing his throat. "You'll be all right," he said, while I sniffed.

So why didn't he sound pleased? And why was he here at all? He wasn't when we left.

As if I'd spoken out loud, he rocked back on his heels. The furrows between his brows deepening. "If you ever do such a lame-brained, naïve, ill-advised stunt again, I'll take my belt to you. You got that."

It wasn't really a question. Not what I expected. Once again I was my hurting seven-year-old self who'd pulled a dumb stunt.

"We did it." My Noziak mule-headed tone layered my words. "We got Aini out and stopped—"

The words dried up. Dad was right, as he often was. How'd we ever think we could go where living, breathing, humans never had gone, stop the unstoppable, and think, for one second, we could escape. . .

I pulled my knees to my chest and sunk my head on them even as I shook it.

"There, there." Dad patted me on the back. "You're too old for the belt."

As if that's what I really worried about.

Piece by piece, I pulled away from my self-horsewhipping, but continued to cradle my head, mostly from sheer exhaustion. When I managed to raise it at last I asked, "Aini? Is she. . ."

"Alive, yes. And out of the coma."

I shuddered, not with dread but relief.

He continued talking, as if aware I didn't have enough left in me to form too many coherent words. "The others are in the infirmary. I thought it best to leave you here until you woke up."

"Why?" I pointed one finger to the floor. "Why are you here?"

His brows drew together like thunderclouds before a lightning storm. "Van, and Ling Mai, informed me of what you were attempting." I heard all the words he left out this time— foolish, mule-headed, suicidal—but he waved his hand as if dismissing what had already been done. "Figured you might need some help returning."

Understatement.

"It was your drum," I whispered, realizing why that last dash felt so much like coming home. It was. Back to the drumbeat my dad used many times in his shamanic work, a sound as familiar as my own heartbeat.

He nodded. "You did a good job with the CD music, but—" he seemed at a loss for words, until he cleared his throat again and swiped a hand through his hair. "Going deep into the Underworld, as deep as you planned. . . don't do it again without . . . without help on this end. Please."

Since all of us Noziaks used the *please* word as much as we used the *I'm sorry* words, I knew the toll my father had taken to be here for me. For us.

"I didn't know how else to help Aini. And stop—him." I didn't even want to say his name again, as if giving voice to it might give life to him.

Before my dad could respond, someone hailed from the doorway. "About frickin' time, Noziak," Jaylene called out, then cast a sheepish look at my dad. "Sorry, Sir, I meant, about time you rejoined us, Alex." She glanced back at me, a big grin splitting her face. Man, I'd missed that smile. "Thought you'd be snoozing for days."

I wish. But right then I was too damn happy to see the rest of the IR team crowding into the gym—Jaylene, Vaughn and Nicki. Mandy and Kelly brought up the rear, looking as depleted as I felt. Kelly especially. Even some of the IR teens—Herc, Beau and Sabina appeared.

Sabina raced forward and pulled me to my feet, wrapping me in a huge bear hug. Almost toppled me back to the floor as I tried to hold off wincing. There wasn't a square inch of me that didn't hurt, outside and inside.

"I'm so glad you made it," she said, holding me tight. "Your dad scared us."

I glanced over her shoulder at my dad and gave him a silent thumbs-up.

"Didn't you trust me to get the mission done?" I asked, meaning it to be a joke, except three of us there knew how close we'd come to never returning. I couldn't even look Mandy in the eye. And Kelly? Damn, she looked bad.

"You okay?" I asked her, releasing Sabina to reach a hand toward Kelly who held her arms wrapped tight around herself as if fearing she'd splinter if she released them.

She gave me a tight nod and wobbly smile but left my hand wavering in the air until I let it drop. "Fine," she said. "I'm fine."

Yeah, right.

Only then did I look at Mandy, swallowing before saying, "Thanks."

"For?" Since only a smidge of attitude colored her words, I knew she was as shaky as I was.

"For going. . .for hanging in. . .for. . .there at the end. You got us out."

"My brother did."

The other team members, those who hadn't gone, cast raised brows and cautious glances at one another, no doubt having more questions than answers so far. I didn't blame them. I still had a number of my own, and I'd been there.

"So the Horned One is gone?" Jaylene broke the awkwardness, with a sledgehammer.

I raised my chin toward Kelly. "Yeah. Kels gets all the credit for that."

She looked like I'd slapped her as she raised her gaze to collide with mine. "We all know what that means."

All gazes ricocheted to mine. I shrugged, knowing if Kelly wanted the truth to be told, she'd need to do it herself. Was it Malik who'd said something about only one of the blood of the Horned One could kill him? So what did that mean for Kelly? Heck, she'd been worried about finding her birth mother. Now?

What a mess.

I scrubbed my hands over my face. "There's a lot to tell." And a lot I never wanted to reveal—the tree called Ygdrassil, how each of us nearly killed the others with our fears being manifested, what I'd given up. Relinquished like it didn't matter, pretending I could bear the cost—all a lie. Bran.

Yup, secrets all around.

Mandy stepped in to help smooth over Kelly's abruptness and my vagueness. "The Horned One *really* is gone." She looked at Kelly and me. "All three of us saw him go down."

"But how?" Nicki asked what I wanted to ask.

Kelly glanced at Mandy, then me, and inhaled a deep breath. "When I came into that. . . that room . . I saw. . . I figured it'd be better if I was invisible."

That made perfect sense. Why hadn't I thought of that as part of our strategy? Talk about a smack upside the head.

"I managed to snag the knife that Mandy carried while she was fighting whatever she fought."

I was nodding, glad one of us had enough presence of mind.

"I didn't think it could do much against. . . against him."

My turn to jump in. "He was huge, Kels. I know I wouldn't have had enough guts to go up against him with that little ol' credit-card knife."

She gave me a wobbly smile. "I didn't want to. . ." Her voice faded away before she spoke again. "But he was hurting you. And sending those horrible souls after Mandy. And Aini—"

"You did the right thing," Mandy said, and I could have hugged her for it. The rest of the team remained quiet, aware how hard it was for Kelly to relive those moments. "None of us would have made it out of there if you hadn't taken the risk."

"I wasn't thinking of the risk," Kelly admitted with a harsh laugh. "I just got so. . . so angry." She looked around as if that had been a bad thing. Not in my book. "I was only hoping to distract him. Especially—" She swallowed again as I watched her fists curl and uncurl. "He said he could smell. . ."

"Of course." The penny finally dropped for me. "*You're* the Clavis. No wonder he went bat-crap crazy there. *You* were the biggest threat to him."

"Didn't feel like it."

I actually laughed out loud. A real one. "That's what heroes really are," I said, meaning every word. "The ones who do the hard things when they don't want to, when no one else can do what must be done, and when they're sure they can't make a difference."

I glanced at Mandy. "It was Mandy dealing the last blow with her make-do candle weapon."

"And your distracting him," Kelly said, "so Mandy and I could get close enough."

"Yeah, with the stupidest ugly momma jokes I've ever heard," Mandy added, shaking her head.

"It took all of us." I straightened. "Good versus evil, and we rocked it."

Kelly's eyes brightened but her gaze skittered away. I could tell she didn't believe me. Not really. Heck, I barely believed me, except for the fact we were here. All three of us and Aini.

"So you skewered him with a credit-card blade." Mandy had a big whole face grin as she raised her hand toward Kelly.

"High-five girlfriend! Way to take down a demon of the Underworld."

"Not just *a* demon," I added. "*THE* demon. One of the big ones." Then added, so Kelly knew exactly what a huge thing she'd accomplished, "And in doing so you released all those souls held by him—all the ones we passed on the way to find him."

Kelly's gaze snapped to mine, a little of the bleakness escaping from her haunted expression. "The children?"

I nodded. "Yup." I glanced at Mandy so she and Kels knew exactly who else I was talking about when I added, "Every single last soul that the Horned One kept around him to feed on their pain and misery."

I stepped up to Kelly and gave her a hug—a little rough and awkward—but hey, I did it.

She wiped her eyes and murmured a soft, "Thank you."

Heck, the thanks were all mine. If it hadn't been for her, I'd probably be hanging from a set of chains being tortured daily. I squelched the shudder that raced through me.

"So he's really dead and gone, Kelly." Mandy stepped up on the other side of her and wrapped one arm around her. "The Realms—spirit and this world—are safe because of you."

"Plus you killed an asshole." Jaylene summed up my sentiments exactly.

"Which could explain why Aini came out of her coma," Vaughn, our team leader, spoke up then raised a hand at my expression. "She's alive but very weak. No telling how much she remembers or not. Let's give her a few days to gain her strength back before she has too many visitors."

Made sense. My gut told me that Aini would be as scared as the rest of us, and it'd take a lot more than a few days to recoup from that.

"I think you all coming back in one piece deserves a little celebration," Nicki tossed out. I could have high-fived her for that. Focus on the win, not the wounds. "In fact, a big celebration!"

My shoulders had just started to relax and a smile crept up on me when my father raised his hand. "There is one problem though."

It felt like I'd been slammed on the Horned One's marble floor again.

"What?" Jaylene braved where I didn't want to go.

"Someone, or something, returned with Alex and the others. Two in fact."

"Two what?" Vaughn asked, assuming leadership in the absence of our director Ling Mai. Who should have been here. So where was she?

One problem at a time. My dad's first. I cleared my throat, waiting for his response.

"I couldn't say for sure," he started, then paused, which wasn't like him at all. "I was so focused on guiding Alex back and the thread was very weak. . . it's hard to be specific, but two beings crossed over with the three IR Agents and the girl."

Crud in a bucket.

How? Who? Then, as if I'd summoned it, a faint mocking laugh rolled over me. Malik.

That son of a b—

I glanced around, aware now of that low level laugh, like the rumble of near thunder tip-toeing across my skin. But no one else seemed to hear what I was hearing.

"I warned you I wanted a plaything, Witch," he murmured as if standing right beside me.

I jumped, earning a few odd looks. "You okay?" Mandy asked, her brows puckered.

"Yeah. Peachy."

Just wait, asshole. If I could bring you here, I can find a way to send you back.

That laugh again, fading into the distance. At least that explained one of what traveled with us to this Realm. So who was the other? Mandy's brother? The Ghost Guy? Or something from the Horned One's Realm?

Since the team was already heading out the door, my father with them, I decided not to call them back. I'd tell everyone about Malik as soon as we regrouped. Malik and the other spirit possibilities. But not right now. He didn't pose a threat to us in the next fifteen minutes, as far as I knew. He could wait.

Mandy, Kelly and I brought up the rear, mostly because we couldn't move that fast, and partially. . . well, partially because we'd gone through so much together, it seemed natural to have one another close.

Sure, we'd survived, but we'd all changed. Hell could do that to a person.

"Ling Mai around?" I asked, not sure if they'd know, but it was a neutral get-back-on-track enough question.

Mandy's gaze rocketed to mine. "Yeah. She's in a meeting."

The way she said it, as if caught with her hand in the cookie jar, had me slowing and asking, "Something I need to know about that meeting?"

She cut a look toward Kelly who nodded, before Mandy spoke. "It's with Bran."

That fast my heart took a nosedive. Bran? Here? This close. I wanted to push the other two aside and race to Ling Mai's office like one of those made-for-TV-historical romances. The ones with misty moors and long, flowing skirts. Neither of which was my style. At all.

Maybe it was time to change my style? If he was here. . .maybe with the Horned One gone it meant the price I paid never happened? Hope or illusion? Only one way to know.

I didn't plan on running, mostly because I couldn't, but I could walk fast. I squared my shoulders, raised my chin and gave myself a mental atta-girl for my voice sounding only a little rusty. "A meeting? Sounds important."

They looked at each other again, those like-we-believe-her kind of glances, and Mandy strode off.

Just as well. I wanted to ask Kelly something privately. "Is Van here?"

I expected him to be. We'd been gone less than a day in this world's time, and he'd been here when we left. Mad that Kels was leaving, but it wasn't like he had anywhere else to go.

Her arms, still wrapped ribbon tight around her, stiffened. What had I said now?

So I pushed, as gently as possible. "You hear from him?" A call? A text? Surely that was to be expected.

She looked straight ahead before answering. "He's gone."

"Gone? Like not at the Compound?" So maybe I didn't expect him lounging around, cooling his heels. I would have stayed though if I'd known he was off on a dangerous mission, one that'd be over almost before it had begun. And if he'd gone with someone I cared for, someone I loved. . . like Bran. . . there'd be no question I'd want to be on scene the minute they returned. So what was up?

Kelly swallowed deeply before answering. "He's off on some hush-hush mission."

"What?" I stopped, putting my hand on Kelly's arm before she looked at me. "Not with the EMA guys?"

Since EMA was the group that had attacked our Compound, and us, just last night, led by Kincaide who'd been possessed by the Horned One, I knew Van wouldn't be with them, if there was even a *them*, anymore.

"Seems he was recruited by a new group." Kelly spoke so quietly I had to lean in to hear her. "He's with them."

That was damn quick. "That's not bad then. We'll hear from him as soon as he can communicate."

I actually started breathing when Kelly unwrapped her arms enough to shove a crumpled piece of paper into my hand. "Here. This is for both of us."

She walked off before I could unfold what looked like a hastily written note in Van's handwriting.

By the time you're back, if you get back, I'll be gone. What we do—

That last word was almost gouged into the paper with enough force it was hard to make out.

What we do has no room for commitments. Best to end whatever we had. Now. Before—

Several words were crossed out with enough hash marks to make them illegible.

It was fun. Tell Alex goodbye for me.

Oh, he did not—he so did not tell Kels *it was fun*. And not even a goodbye to her? When I got my hands on him, there was going to be a reckoning—Noziak style.

Then—before I could finish the thought, a voice hailed me. Ling Mai's voice.

"Miss Noziak, I am glad to see you back with us."

That was the Director all over, her tone as casual as if I'd been off running an errand at the nearest mall. Except that might be worse than Hell.

I looked up to offer her a yes-I-have-returned smile before I caught sight of who was behind her.

Bran.

Tall, dark and sinfully handsome. Black Irish in coloring—thick black hair, and eyes so blue there ought to be a law against them.

My breath caught and held, a tremor snaking through me as I struggled with the emotions racing through me—exhilaration, relief, desire.

Here. He was really here. He towered behind the Director, his face in the shadows so I couldn't see his expression.

Probably looking like the consummate business professional he was—all controlled and private. No hint that the last time we'd met. . .well, not the last time we'd talked because that was an argument, but before then. . . I found myself growing warm, too warm for the cool gym interior.

That's right, focus on the past, not what I'd done—to him, to me, to us.

Ling Mai must have continued speaking as I scrambled to catch up with what she said.

"Pardon," I mumbled, "You were saying?"

"I said this is Bran. You haven't met—" She cantered her head, like one did to a slow child. "—however, there's a very vital mission I wish you to consider, as soon as you are recovered, that is."

My thoughts tumbled and roiled. Why was she introducing the man who'd been my lover almost since we'd first met?

What was going on? Mission? Now?

Bran stepped forward, one hand outstretched, his face a blank mask, his eyes intense and focused, but unfathomable. "Miss Noziak, pleased to meet you."

I almost snorted. He'd never been pleased to see me before, especially when I hadn't been willing to help him not that long ago. . . so why now?

I took his hand, an automatic gesture. Sure I'd play along with the ruse. Until I could get him alone to talk with him.

His touch, the calluses on his fingertips, strength of his hold sent the familiar heat curling through me but by the lack of expression creasing those Celtic eyes, I alone felt it.

His hand swallowed mine, which meant I was close enough to look closely at him, look deeply into his gaze, and only then did I realize he really didn't recognize me. Didn't know me.

Noooooooo!

I must have paled as the shock slammed against me.

Strangers. Complete strangers.

He tightened his grip on my hand and stepped closer. "Are you all right, Miss Noziak?" he murmured in his familiar voice, one that layered a French accent over deeper, darker, richer tones. "Maybe this is too much, so soon after whatever you've returned from."

As if he didn't know where I'd been. But if he'd forgotten who I was. . . is that what happened? Love not lost but wiped clean? Gone, as if it'd never happened.

I pulled my hand from his. Staggered backwards.

"Alex?" Ling Mai's voice cut through to me. She so rarely used our Christian names—not when speaking directly to us—that she startled me. I shot a wary side-glance her way. "When you are . . . later. Today if possible, we'll meet again. If you need more time—"

"She must come. There *is* no choice." Bran spoke up, the tone brooking no argument. So familiar, so like him I wanted to melt into a puddle of misery. Because it was also so impersonal. The voice of a man talking about a commodity—me—he needed. That's all.

So this is what the Guardian of the Gate meant about giving up what I valued most. It was as if everything Bran and I had been through together—our memories, our feelings, our connection—had never happened.

Now, only now, did I really know what Hell meant.

*** The End **

DID YOU LIKE
INVISIBLE JOURNEY?

Thank you for reading about Alex Noziak in this novel and I hope you enjoyed her story! Let the world know by posting a review on Amazon, Goodreads or Shelfari. Write a Customer Review. You = Awesome. Me = Grateful.

I also love hearing from readers! Find me on Goodreads or Facebook or Twitter !

Questions? Comments?

Help make the next edition of this book even better. If you've found a pesky typo in this book, here's your chance to let me know. Email suggestions to:
Assistant@MaryBuckham.com

WHAT READERS ARE SAYING ABOUT
INVISIBLE RECRUITS

"Not since Kate Daniels and Mercy Thompson have I fallen in love with a female character like I have with Alex Noziak."
~Urban Girl Reader.

"This is a definite must read for anyone who enjoys a bit of a thrill, a good laugh, and great characters with attitude."
~ Parchment Place

"I … encourage those of you who like action, magic and sassy heroines to snatch up this series."
~ Romancing the Genres

WANT TO READ MORE ABOUT THE
INVISIBLE RECRUIT TEAM?
CHECK OUT:

INVISIBLE PRISON (novella, free on Amazon)
On her first days with the Invisible Recruit Agency, Alex
Noziak learns she's not the only recruit with secrets to hide.
But hers could get her kicked off the Team even before she
begins. Or they could get her killed.

INVISIBLE MAGIC (full-length novel)
On her first official mission for the Invisible Recruit Agency
Alex Noziak discovers that to save the innocent she must call
upon her untested abilities. But at what cost? She has nothing
to lose, except her life.

INVISIBLE DUTY (novella)
The mission sounded easy for Alex Noziak, part witch/part
shaman. And easy is what she needed. But in the heart of
Africa, she finds something so deadly it will test her in ways
she never expected.

INVISIBLE POWER (full-length novel)
When Alex has a chance to save her brother and expose the
Weres who held him hostage, she must make a hard choice
with lives at risk, including her own.

INVISIBLE FATE (full-length novel)
Forced to choose, will dark magic be the only path. Hidden
from a world unaware of magic, a recently and only partially
trained group of operatives known as the Invisible Recruits are
the only ones willing to stand between mankind and those
powerful preternatural factions seeking to change the balance
of power and gain world domination.

BE THE FIRST TO FIND OUT WHEN THE NEXT BOOKS IN THE INVISIBLE RECRUITS SERIES COME OUT.

Sign up for my newsletter on:

MaryBuckham.com or **http://bit.ly/1aVMvtU**

THE KELLY MCALLISTER BOOKS

INVISIBLE ALLIES (novella)
Juggling with the side effects of her developing powers, patience isn't Kelly's current strong suit, especially around Alex Noziak, once a best friend, who has become a constant rub since realizing Kelly has an interest in Alex's brother. Now they're stuck together on an off the record assignment. Two IR

operatives should be able to track down a runaway witch in a small Missouri town without breaking a sweat, but even if they survive working together Alex is hiding a secret that might rear its deadly head and get both of them killed.

INVISIBLE FEARS (full-length novel)
He's a preternatural fighting for the humans.
She's a human fighting for the preternaturals.
Kelly McAllister's Invisible Recruit mission in Sierra Leone is to locate and secure a threat to humans and preternaturals. Van Noziak is also there, with his own secret mission, one that's on a collision course with Kelly's. In deepest Africa the race against a deadly bloom reveals secrets, exposes fears, and forces unlikely alliances.

INVISIBLE EMBRACE (novel – coming 2015)

ABOUT THE AUTHOR

A USA Today bestselling author, I started my career writing romantic suspense novels. Nothing like bombs and gunfire making a relationship more complicated. Between publication dates I was also fortunate to become a writing craft instructor, offering live workshops around the US and Canada as well as online workshops to writers throughout the world. As fun as the travel, and getting to know so many writers of all genres was, my first love has always been fiction. Thus the Invisible Recruit series was born and took off running!

I love conflict. On the page. The conflict between dark magic and white. The conflict between beings created with different needs and wants. Witches. Mage warlocks. Shifters, Weres, and demons all trying to co-exist against their natures. Bring it on!

I'm a huge paranormal and fantasy lover. Especially Urban Fantasy and any paranormal fantasy series that allows me to throw myself into magic and mystery page after page, book after book

The paranormal world of the Invisible Recruits is built on women who must learn to embrace their preternatural talents to fight good and evil. Talents that they've hidden from the human population for fear of being different.

But because I love conflict I've dropped these women into a world where magic and fantasy exist side by side with humans intentionally kept in the dark about Shifters, Weres, warlocks, witches, and especially about magic.

Throw in a strong dose of romantic suspense, emotional relationships to add more conflict, and paranormal beings you've never heard of before, and you'll know why readers can't get enough of this fast-paced paranormal thriller series.

www.MaryBuckham.com
www.InvisibleRecruits.com